LONE STAR
RENEGADES

By

Mark Wayne McGinnis

Cover design by:
Eren Arik

Edited by:
Lura Lee Genz
Mia Manns

Published by:
Avenstar Productions

ISBN: 978-0-9861098-1-2
www.markwaynemcginnis.com

Preface

Relatively close, at least in terms of distance from Earth … there are two highly unique dual galaxies. Actual satellites of the Milky Way galaxy, they're called the Magellanic Clouds.

With a fundamentally different structure and lower mass form, life differs in this region of space … again, compared to life found on Earth and within the confines of the Milky Way galaxy. The two dwarf galaxies are gas-rich and a higher fraction of their mass is both hydrogen- and helium-based. They are also deficient in even the most common metals found within the Milky Way.

The smaller of the two galaxies, dubbed the Mini Magellanic, is teeming with planets sporting a wide variety of advanced life forms. One particular world, Corpus 956, is the most technologically advanced civilization in the entire sector. Thousands, if not tens of thousands, of years ahead of Earth in virtually all aspects pertaining to technology and the sciences, the Notares, inhabitants of Corpus 956, are feverously hungry for metals such as aluminum, iron, magnesium, and titanium—to name just a few—all necessary to support their ever-expanding presence in outer space. But metals that are already processed hold the highest interest to the Notares. For thousands of years, magnificent transport vessels called sim-rovers have been traversing the dual Magellanic galaxies to meet the Notares' ever-growing dependence on metal. Only now, to obtain more of the metals their society requires, they have been forced to explore worlds outside their own dual galaxies.

With the exception of a handful of Notares technicians,

along with a small command crew, a highly automated sim-rover has crossed into the nearest regions of the Milky Way. The vessel has two directives—first, to explore all the planets within the region and those that maintain civilizations advanced enough to have adequate quantities of processed metal. Second ... to extricate and return with those processed metals.

Now, venturing well into the Milky Way, sim-rover ship 1229, detecting vast quantities of processed metal, slowly moves into a high orbit above Earth.

Chapter 1

Collin Frost sat in silence as John Bubba Washington repeatedly punched his upper left arm. Apparently, this was the price Collin would have to pay for taking the only remaining open seat on the Middleton High School Athletic Association's bus back to school.

To say Bubba was a bully was a ridiculous understatement. Collin wasn't alone with his opinion that Bubba was a raging psychopath in the making—he liked to hurt people, got off on it. With that said, the degenerate would still be allowed to finish up his senior year. He was too important. At two hundred and sixty-five pounds, nineteen and a half years old, the starting defensive tackle was not only the baddest son of a bitch on the bus that evening, he was a college athletic recruiter's dream come true. Easily the most sought after high school senior in the entire great state of Texas.

Collin continued to stare straight ahead, looking at his teammate's Lone Stars jersey: white with blue numbers. He kept his expression neutral—as neutral as possible, considering his arm was being socked over and over by a fist nearly the size of Collin's own head.

"I told you, Sticks, don't even think about sitting here."

Collin braced for the inevitable, thunderous, jaw-wrenching next punch to the exact same location on his fairly unsubstantial upper right arm. When it came, Collin was physically transported up and out of his seat into the narrow aisle. As he sat on the mud-crusted linoleum, between grass-stained football pants and bloodied knees, a cleated foot, from God knew where, kicked into Collin's middle back.

Sticks was a nickname Collin had picked up three years before, as a freshman. Where Bubba was two hundred and sixty-five pounds of hardened muscle and brawn, Collin was a tall, lanky, skinny kid who barely tipped the scales at one hundred and sixty pounds.

"Stay down, fuckface," Bubba spat. "Don't make me hurt you."

"Yeah, stay down, Sticks," came the annoying voice from the seat directly behind Bubba's. Collin glanced back at the smaller, white version of Bubba, Mike Humphrey. Humphrey was Bubba's best friend. His hair typically looked unwashed and always seemed to hang in his face. When not playing football he exclusively wore his father's old army jacket. Bubba and Humphrey had always hung together—an obnoxious duo, they cut a swath of misery wherever they went, and toward anyone who crossed their path. Unfortunately for Collin, today was his turn. "Hey, Sticks ... tell me how you could miss a field goal from fifteen yards out. That must be some kind of high school record, don't you think?"

Collin didn't answer. Truth was, he wasn't completely sure how he'd missed it.

The fact that Collin was considered an egghead, smart, only increased the level of torment he'd endured since he'd first tried out for the football team. But what had amazed more than a few coaches that early fall afternoon when he'd tried out for the team was that he had a pretty good kicking leg on him. Collin suspected he'd have a fair chance as a kicker; he'd played soccer as a little kid and knew for a fact he wasn't all that bad.

Still on the floor, Collin debated the perils of sharing a seat with Bubba again. He could see the bus driver was already looking back at him from the overhead mirror. Scowling, the driver yelled over the loud chattering of the other kids, "Back on your seat, now!"

Toward the front of the bus Collin heard the distinctive higher-pitched voices of the female cheerleaders. They were singing—actually, they were rapping along to a song Collin was somewhat familiar with … Club goin' up, on a Tuesday

Got your girl in the cut and she choosay …

Club goin' up, on a Tuesday

Got your girl in the cut and she choosay.

That's when Collin saw Lydia casually glance back at him over her shoulder while she pulled her long dark hair away from her face—their eyes momentarily locked. Was that a smile on her lips as she sang along? … "Club goin' up, on a Tuesday Got your girl in the cut and she choosay …"

There was a lot Collin could put up with at that moment: a detention slip from the bus driver, whatever … fine; more pummeling from Bubba, okay, sure … But Lydia seeing him looking like an ass wipe, wedged down in the aisle? No flippin' way.

Collin pulled himself back up onto the bench seat and looked over to a surprised Bubba. "Hey Bubba, I heard Humph talking about you in the locker room."

Out of his peripheral vision, Collin saw Humphrey's snarly face jerk angrily in his direction. "You gunna die, Sticks," Humphrey said.

Collin continued: "He was telling Clifford Bosh you've got the tiniest baloney pony he'd ever seen. That must be like … really embarrassing, Bubba. But hey, forget it. Why's Humph watching you in the shower anyway? I guess that's a whole other issue."

Collin saw and heard Lydia laugh out loud. But whatever redemption Collin hoped to earn was short-lived. She'd turned around in her seat in time to see both Bubba and

Humphrey's fists make solid connections—one to the side of Collin's head and the next to the back.

Collin was back down in the aisle again and seeing stars. He was barely conscious of the fact the bus was coming to a stop. His head throbbed and he felt like he might throw up. The *ding ding ding* of a railroad crossing put them at Mills Country Road. **Crap**, they were only halfway home. As the train drew closer, Collin heard its whistle scream in three long bursts and then the *ticketty clack ticketty clack ticketty clack* of metal wheels rolling by on metal rails.

While debating if he should move back to his seat, Collin was aware of another sound. Actually, it was the lack of sound. Had the two punches affected his hearing? Collin rubbed at his ears and heard his fingers moving back and forth in stereo … hearing's okay. Collin looked to his right and saw Bubba looking out the window. Hell, everyone was looking out the windows. Next came voices of trepidation—of fear.

"Do you see that?"

"Oh my God!"

"Help them!"

"I need to get off … God … let me off!"

Then the screams started. Boys and girls and, in Bubba's case, a full-grown man, screamed out with terrified voices.

A green light had replaced the darkness outside. "What is it?" Collin asked, frustrated, still trying to get his feet underneath him. "What do you see?"

No one paid any attention to his questions.

The former swish of the passing train was replaced by the wrenching-twisting sounds of metal … and now, other distant screams. As Collin finally made it to his knees and was able to peer out the left side of the bus, he saw firsthand what had everyone in such a frenzy.

Collin blinked three times in rapid succession, hoping to

clear his vision from what must be, he figured, an illusion. But it wasn't an illusion. It was a horrific scene that had no place in his logical, highly intelligent brain. Before them was the train's engine, still attached to six railroad cars, which dangled beneath it, at an elevation of one hundred feet above the ground. People had started to jump from passenger car windows to what would surely be an inevitable death onto the flat farmland far below. Several autos and a pickup truck, on the far side of the track, were suddenly lifted into the air simultaneously. Slowly at first, then picking up speed, the cars, the pickup truck, and the train—engine and dangling passenger cars—moved higher and higher up into the air.

But Collin's eyes were no longer on any of those things. What grabbed his attention, as well as everyone else's on the bus, was the gargantuan, egg-shaped space ship. Bigger than anything Collin had ever seen—bigger than the Sears Tower he'd visited two years ago in Chicago or AT&T Stadium, where he and his dad watched the Dallas Cowboys defeat the Bengals. For a brief moment, Collin saw the cars and pickup truck lowering back down to the street. But that wasn't really what was happening. No ... the bus, too—their bus—was now also rising into the air. Students were scrambling to open up windows, only to find they were already too far off the ground to jump out. Shrieks and screams filled the cramped space.

Collin was on his feet and, like the other kids, looking for a way out. Bubba, still crouched on his seat, had been reduced to a blubbering child—his eyes wide and frantic. Toward the front of the bus, Collin saw Lydia standing and staring out the window, both hands covering her mouth. It was then Collin felt the pull—like the G-forces he recalled feeling on a Six Flags roller-coaster—only this force was pulling him, and everything else, straight up toward an open orifice at the bottom of the ship.

Chapter 2

Collin watched as the mayhem around him continued to elevate. He sat back down next to Bubba. Was Collin scared shitless? Of course, but the logic-deducing part of Collin's brain had already come to terms with the simple fact there was zero he could do about any of it … things did not look promising for a long and healthy life. On the other hand, the experience was beyond amazing.

"We're going to die … we're going to die … we're going to die …" said Bubba, the words coming out in a rapid, murmuring succession. Even taking up three quarters of the seat, Bubba somehow seemed smaller. His tough-guy bravado was replaced by a vulnerability Collin never guessed was there.

"You want to know something, big guy?" Collin asked, in a tone that betrayed none of his own fears.

Bubba, looking momentarily awed by Collin's seeming nonchalance, stopped his blathering. "Wha … What?"

"If … and I'll give you it's a big if … but if we live through this, you might want to try to pull yourself together … some. You never know what's going to happen."

But Bubba's attention was drawn back out the window and Collin spotted the yellow stain where he'd wet himself. The big defensive tackle held his two meaty hands tightly clenched in his lap.

The now frantic bus driver was still seated behind the wheel. Every so often he put his hands at ten and two and attempted to steer the bus away from their inevitable destination. It almost would have been funny, if their lives hadn't been in such peril. Looking on the brighter side of their ongoing ordeal, Collin noticed there was another interesting aspect to their continuing ascent. While the train, cars, and pickup truck had changed their orientation, now rotating vertically as they rose, the school bus had stayed relatively horizontal, as if traveling on some invisible, unseen highway into the ever-nearing glowing green aperture above.

Collin realized he didn't want to be alone when they entered that big ship. If he was going to die, which Bubba was all too sure of, he should go out with someone he cared about. He scanned the front of the bus for her long hair. She wasn't where he'd last seen her. Collin stood up, fear gripping him tightly around the throat. He spun to his left and then looked behind him. *How'd she get behind me? …* Collin saw her, her head buried into the chest of Darren Mallon … varsity starting quarterback, almost as much in demand as Bubba, and rock-star handsome. Of course she'd find him. He'd been her boyfriend as long as Collin had known her.

The bus shifted backward and Collin momentarily lost his balance. Surprisingly, there was a voice yelling over the intercom: "Everyone back in your seats. Sit down!"

Apparently the bus driver still had the presence of mind to act and say something constructive. No one paid any attention, but Collin appreciated his effort to control the bus just the same.

"Hell if I'm going to stay here," Collin said, moving forward in the aisle. He had to squirm past several colossal-sized teenagers before reaching the bus driver's side.

"I told you to sit the hell down, kid!" the driver spewed, hands still gripped tightly on the wheel.

Shrugging, Collin said, "I don't want to miss this," gesturing to the rapidly approaching opening, easily the size of several city blocks. He could now partially see inside the ship. Everything in there was bathed in emerald green, and

11

he could discern movement inside. The bus driver and Collin leaned more forward to get a better perspective of what they were seeing through the windshield.

Both suddenly leaned back and gasped. "Robotic arms … they're sorting what's coming into the ship," Collin said flatly. What was even more apparent to him was that their relatively smooth travel into the ship so far was about to end. There was nothing gentle about the way the large, articulating arms were handling what was coming in. He watched as the red pickup truck rose into the aperture and was abruptly plucked out of the air by a three-fingered claw. Without hesitation it tossed the truck hundreds of feet, like a discarded toy, onto a pile of like-sized objects.

Collin and the driver looked at each other. The driver yelled into the microphone: "Sit down and hold on … do it, now!"

This time everyone did as told. Collin moved into the seat behind the driver. He looked for something to grab on to, deciding the back of the driver's seat was his only real option. The G-forces were increasing and Collin was having an extremely hard time staying in his seat. Arms and legs, and the flesh on his face, were being pulled forward. Abruptly, something brushed by Collin's right shoulder. Before his brain could make sense of it—a short white skirt—a white and gold sweater with the school emblem—a cheerleader careened through the windshield backwards. Her face contorted in a perpetual, soundless scream. Instinctively, Collin reached for her—almost releasing his precarious hold on the driver's seat back in the process.

The bus changed its angle again, becoming nearly straight up and down as it vertically ascended into the ship's opening. With a quick glance behind him, Collin saw elevated feet—bodies held high, as if caught in a hurricane-force wind tunnel. Another body, a football player, flew past him and out through the now non-existent windshield.

Without warning the bus driver too was gone. Collin didn't see him get yanked from the bus—one second he was there, the next he was gone. The bus entered the opening, into the ship itself. There were hundreds of large articulating arms at work around the periphery of the open expanse. Everything entering was forced to the side, into the constantly moving arms. Collin felt the G-forces on the bus change direction—they were being pulled sideways. Two arms rose in unison to catch the entering bus. The forward-most arm, with its outstretched claws, penetrated the bus. One of its claw fingers tore into the two seats behind Collin, one tore through the ceiling directly overhead, and another took hold of the engine section. Collin listened to the screams around him. Some were from fear—others from agonizing pain. The bus shuddered and was jerked about with tremendous force and then, as it left the clutches of the articulating arm, sailed through the air for several agonizingly long seconds. Upside down, and moving with way too much speed, the bus impacted something significantly larger than itself.

The bus landed hard onto its right side and then rolled. Collin lost his grip on the driver's seat back and landed atop the big blue numbers on the jersey of Alan Baker—a talented running back whose skull, somewhere over the last few moments, had been crushed.

As Collin continued to lie still he took stock of his own self. His right arm hurt but he didn't think it was broken. He slowly moved his left arm and then his legs. Considering what had just transpired, he'd come through it relatively well. He wondered if he was the only survivor. He listened and heard nothing but the continual crashing of metal objects being tossed about by the articulating arms. Collin wondered if Lydia had survived … perhaps it would be best if she hadn't. Perhaps it would have been best if he hadn't either.

Pushing himself up off the dead body, he averted his eyes from poor Alan Baker's mangled head. Collin was surprised he was able to sit upright. Apparently the bus was now sited right side up on its tires.

Without warning, the loud banging and crashing came to an abrupt end. An eerie quiet pressed in around Collin. The dead silence was almost worse than the interminable racket. In the distance, Collin saw the huge opening rapidly disappearing. Like a constricting camera lens aperture, it grew smaller and smaller until he saw it seal tight … completely closed. They were—he was—trapped inside the ship.

Collin wasn't sure he wanted to see what lay behind him. Slowly he turned in his seat and took in the carnage.

Chapter 3

Movement. Some of the kids were coming around. Others stayed where they lay. Even in the bus's battered condition, with most of the interior lights shattered, there was still enough illumination to see who was who. Collin did a quick mental calculation. There were twenty-four seats on the bus, twelve per side. Each seat held two people. Forty-eight kids … half of them were either unconscious or—

Dana Stoker screamed as she realized her best friend, Lisa Cole—seated next to her—was dead. Linebacker Bill Myers started to cry when he tried to stand up but couldn't … apparently he was paralyzed from the waist down. Collin continued to watch them all as the scene behind him quickly unraveled.

As the screams and crying hit a new crescendo, of course it was Darren Mallon, Lydia's boyfriend, who took control of the situation. He was standing near Lydia, who was hunched over, crying into her open palms.

"Everyone just shut up! We lived through this crap, so just shut up!"

The noise-level decreased by half. "We've been abducted. But we're going to be rescued. We just need to sit tight and wait."

Collin had no particular problem with Darren—other than he was Lydia's boyfriend … that, and the fact he seemed to live a charmed life. Athletically speaking, he was a God … he had Brad Pitt good looks … and he was an eventual heir to the Mallon family fortune. A trifecta. And now, just like on the playing field, he'd be the guy these kids would turn to as their leader—the one they'd follow.

"You heard him, sit the down!" came Bubba's thunderous voice. Darren and Bubba reached across a row of seats and bumped fists.

Those standing sat back down. Darren continued, "We'll need to move everyone that … didn't make it … off the bus. Anyone here know first-aid?"

Two people raised their hands—a cheerleader, Collin didn't know her name, and Paul DiMaggio.

"Cool," Darren said, nodding his head. "Go help everyone who's injured. Bubba, Humphrey … um, we need to get the … um, ones that didn't make it, and move them off the bus."

The noise level rose again as fuller realization of their situation took hold.

Collin turned his attention to what was outside the bus. They were situated high up, atop an enormous mound of twisted and gnarled metal—numerous eighteen-wheelers; what looked like girders, the kind that held buildings together; and the same locomotive engine, along with six or so passenger cars he'd earlier watched get sucked up into this spaceship. He did a double take when he saw the tail section of what must have been a commercial jetliner. Off in the distance, there were countless small mountains of similar objects. Mostly everything was made of some kind of metal. The whole space was illuminated in a bright green light from high above. Collin turned to look out the opposite window—the spacecraft they were in was vast, easily reaching a mile in circumference.

Darren was wrong. They hadn't been abducted. Whatever they were, the aliens who'd sucked them into this spaceship were after the raw materials … not humans. The humans were nothing more than collateral baggage. Again, Collin took in the huge quantities of metal objects piled within the ginormous outer compartment. One thing was evident—it was filled to capacity. *What happens when you've got a full load?*

"Where the hell you going, Sticks?" Bubba roared. "What … you didn't hear the man?"

Collin moved to the front console and pulled up on the large protruding handle that operated the opening and closing of the tall double-doors. The doors opened. When Collin turned back toward Bubba, he saw everyone was looking at him.

"We weren't abducted."

"What the hell do you know, Sticks?" Bubba snickered.

"Let the geek go," Humphrey said.

"Where you going, Frost?" Darren asked, looking surprisingly interested.

"Look … Whoever took us? Aliens … whatever … they aren't remotely interested in us … what they're interested in is the raw materials. Just take a look outside. Also, nobody is going to rescue us. Not with what's going on with trains and planes and cars and trucks being sucked up. Things are crazy down there." Collin momentarily thought of his mother and wondered if she was okay. His heart tugged in his chest as he thought of her; she'd be devastated at his disappearance.

"I'm getting out of here. Sitting tight, as you put it, will only get you dead."

"Why's that?" Darren asked.

"I'm guessing we're breathing some air, oxygen, because that opening sucked up atmosphere from Earth. Remember, they didn't come for us … they came for the metal crap piled outside the bus. What happens when they vent the air out of here or that opening opens on another planet or to outer space?"

"I told you, Sticks, you need to shut your—"

"Hold on, Bubba. Where are you gonna go that the same thing isn't going to happen to you?" Darren asked.

Collin saw Lydia looking at him, leaning forward in her seat—taking in his every word.

He shrugged. "I don't want to just sit here and do nothing. I'd rather die trying to survive than die waiting around."

"There's no magic place out there, Sticks. You're a fool," Humphrey sneered.

"See that tail section over there? It's from a jetliner."

"So what … a bus, a jetliner, there's not much difference when it comes down to it."

"I know one big difference. Oxygen," Collin said, letting that bit of information sink in. There wasn't a person on the bus who hadn't sometime watched an airline attendant demonstrate the use of small yellow oxygen masks.

Collin saw the comprehension on Darren's face. On all their faces.

"So … what … you were just going to leave us? Save yourself?" Darren asked, looking mystified.

Collin wasn't prepared for that. "Hey … everyone can do what they want. The rules have changed … we're not on the field anymore, Darren. Truth is, I don't owe any of you anything." His eyes went from Bubba to Humphrey and then back to Darren. But it was only when he looked at Lydia that he regretted his harsh words.

Bill Myers looked like he was having trouble breathing. When he spoke, his voice was full of fear and came out in rapid short bursts: "I can't … move … my legs. How would I … get off the bus?"

Collin's mind reeled—*what the hell just happened? Since when am I making decisions for anyone other than myself?* "I guess someone would have to carry you, man. Sorry." Collin looked to Humphrey. "Maybe Humph here … and Bubba. They can carry you. Staying here is simply not an option. At least for me it isn't." Collin shrugged. Then he turned and hurried down the steps and walked out of the bus.

The first thing he noticed was the smell. A mix of chemical scents—the most prevalent was diesel fuel. There was also the sweet sickening stench of blood and decay. Obviously, there were a lot of dead bodies strewn around in the wreckage.

Behind him other kids started to exit the bus. Collin looked down at what lay beneath his feet. The train engine. It was upside down, its wheels pointed upward. Below, and to his left, was a passenger car—it was lying on its side, positioned parallel to the locomotive. Its upward facing windows had either shattered or were broken out.

One by one the students emptied out of the bus. The last to exit were Bubba and Humphrey carrying Bill Myers.

Humphrey looked ready to kill someone. "There's no way I'm dragging Myers' ass around like this." He tilted his head at an angle and peered down and around Myers. "Yeah ... no way ... the guy just crap his pants. I'm done ... Bubba, put the dude down."

The other kids took a step backward as the acrid smell reached their noses.

Paul DiMaggio knelt down beside Myers, who seemed to be unconscious. Paul placed two fingers on Myers' neck. He shook his head and quickly stood up, stepping away. "Holy hell ... the guy's dead."

Bubba, still holding Myers semi-upright, let him go, after taking a quick step back. Myers flopped backward with a thump.

"I can't believe you just dropped him like that," Lydia said, moving forward from the back of the crowd—her forehead creased in a scowl. "For God's sakes, he was your friend." Lydia knelt down next to Paul. She too checked Myers' pulse and let her hand rest on the teen's chest for several moments.

Darren, who'd been walking atop the mountainous

plateau of accumulated rubble, said, "All right, to get down to the plane we'll need to climb down from here." He stood with his hands on his hips and gestured with his chin. Below him was the path that looked to present the least precarious descent. "It'll be a little dicey; we'll have to watch our step … we'll have to climb from one section of the mound to another." His eyes moved over the scared faces and eventually looked over to Collin.

"Better to go through the passenger car over here. I think the plane is directly beneath it. Safer … easier," Collin said.

"Yeah … well, I think we'll do things my way, Sticks. No offense."

It wasn't lost on Collin that Darren had started using the same derogatory nickname Bubba was so fond of calling him.

Again, Collin simply shrugged. "Good luck with that." He turned and began climbing down the side of the locomotive toward the passenger car.

Chapter 4

As he climbed down, Collin had to avert his eyes several times. Once, it was the long gray hair on a decomposing woman's head, facing away from him in the heap of junk. Another was a simple street sign—a sign that he recognized from his own neighborhood. He wondered if the other way, Darren's way, would have worked just as well. Collin wondered too if he was purposely being obstinate. Maybe it was because of all the crap he'd had to put up with from Bubba and Humph, and their ilk, over the past few years. Or, maybe it was because Darren really was a pompous blowhard. But Collin knew the real reason was Lydia. Why was she with him? ... *Because he's a hell of a lot cooler than you are,* Collin's inner voice mockingly retorted back.

The locomotive's thousands of rods and gears and other steel components were making hissing and ticking sounds as parts cooled in the chilly environment. By the time Collin climbed all the way down and was standing next to the train's passenger car, the first of the students had started to climb over the edge of the locomotive above him. He heard Bubba's voice somewhere above, but couldn't make out what he was saying. Maybe Darren's way down the mound hadn't worked out well after all.

Collin walked several yards farther to his left until he reached the end of the turned-over railcar. Three feet above him were metal steps, leading into the passenger compartment. He wouldn't need them. He used various hand- and foot-holds on the car's exposed underside to climb to where he could pull himself up to the compartment's doorway. It was open. Before dropping inside, he made sure some of the

21

others, now climbing down the locomotive's side, had seen him and where he was heading.

He started to gag and retch before his mind could fully register what he was actually seeing. The smell of bodies, which had released urine and excrement in death, was overwhelming. The bodies were stacked one atop another, in some places three deep: a businessman in a three-piece suit, a woman wearing shorts and a tank top, and a bald, elderly man, his aluminum walker nearby, lying on top of both. There were others—many others. Collin averted his eyes and stepped between sprawled legs, awkwardly contorted torsos, and an accumulation of personal items—attaché cases, backpacks, and small suitcases, designed to perfectly fit on overhead racks. Collin grabbed a well-used rucksack next to a teenager who looked about his age. Checking inside, he found it primarily full of books—books and snacks. He ditched the books and kept the snacks. Football pants had no pockets and he'd need to carry such things with him.

It occurred to him that food would become an issue … a huge issue. He backtracked and started to check all the bags, attaché cases and backpacks. By the time he'd check them all, he'd accumulated seven energy bars, nine bottles of water, a ham and cheese sandwich, and a handful of candy bars. As he turned back toward the other end of the compartment, some of the first students to arrive had begun to drop inside the car.

He heard someone retch and then scream a string of obscenities. It was Humphrey. "Great plan, Sticks … really glad we decided to follow in your footsteps."

Collin was already nearing the far end of the compartment. He opened the door to the lavatory. He was relieved to see it was empty. Empty, but a mess. There were three full rolls of toilet paper lying on what was now the new floor. He snatched them up and placed them in his rucksack.

When he stepped back out to the main compartment, Humphrey was standing there. "Stealing from the dead, Sticks? You sick mother-fu—"

"You going to wipe your ass with your hand, Humph? Or maybe you'll have Bubba do that for you?" Collin snickered back.

Both Lydia and Darren were halfway into the car.

"I have to agree with Humphrey; this is beyond gross, Frost," Darren said.

"No one twisted your arm to come here. But you might thank me later." He fished out a bottle of water and an energy bar from the rucksack and held them up. "What were you planning on eating as long as you were trapped in here? My suggestion … have everyone find a pack or something like what I have, and start looking for items we can use. Primarily: food and water. Pass that on to those coming in behind you." Collin reached out and placed the water and energy bar in Lydia's hands.

"Where are you going?" Lydia asked.

"There's still four more railcars to explore before we try to enter the plane."

Collin had difficulty opening the door to the connecting railcar, but eventually he managed to hold it open enough to wedge beneath it and push himself into the next car. It was almost an identical, grisly scene to that of the previous compartment. He immediately went to work snatching up bags and packs and discarding everything but the essentials. He made a pile of them in an open space in the middle of the car and continued forward. Again, he checked the lavatory and collected more toilet paper.

Bubba was bent over the pile of packs and satchels. "Distribute these," Collin said. One after another, he threw the rolls in the air toward Bubba's direction. Not waiting to see if he'd caught them, Collin wrestled with the next inter-railcar door.

★ ★ ★

By the time all sixteen JV and varsity football players, and the eight varsity cheerleaders, raked through the dead passengers' personal baggage, Collin, with the help of DiMaggio, found a section of the airliner beneath a window in railcar number four. Unfortunately, they'd have to tear into the plane's aluminum fuselage to get inside. Collin looked around for something sharp and heavy enough to do the job. Then, he remembered something he'd seen in railcar number three.

"Paul, mind going back to car three? There's a pipe attached to a ragged piece of metal. It's a heavy thing, lying about two-thirds back in the car."

"No problem, I'll get it."

"Um … can you see if Bubba wants to come back with you?"

Paul left and Collin continued clearing debris away from the window and surrounding area. There was an iPhone lying beneath an overcoat and Collin slipped it into his rucksack.

DiMaggio was already on his way back, but he was empty handed.

"You didn't see the pipe—"

Before Collin could get the words out, Bubba's voice thundered from two paces back. "Now you think you can summon me like some kind of damn dog? You're lucky I don't beat your head with this thing."

DiMaggio scooted behind Collin and moved to the other side of the window. Bubba, looking angry in his pee-stained football pants, crouched down next to Collin.

"What the hell am I supposed to do here? You think I'm like superman, I can rip through metal?"

"It's aluminum. Stuff's lightweight," Collin said.

"Just get back. Further! Come on, I'll need room to swing this bad boy."

Collin and DiMaggio cleared out of the way. Bubba used the business end of the pipe, the end with the thick ragged piece of metal connected to its end. He stood, ensured no one was close by, and brought the makeshift hammer over his head, swinging it down like he was Paul Bunyan. The fuselage tore open, creating a hole the size of a soft ball. Bubba peered down at the damage he'd caused. "This needs to be big enough for a person to crawl through?"

Both Collin and DiMaggio nodded.

"Stay back." He swung again, and then again a dozen or two more times. Slowly, but measurably, progress was made and the aluminum skin of the jetliner opened into a two-foot by three-foot-wide opening. When Bubba finally stopped, he was sopping with sweat. His dark, nearly black skin glistened in the dim light. "That should do it. Even I can squeeze through that."

"Yeah, that's pretty good," Collin answered.

Bubba glanced behind him and saw a crowd watching. He tossed the pipe out of the way and stood back.

Darren moved up and stood over the ragged, gaping hole. "Can't see a thing down there. Smells just as bad, though."

Collin suddenly remembered the cell phone. He dug through his rucksack and came out with the new iPhone 6 he'd found. The previous user had evidently disabled the auto-lock feature that would require a pass code, and the cell phone came alive in his hand. He thumbed through several screens of apps. "Here we go." He tapped the screen and the flashlight feature came alive with a beam of bright white light.

"That'll work; here, hand it over," Darren said, holding out his hand expectantly.

Collin ignored him and positioned himself over the opening. He reached his arm and the iPhone down into the blackness. Darren, Bubba, and DiMaggio brought their faces down close to Collin's as they peered together into the jetliner.

"I think that's the kitchen area," DiMaggio said.

"What was your first clue … the banks of coffee pots or the food cart?" Bubba asked.

Collin pulled his arm back and handed the phone to DiMaggio. "Hold this for a sec."

Before anyone could say anything, Collin was already lowering himself, legs first, into the hole.

Chapter 5

What Collin noticed first was the airliner was lying upright. The second thing he noticed was that it was empty—at least empty of passengers. He'd assumed the spaceship had plucked the jet right out of the air, but it was just as conceivable it had been parked on a Dallas/Fort Worth Airport runway.

The ceiling, the outer hull of the plane, was crushed inward several feet from the weight of the passenger railcar that lay perpendicular across this section of the jet. Leaving the kitchen zone, which was in the rear of the plane, he moved into the main cabin—coach. He discovered the plane was a wide-body Boeing 777-328 from a laminated information card protruding up from a seat pocket. The light from his iPhone app cast long shadows across the expansive compartment.

Others were now dropping into the plane's kitchen compartment. Tina McBride and Humphrey entered the main cabin behind Collin, but entered it down a different aisle.

"Tight!" Tina said. "Like this is the biggest jet in the world … right?" She stopped and counted the seats with a bobbing index finger. "Three seats on each side and four in the middle. And look at the little built-in TVs." The waif-sized cheerleader had the high-pitched voice of a cartoon character, which had garnered her the nickname Tink, for Tinkerbell, by all her friends. Collin appraised the chipper teen with amazement … was she totally oblivious to the fact they were all perilously close to living the last few hours, maybe only minutes, of their young lives?

As more and more students filed in, more cellphone

flashlights illuminated the cabin. Apparently, a number of them had been found back in the railcars. Kids started to plop down onto the plush leather seats.

Darren appeared from the kitchen, with Lydia trailing behind holding on to his hand. "Okay, Frost …" he said, "I have to give it to you … this'll be a much better crib than the bus."

Collin didn't say anything as he continued up the aisle. He passed by a center grouping of lavatories and then into a similar-sized seating compartment he guessed was business class. He held out his hands and let them bounce off opposite headrests as he moved down the aisle. Up ahead was a bulkhead, with a closed curtain. He passed through it and whistled. Nice! He'd entered first class. Here, the thirty or forty seats were significantly larger and were capable of extending into bed-like configurations. He continued on, passing another bulkhead. *What's this?* Apparently he'd been wrong; here was another, smaller, more intimate compartment, with eight extra-large, even plushier seats. Upper first class?

He was finally getting to the front of the plane. The forward section was a double-decker affair: The first class compartment and the cockpit were located on the upper level. Collin found the stairway and made his way to the upper section. Up here, the twenty or thirty first class seats were more luxurious than those on the rest of the plane. The second galley, at the farthest back section of the compartment, was big and well appointed.

He continued forward. Seeing that the cockpit door was closed was initially discouraging. Collin surmised breaking it down wouldn't be a small feat—not since 9/11 and the FAA's requirement for installing more strictly reinforced security measures.

Trying the latch anyway, he was surprised when the door

opened right up. Standing inside the doorway into the ultra-advanced-looking cockpit, he moved his cellphone light and saw four cockpit crew seats, two up front, two behind, and the myriad of dials and controls. So the 777 was significantly different from the 747! It had been a while since he'd played *Flight Academy* on his Xbox. He'd gotten fairly proficient at takeoffs and landings on the Boeing 747. He knew well, at least on the 747-jetliner, the instrumentation—where everything was located. He wasn't so sure he'd be able to make heads or tails, though, out of what he was seeing here.

One thing he was sure of—there had to be a manual—a binder with locations of things and basic instructions. It was a requirement on all passenger and probably other commercial jets as well. *There you are.* He found the two-inch-thick binder in a shelf next to the rear seat to his right.

Binder in hand, he took a seat in the left-hand pilot's chair and moved the light over the dashboard controls. There were so many more switches and dials here that he had no idea what some of them were used for. Collin opened the binder and started reading.

"What are you doing?"

Startled, Collin spun to see Lydia standing at the doorway.

"Um … trying to find auxiliary power unit switches. Maybe we can get some lights on. We'll also need power for the oxygen … at least, I think we will."

Lydia took a seat to his right, in the co-pilot's seat, and leaned forward. She had her own cellphone flashlight on and was moving it across her side of the control panel.

Collin realized he'd let his eyes linger on her face a bit too long and resumed his own search.

"Wait … is this it? It says battery right here."

Collin leaned to his right, bringing his face within several inches of hers. Sure enough, there was a small panel—about eight inches wide by eleven inches long. There was a small button labeled Battery, and next to that a three-position APU dial with the words: OFF / ON / START. Beneath that were a half-dozen other switches: SECONDARY EXT POWER … PRIMARY EXT POWER … L MAIN … L XFER … R XFER … R MAIN.

Collin inspected the panel. When he looked back at Lydia he saw she was staring at him. This was the closest he'd ever been to her. He noticed she had a dusting of faint freckles across the bridge of her small, upturned nose … and she had the most perfect lips—lips that continually expressed her thoughts and emotions. He saw the corners of them turn slightly upward.

"Hello? Collin … is that what you're looking for?"

"Oh, yeah … I think so." He brought his attention back to the panel. He turned the spring-loaded switch from OFF all the way over to START. It was faint, but there was a slight vibration—one he knew was caused by a small turbine engine firing up in the tail section. "With this up you can provide all electrical power to the plane and pneumatic air for pressurization and air-conditioning. As long as there's enough fuel, the batteries will charge and we'll have power … probably for a few days." He ensured the BATTERY switch was flipped up.

"You really are smart. I mean … we're the same age and I don't know anything about stuff like this."

Collin felt his face flush. "Okay, now we need to find the switch where the cabin lights are controlled."

They both pointed to the panel at the same time. "Here it is," they said in unison.

Under the panel heading PASS SIGNS, a grouping of switches and dials, including those marked NO SMOKING … SEAT BELTS, Collin found the dial for OVHD/CB. He turned the dial and the cockpit lights came on.

"You did it!" Lydia said excitedly.

Collin found another tiny switch labeled OXYGEN and ensured that was flipped on as well. "I think that will do it … for now, anyway," Collin said self-consciously. "The rear cabin lights are controlled from the various flight attendant stations."

"I can do that," Lydia said. She got up from her seat and patted Collin on the shoulder. "You rock, Collin." With that, she left the cockpit. Collin took one more look at the controls and stood to leave. He left the cockpit and entered the now-illuminated upstairs first class section. The group had all moved forward; some kids were stretched out on the lounge-like seats. Collin arrived in time to see Darren pull Lydia down onto his lap and envelop her in his arms. Collin averted his eyes.

"And the Frost man comes through again," Darren said with a broad smile. "Hey, any way to get the heat cookin' in here?" he added. "Is it only me or has the temperature dropped like twenty degrees since we arrived?"

First class was feeling claustrophobic with the twenty-four of them all huddled into the smallest one of the four passenger cabins. Collin chewed the inside of his lip. "I think the plane will start warming up now that the auxiliary power unit is going."

"Dude, I have no idea what you just said. But if it means we'll be toasty soon … I'm down with that," Darren said optimistically.

DiMaggio entered the cabin with his arms piled high with folded blankets. He dropped them onto an open seat. "Help yourselves."

"Hop off, sweet cheeks," Darren said, pushing Lydia off his lap. "I need to drop a major deuce. Hey Frost, what's the story with the bathrooms? You got all the shitters operational in here? Or maybe you gotta go flip some more switches for that?" Darren sat forward on his seat with his eyebrows raised.

All eyes turned to Collin. "I don't know. I'm no expert on how the toilets work. They'll probably work, though."

The girls looked first at Darren and then at each other, disgust registering on each face.

All of a sudden the jetliner abruptly and violently shook. Anyone standing was thrown to the floor. Like being immersed suddenly into ice-cold water, the temperature plummeted to well below freezing in a matter of seconds.

Collin tried to stand only to find himself suddenly struggling for breath. **Crap.** The very thing he'd been worried about was happening. The spaceship's vast aperture must have opened—perhaps their oxygenated air was now venting out to open space. Collin saw everyone's eyes go wide as hands grabbed for throats—mouths opened and closed, like fish out of water—all gasping, struggling to inhale.

Bubba, who'd made it briefly to his knees, toppled over sideways, unconscious.

The cold was absolute. Collin felt his life slipping away. As oxygen left the big Boeing 777-328, wide-body jetliner, everything went quiet. As the effects of suffocation reduced Collin's eyesight into an ever-narrowing tunnel-effect, he looked about and found Lydia's still form sprawled on the aisle carpeting, on the other side of the cabin.

Chapter 6

The jetliner jerked violently and all at once oxygen masks dropped from overhead panels around the cabin. *Too little too late*, Collin thought. He knew he was dying. Feeling detached from his own body he was already resigned that he was falling away … slipping deeper and deeper into the void.

★ ★ ★

He awoke, lying back in a seat. A mask was strapped securely over his nose and mouth. A blanket was spread across his body. As awareness of his surroundings returned, Collin noticed the temperature in the cabin wasn't nearly as frigid. It was bearable. He tried to sit forward but his head throbbed to the point he had to lean back again.

Turning his head, he saw he was still in the upper first class section. Someone had gotten him onto a seat. Collin pulled the mask away from his face and tested the air. He could breathe normally.

DiMaggio and Tink, standing and talking to each other, were near the forward bulkhead.

"What happened?" Collin asked them, his throat dry and raspy-sounding.

DiMaggio crossed in front of two center aisle seats and knelt down next to Collin. "The oxygen masks are what happened. Thanks to you. A few of us got to them just in time."

Collin noticed others lying prone throughout the cabin; most still had oxygen masks over their mouths and looked unconscious. "How did you move them? Most of these guys are huge," Collin asked, eyeing little Tink, who'd joined DiMaggio's side.

"Believe it or not, it was Humph. The guy did almost all the heavy lifting ... although moving Bubba took both of us to get him up into a seat."

"And there's air again?" Collin asked, slowly getting to his feet.

"We were just talking about that. Just guessing, but we think the spaceship moved into space for a while ... where it opened like it did when it sucked in half of Texas. After that, the ship must have come back down to Earth ... maybe to suck up more metal."

"The air we're breathing isn't ... right," Tink said, scrunching up her nose.

Collin noticed there was something funky about the air too. "Maybe the ship didn't return to Earth. Maybe we've moved on to some other planet."

"That's the other thing we were talking about. The constant screeching," DiMaggio said, his eyes looking upward as if searching for something beyond the confines of the cabin.

Before he could respond, Collin heard something. It was muffled and far-off sounding, but he definitely heard it too: a series of sounds that were a cross between a lion's roar and the screech of a hawk.

"I don't like the sound of that," Collin said. Maybe they really had stopped at another world. One thing was for sure ... there were other survivors out there.

"And I'm going to cap its ass if it comes anywhere near me." Humphrey had entered the cabin and was brandishing a handgun Collin recognized as a Glock 19. His father owned the same model; Collin had fired it hundreds of times at the firing range—something he and his dad had done together on Saturday mornings.

"Don't point that thing at me," Tink spat.

"Where'd you get the gun, Humph?" Collin asked, eyeing the weapon warily.

"Found it in some dead dude's satchel in one of the railcars. And don't call me that, Sticks."

"You know how to use it? It's not a toy—"

"You just don't know when to shut up, Sticks. Any douchebag knows how to shoot a gun … you just point and pull the trigger." Collin nearly jumped out of his skin when Humph suddenly fired off two rounds toward the back of the plane.

Kids shot up in their seats while others rushed in from the other cabin.

Bubba filled the bulkhead opening, looking ready to kill. "What's all the mo-fo shootin' about?!"

Humph smiled and blew onto the end of the pistol. "There's a new sheriff in town, folks. I've got us covered."

"And that's two rounds lost that we might need. You're truly an idiot, Humph," Collin said, leaning forward—his right fist clenched so tight his knuckles looked white.

Humph turned the gun toward Collin and everyone went quiet. Collin kept his eyes on Humphrey's face—his arrogant, condescending smile; his brooding hate-filled eyes.

"Bro … you need to put that piece away. Sticks is right. There's something out there and you takin' pot-shots in the plane is dumb-ass." Bubba took a step forward, his towering hulk looking far more threatening than the gun held in Humphrey's hand.

Humph continued to smile as he slid the Glock into the waistband at the back of his pants.

"You might want to think about putting the safety on that weapon, Humph … unless you want to have two ass holes,"

Collin said.

Humphrey laughed it off while pulling the Glock free and setting the safety. He replaced it back into his waistband and smiled over at Bubba. He held a fist out in front of himself. "It's put away. We cool, man?"

Bubba hesitated and then reluctantly bumped the outstretched fist with his own. "Yeah … sure … we cool."

"Um … we need to eat," Collin said, getting up out of the seat. "With auxiliary power going, we can start warming up some of the ready-made meals they offer folks in first class."

Collin entered the galley kitchen where three teen boys were leaning against the counter tops, blankets draped over their shoulders, and drinking from an assortment of little liquor bottles. Apparently someone'd said something funny because all three were laughing hysterically.

"Hey, Frost, you come to party?" Clifford Bosh, the Lone Stars' high-scoring wide receiver, asked, holding up a small, unopened Smirnoff bottle. The other two, Owen Platt and Garry Hurst—both running backs—let their laughter subside as they brought their attention to Collin.

"Maybe later. Hey, Hurst, let me get by you. I think there's some ready-made meals in that cart behind you."

Hurst used a forearm to slide his collection of still-unopened bottles down the countertop and took a possessive position there. Collin found the top handle on the recessed cart and gave it a pull. It shook but didn't come free.

"Wait, you gotta unlatch it, man," Owen said, leaning over to the red latch mechanism at the top of the cart. Unsteady on his feet, he needed several tries before the lever finally turned sideways, out of the way.

"Thanks," Collin said, rolling the refrigerated cart free and out into the galley. He opened the top drawer and found a row of foil-topped meal containers. He touched the first one. "Still cold."

It took him several minutes to figure out the controls for the row of top-mounted ovens. With the help of Clifford, Owen and Garry, they got the cold meals loaded into the ovens and the meal heating process started.

★ ★ ★

Collin ate with DiMaggio and Tink and several cheerleaders he didn't know very well.

"So what's next?" DiMaggio asked, his mouth full of chateaubriand steak and gravy. "We can't stay here forever."

Tami Drake said, "We're going to need a change of clothes." She and the other girls were wrapped in blankets. "You guys have pants on … we're wearing miniskirts."

"It's not like we can pop down to Macy's for a new wardrobe, Tami," DiMaggio said.

"There may be clothes below," Collin said. "I'm guessing this plane was in the process of pre-boarding … I mean, it makes sense since the food carts were filled. You never know, we could check to see if they'd started loading luggage into the cargo section."

"What we really need is another weapon," DiMaggio said. "You saw it … Humph's not going to give up his gun and he's probably not the best person to protect us all …"

Collin remembered seeing a diagram of the jetliner in the pilot's manual. There was an access door in the rear galley at the back of the plane. "What do you say we do some exploring? Probably best not to mention where we're going to Humph, or any of his friends."

Tina and Tami said they wanted to come with them. "Let's make our way to the back of the plane … but let's not go in a group," Collin added. "I'll meet you all there in a few minutes."

Collin was the first to stand and head down the stairs. He moved through the plane's business, then economy, compartments. He was surprised when he entered the galley to see the ceiling drooping at least another foot. The weight of the passenger car on top of this portion of the plane's fuselage was taking its toll. He figured it was only a matter of time before this section was flattened like a pancake.

Hunching over, he'd missed it earlier when he'd first entered the galley. There it was on the carpeted floor: a two-by three-foot door panel with an inset handle. Tami and Tink arrived together, followed by DiMaggio a minute later.

Collin tugged the metal ring out from the inset on the panel, turned it and pulled upward. The panel opened on its hinges. He swung the panel all the way back and the four of them stared down into the darkness. Cold air rose up from below, into the galley.

"I'll go first," Collin said. He turned on his flashlight app, placing his iPhone between his teeth, and stepped onto the top step of the metal-wrung ladder. He tried not to think about what was below him, in the cold, dark, cargo hold. He descended into the hold, one cautious step at a time. By the time his feet hit the cargo compartment's floor he already knew two things: one, there definitely was luggage there—two, the cargo doors were wide open.

Chapter 7

What looked to be a late model combine machine was pressed up against the outer hull of the jetliner, where the cargo doors once stood. Collin stepped closer and was able to see a myriad of other things packed in behind it, including an old, rusted-out Chevy Ranchero; a segment of a Ferris wheel; wide blades of a windmill; and the cab section of a fire truck.

Collin turned back to see Tink already going through a large Samsonite at the top of a heap of suitcases. She held up a pair of silk underpants and pulled them wide between her open arms. "Someone's grandma is missing a parachute," she exclaimed, closing the lid and moving on to another suitcase.

Collin turned and sidestepped past Tami Drake's own five-foot-high stack of suitcases. DiMaggio had already torn into half the suitcases in his stack and had a separate pile of items set off to the side.

Collin went farther back in the compartment where there were larger items, including hooded golf bags, several sets of skis, and some oversized duffle bags. Right off the bat, Collin hit pay dirt. He found two long, one short, green and tan camo hard cases. Each was individually locked. He'd seen these types of cases before at the shooting range—often used by serious gun enthusiasts. As Collin continued to separate out the items in his stack, he found several cases that matched the other camo cases. He put them aside, in their own pile, and continued to seek what else could be of use.

He unzipped a large black duffle and found neatly stacked T-shirts, boxers, socks, and green army-issue pants inside. He pulled out a pair of pants and held them up. Might be a little big, but looked long enough. He looked over to the others and saw they were still busy digging through their own stacks of luggage. Quickly, Collin pulled off his football pants, jockstrap and cup, and pretty rank-smelling jersey. He then pulled on the clean boxers, T-shirt and army pants. He found a belt for the pants in the duffel, as well as a pocketknife, a small first-aid kit, and a pair of well-used boots.

The boots were a pretty good fit. He checked the duffle one more time—he'd almost missed the most important item … a set of small keys tucked into a side pocket—the kind used for unlocking weapon hard cases. Collin suspected the duffle, and the clean clothes he was wearing, were owned by the same person owning the set of gun cases.

Collin's attention was pulled away when he heard other voices entering the dimly lit cargo hold. Two were unmistakable—Humphrey's and Darren's. Crap. There was no way he was going to hand over more firepower to those two idiots.

Collin hunched down lower, doing his best to keep out of sight. But it was too late—Darren was quickly making his way through the stacks of suitcases.

"He's over here," Darren yelled back over his shoulder, picking up his pace.

Collin tried the first of the keys on the small hard case. Not the right key. He fumbled to get the second key into the lock. It worked. He turned the lock and opened the lid. Inside were three secured handguns—two Glocks, similar to the one Humphrey was carrying around, and a Beretta. One by one, he checked the weapons—all unloaded. That made sense. Collin was pretty sure there were strict airline transport regulations for firearms. Noticing the various official-looking tags affixed to the case's handle confirmed as much. Fortunately, the weapons' magazines were stored in the box as well.

"There you are ... what are you doing hiding back here, Sticks?" Darren asked.

Collin didn't look up until he heard the other voice.

"Step the hell away from that, Sticks," Humphrey demanded, his voice deep and threatening. He was two paces behind Darren and was reaching for the Glock at the back of his pants.

Collin, still holding the Beretta in his right hand, grabbed the matching magazine with his left. He slipped the clip into the butt of the handle, locked it home with the heel of his palm, then pulled the slide and chambered a round.

Collin brought the gun up and pointed it directly at Humphrey's forehead. Humphrey had his gun out but hadn't had time to aim.

"Don't!" Collin said.

Humphrey froze.

"Hey, man, we're all on the same side," Darren said, holding his palms up in a gesture of friendship. He smiled and turned back to Humphrey. "Put your gun away, Humphrey. Let's keep things cool here."

Humphrey hesitated, then did as he was told. Collin debated whether to relieve Humphrey of his weapon but decided, instead, to just keep a close eye on him.

"So, ah ... what have you got there, Frost?" Darren asked, his eyes locked on the open hard case and the other handguns lying in front of Collin.

"A way to defend ourselves. That is, other than Sheriff Humph there and his Glock."

It started with a wobbling motion. Collin reached out for something, anything, to grab on to. The cargo hold began to tilt—the far tail section dropped as the nose section, where they were standing, rose up several feet. Everyone was thrown to the floor. Sounds of bending and twisting metal increased, soon culminating in a loud crash. Everything came to a shuddering stop. The sounds—the tilting of the plane's angle—spoke for themselves: The tail section of the plane had collapsed under the weight of the passenger car above.

Getting to his knees, Collin saw that more than the tail section had collapsed—nearly half the plane was gone. He got to his feet and yelled, "DiMaggio! Tink … Tami!"

Darren and Humphrey got to their feet, too, and stood looking back at the jet's significantly reduced cargo hold.

"I'm okay," came DiMaggio's voice.

"What happened?" asked Tink weakly.

Collin let out his breath in relief.

"Tami … Oh God. She was farther back. She's under there," DiMaggio said, the emotion heavy in his voice.

As much as Collin liked Tami, all he could think about was Lydia. How far back in the plane above had she been when everything collapsed? Was she lying dead beneath tons of twisted metal above them?

"We're trapped. We're fricking trapped!" Darren said angrily. He spun toward Collin. "It was your brilliant idea to come down here. Now we're going to die in this little hell hole and it's your fault."

"I didn't ask you to come down here. In fact, we purposely didn't tell you where we were going. Have you even thought about who might be dead up in the passenger area?"

Darren's expression went from anger to fear in a millisecond. "Crap! Bubba … all the guys … the team."

"Yeah … and how about Lydia … you at all worried about her?"

Collin's question stunned him. "We have to get back up there. Maybe there's another access panel." Almost frantic in his movements, Darren started pacing and looking upward toward the ceiling of the cargo hold.

"There's no other access to above. At least not where you're looking," Collin said.

Humphrey's cold stare bore down on Collin. "Then where, Frost? How do we get out of here?"

DiMaggio and Tink, a layer of white dust covering their hair and faces, joined Collin's side. Collin knew DiMaggio was close to Tami; he'd wanted to ask her out ever since their freshman year—but lacked the courage.

"I'm sorry, Paul. Tami … She was …" Collin didn't know what to say. He didn't know how to put words to something so terrible.

DiMaggio simply nodded, his eyes beginning to well up with tears.

"You can cry about her later," Humphrey said. "Frost, stay focused! Did you have an idea how to get us out of here?"

Collin smacked a magazine into one of the Glocks and handed it—along with one of the holsters—over to DiMaggio.

"You giving that last one to me?" Darren asked.

Collin stood and appraised Darren with disgust. He looked over to Tink, who shook her head.

"Not me … I hate guns."

Minutes earlier he'd had no intention of giving Darren or Humphrey another weapon. Now things were obviously different. Leaving any of the weapons he'd found behind would be crazy. Collin picked up the remaining Glock, slid in the last remaining magazine, and handed it over to Darren.

He took it and nodded, "Cool."

Collin handed him the last remaining holster. "You'll need this too."

"We'll each need to carry a load." He looked over to Humphrey. "That means you too, Humph."

"What the hell you talking about? I'm not carrying crap…

if there's a way out of here, I'm gone ... before I'm flattened."

"Whatever ... Help me out here, DiMaggio," Collin said, pointing to the two longer hard cases on the floor. DiMaggio passed one of the cases, and then the second, to Collin, who placed them on top of the waist-high stack of remaining satchels and suitcases. Collin used his keys to open the first of the cases and flipped up the lid. The five inhaled.

"Nice," Darren said.

Collin opened the next case. Now there was little doubt the guns, one a Heckler and Koch MP5, the other an MK48—both machine guns—had belonged to someone in the military. The weapons looked to be fully automatic and neither one was legal to own by civilians—strictly for use by the military.

Chapter 8

Collin, Tink and DiMaggio began transporting the stash of weapons over to the now significantly smaller cargo opening. Five of the largest duffle bags were quickly repacked with various needed clothing items. Darren and Humphrey reluctantly hefted them over to where the weapons lay.

"We'll have to go through here," Collin said, gesturing to the blocked cargo opening.

"No way. Have you looked at that wall of crap? Stuff's packed together way too tight," Humphrey said, shaking his head.

Collin stepped over to the opening and knelt down. "We'll have to go down first, then go up again. We're standing right below and behind the left wing. I'll go first … find a pathway in this mess and get up on the wing. There's a cabin door there."

Tink was already on the move. "I'll go with you, I'm small."

Collin turned to DiMaggio and said under his breath, "Watch the weapons."

"How do we know you'll come back for us?" Darren asked, his voice sounding more shaky than he'd probably intended.

"Because I wouldn't leave DiMaggio," Collin said flatly.

Tink, crouched down low at the forwardmost part of the cargo opening, said, "I don't see a way out through here, Collin."

"This is where we'll need to work as a team." He turned to Darren, the biggest of the four of them. "We need you three to help lift and separate the closest metal items here."

"Like hell," Humphrey said. "Stuff's too tightly packed."

Collin moved close to Tink and used his boot to kick at what looked like an old bicycle frame. It moved. "There's a significant amount of play between everything. Looks like things are clustered mostly here, at the opening. Help get us through here and we should be able to maneuver around in there … at least that's the plan."

"Found this. You'll need it more than we will here." DiMaggio handed Collin a small bright red Maglite.

Collin moved the Beretta from the back of his pants to one of the pants' oversized pockets. "DiMaggio … you lift here, at the back of this freezer unit. Darren and Humphrey, you'll actually need to push up on this and down on that," Collin said, gesturing.

DiMaggio moved into place, got a good hold on the metal coils at the back of the freezer, and lifted. It moved. He looked over to Darren and Humphrey. "Are you going to help or just stand there?"

They both took up the positions where Collin had indicated and got their hands firmly situated.

"You're going to die in there, you know. Just letting you know," Humphrey said.

"Shut up and push, Humph," DiMaggio said.

The three began to push and pull. Tink hesitated, as if having second thoughts, then moved headfirst into the now two-foot-square opening.

Collin waited until her feet disappeared into the darkness beyond.

"Move it, Sticks, this is heavy!" Humphrey yelled.

DiMaggio nodded his agreement. Collin, like Tink, crawled in headfirst. There was enough light to see Tink moving around. She'd come to a stop. "I think you were right. We'll have to move down first before we can move back up.

There's a big metal shed blocking the way."

"Yeah, try going down." Collin watched as she moved a few smaller items—a plastic lawn chair and a mailbox—out of the way. This time she went through the opening feet first, slowly lowering herself until she found something unseen below to stand on.

Collin transferred the Maglite from his hand to between his teeth and began to follow her. Only her head was now visible. Looking back at Collin, Tink's eyes widened to the size of silver dollars. "Oh my God!"

"What? Did you cut yourself? What is it?"

"I felt something move."

"There's a lot of stuff … things are going to move … shift around."

"No, Collin! Something alive. It had fur."

He saw Tink trying to look down at her feet through all the clustered stuff.

"Just keep going. Probably a squirrel or something."

"It's the 'or something' that scares me."

Collin watched as Tink disappeared. The sound of metal objects being pushed aside let him know she was okay. "Finding a way through down there?" he asked, maneuvering his own feet into the narrow opening.

"Yeah. There's actually more room to move around in, once you get down here. Come on down."

Collin wasn't having quite as easy a time maneuvering as Tink, but he eventually got into the open space where she was waiting. He took the Maglite from between his teeth and played the beam around them.

"There. We can crawl back up the other side of the shed, right there," Tink said.

Collin saw what she was referring to. "What is that?"

"I think it's a jungle gym, lying on its side." Tink half

crawled, half slid, over to the metal bars and began pulling herself up through the lattice of rounded metal. "It's like a ladder … easy-peezy."

Collin followed right behind her. As she climbed nearly straight up, he was prepared to follow when his flashlight caught something in its beam: two intensely bright green eyes thirty feet away.

"You know, it might help if you'd shine that light in front of me so I can see where I'm going," Tink said, looking down at Collin. Curious, she followed the beam of the light. "Oh crap. What the hell is that?"

"Probably a cat. Just keep going." She began climbing twice as fast as before.

Collin too climbed fast. What he hadn't mentioned to Tink was that he'd seen, in the dim light, more than something with two eyes. The partial face wasn't that of a cat—or a squirrel—or any mammal he was aware of on Earth. This creature looked like a person … a man—but one covered in fur. A wolf man. His mind flashed back to the old black and white Lon Chaney movie. "Keep going, don't stop," Collin urged.

"You think?" Tink retorted. "We have a problem," she said.

You have no idea, Collin thought. "What is it?"

"The wing. It's right above me and I can't see a way … wait. Okay, I can crawl off to the side here."

He heard her kicking again and then the sound of something heavy falling. "Tink?"

Nothing … Collin's body tensed. "Hey Tink … you okay?"

Still nothing.

Finally her voice came, "I'm fine. I think I found a way through here."

"I'm coming." Collin got to the underside of the wing

and listened for Tink. He again held the flashlight between his teeth and noticed the beam was vibrating. Had he ever been this scared in his life? There was a creature lurking nearby, probably hungry, and Tink had chosen a path that went right in its direction. Collin crawled through the debris around him double-time. His knee hit something hard and an intense pain shot through his leg. He looked down and saw his pants were ripped and there was blood. *Crap!* He touched the wound with his right hand and assessed the damage. Probably could use a few stitches, but he'd live.

There was a noise to his left. He pointed the Maglite in the general direction. All he saw was more junk.

"I'm on the wing! I made it!"

"Good, hold tight … I'm coming." He wiggled through an area that wasn't much wider than his own body and wondered how the other guys, all quite a few pounds bigger and heavier than he was, would make it through here. Eventually he pulled himself through and, sure enough, found the back edge of the wing.

"What was that down there, Collin?" Tink's voice was barely a whisper. He saw her feet. He wiggled out of the shaft he'd just maneuvered through and held up his hand. "Give me a hand, will you?"

Using two hands, she pulled until Collin was able to crawl up onto the wing.

"Answer me!"

"I don't know." He got to his feet. The plane was crushed—at least half of it was. The passenger railcar took up the space where the rear of the plane used to be. Collin and Tink exchanged glances.

"They might all be dead, Collin. They may have all moved toward the back of the plane and gotten crushed."

Collin had to duck his head. Above them, an eighteen-wheeler's big aluminum trailer lay on its side. It slanted upward, propped onto the top of what remained of the 777's fuselage.

"Let's see if anyone's home." Collin sidestepped a metal file cabinet and moved over to the jetliner's emergency exit. He looked in through the little porthole window. There were still cabin lights on. He pounded his fist against the door … bang bang bang.

Within seconds there was movement inside. "I see movement," he said. It was still too dim inside to see who was in there. "It's me … Collin. Open the door!"

He heard excited murmuring—elevated voices inside. Then came a series of sounds, like the latch mechanism being worked, and the door, now unsealed, was pushed outward. Collin and Tink stepped backward as the big door swung open. The first person to greet them was Lydia. She rushed into his arms.

Chapter 9

Lydia pulled away. "Are you the only one left? Did the rest …" Her eyes welled up with tears. "Did Darren … die down there?"

Collin's heart sank, but his face gave no indication of his disappointment. "No, Darren's fine. Same with Humphrey and DiMaggio. As you can see, Tink is fine, too. We lost Tami, though."

Lydia brought a hand up to her mouth as if choking on what she had to say. "There were a few back in the tail section. They were getting ready to go below. Bobby Lopez, Ryan Mansfield, and Brianna Gould … all are dead. They'd have to be dead, right?"

Collin nodded and did the quick math in his head. They'd started out with somewhere around forty-eight kids. About half of those didn't make it off of the bus. Now, with Tami gone, along with the three in the tail section, there would be twenty kids left. At this rate, it seemed all of them surviving the day would be a stretch.

Collin noticed that although she had taken a half-step back, her palm was still resting on his chest. She looked so scared and vulnerable, he wanted to pull her in close … tell her everything was going to be all right, even though he knew things couldn't get much worse.

"I'm scared, Collin. We're all scared … I miss my parents. Are we going to die?"

"Nah … we'll be fine. Someday you'll be able to tell your grandkids about your adventures in space."

She nodded but clearly didn't buy the mini pep talk. "What do we do now?"

"We need to get everyone out of the plane. There's too much heavy crap on top of it … sooner or later, it'll cave in, like the tail section. Can you have everyone collect their stuff and gather here on the wing? I have to go back down … help the others come up from below."

"You're going back down there?" she asked, looking somewhat exasperated.

"Believe me, there's nothing I'd rather do less."

★ ★ ★

It took the better part of an hour to get Darren, Humphrey, and DiMaggio, as well as the weapons and duffle bags, transferred up to the wing. The latter aspect was pretty much left to Collin and DiMaggio to do on their own, since Darren and Humphrey said they'd rather leave everything behind than take on that extra work. While Collin checked out his still-oozing knee, which had begun to throb, he told DiMaggio what he'd seen—what he thought he'd seen, anyway. At this point he was less and less sure. He was fairly sure the mind played tricks on someone under this kind of stress. Just the same, they both kept an eye out for something furry and green-eyed.

Collin, thankful for his own forethought, brought the automatic weapons up last. There was no way he was going to leave them lying around for Darren and Humphrey to grab up while he was climbing around under tons of junk metal. What the survivors had done, though, was rifle through the bags of clothes—much of which were now haphazardly strewn all over. Tink was in the process of repacking things when Collin lifted himself over the top of the wing and sat with his legs hanging over the edge. DiMaggio passed up the heavy duffel, holding the weapon cache. Collin looked up when he noticed someone standing behind him. Surprised, he saw it was Bubba. He had on a pair of green army pants from the baggage supply, but they were clearly too snug for him around his thick legs.

"Hand it up," he said.

Collin momentarily debated if he should oblige him but figured the big guy had little idea what was in the duffle bag anyway. Bubba took hold of the handles with one hand and lifted the duffle up and away.

"What the hell you got in there?" he asked, now using both hands to carry the bag to the center of the wing.

Collin waited for DiMaggio to reach his hand up and, when he did, Collin pulled him up next to him on the wing. DiMaggio was sweating and out of breath. In the background they heard Darren's voice.

"Listen up, everybody. Gather round … chop chop," he said, waving his hands in toward his body.

Collin and DiMaggio ignored the directive, preferring to stay seated where they were. Lydia moved in close to Darren and he swung an arm around her shoulders. Several of the guys who'd been inside the plane came out and were now huddling around their quarterback. Collin noticed Bubba stayed where he was. He crossed his arms over his broad chest. "What's this about, man?"

Darren combed his fingers through his long hair and smiled. "It's about what we're doing next. We can't have everyone going off in their own direction … we just need a few minutes to strategize." Some of the cheerleaders were speaking among themselves, which brought a loud shush from Humphrey.

Darren glanced over to Collin and continued: "The jetliner isn't safe, as we've discovered. So we need to move our base to a new location. For now, we can stay back in the railcars."

"Uh … railcars are full of a bunch of dead guys," Clifford Bosh said, looking like he wanted to vomit.

"Well, we'll have to move them out of there … won't we?" Darren said.

"What about food? All the food's still here … on the plane," Garry Hurst added.

Darren chewed his lip for a second before looking over to Collin.

After several long beats, Collin said, "If we limit the number of people going in and out of the plane, that might be okay."

"And to drop a brick?"

"Yeah, same thing. Get in and out of the heads fast. Limit the amount of people inside the plane at any one time. That's my suggestion, anyway."

"Good. So that's what we'll do. Let's get moving. Everyone needs to help," Darren barked.

As the group started to disperse, Collin, DiMaggio, and even Bubba stayed put. Humphrey took a step closer. "You got a problem, Sticks? You too important to heft a few bodies?"

Collin said, "I need to take care of something else. I'll take DiMaggio, if he wants to come with me."

"And where's that?" Humphrey asked.

"To do a little reconnaissance. Back up to the top of the pile. I'm thinking at some point we'll need to take control of this space vessel … at least try to. That, or wait to suffocate the next time that big aperture opens up to outer space again."

"Did you forget you're just a skinny teenager, Sticks? Do you really think you can go up against a bunch of advanced aliens?" Humphrey asked, shaking his head.

Collin shrugged, but stayed quiet.

"I'm with you, Frost," DiMaggio said.

"Yeah … I'm with them, too," Bubba said, looking bigger and meaner than ever. He stared back at Humphrey, as if daring him to say something. Collin was surprised Bubba wanted to come along. He unconsciously rubbed his upper arm where, not so long ago, Bubba had been mercilessly punching him.

Collin spent the next few minutes familiarizing himself, DiMaggio and Bubba with the automatic weapons they'd collected. What they really needed was practice shooting the damn things. But with the limited amount of ammunition they'd found, that wouldn't be a good idea. They determined Bubba would carry the MK48 and Collin the MK5, and each would bring along a small rucksack, holding food provisions and other odds and ends.

Most of the group had already left to deal with the bodies in the railcars. Darren and Humphrey were still on the wing, talking between themselves. Collin seriously doubted either one of them would get anywhere near a dead body. They both looked up as Collin approached.

"We're heading out."

"You're taking those weapons with you? Don't you think that's a little selfish, Sticks?" Humphrey asked.

"You both have weapons. Speaking of which, there's something you should be aware of … I think I saw something down there, in the pile."

"Saw something like what?" Darren asked.

"It may have been nothing. It may have been my eyes playing tricks on me."

"Just spit it out, for God's sakes," Humphrey spat.

"I think I saw something alive. It wasn't a squirrel or anything like that. It was the size of a man and covered in fur."

Both Darren and Humphrey simply stared back at Collin for a long moment. Eventually Darren said, "You better not be pulling my chain—"

"I'm not. I'm just telling you so you'll keep an eye out. It's one more reason I'm going to look for a way out of here." For the first time, Collin saw the two teens not as thugs, but as what they really were—two scared boys in way over their heads.

Chapter 10

Collin took up the lead and together the three made their way again into the mass of junk. They headed straight up from the edge of the wing. Collin and Bubba had their rifles strapped across their backs, leaving both hands free to climb. DiMaggio, bringing up the rear, was in charge of marking their course. He'd ripped small strips from a bright yellow Hawaiian T-shirt and was tying them on to whatever was handy as they went along.

After climbing for close to an hour, Collin stopped and rechecked his leg. He saw that it was getting infected—yellow-white puss was forming around the outer edge of the open gash. He retied a piece of cloth around the wound and looked down at Bubba and DiMaggio.

"There's a lot more than when we first got here. They must have made another stop."

"They definitely did," DiMaggio said from below. "Look at this." He held up an automobile license plate—only this one was significantly different from anything they'd seen in Texas. "It's got RUS on it ... I'm betting this is Russian. They probably stopped there for another load."

That made sense. For the past ten or fifteen minutes, Collin had noticed the metal items he'd been crawling around were not typical of what he was used to seeing. He'd seen the tail end of an automobile that definitely wasn't produced in Detroit.

They continued upward for another twenty minutes before Collin, his voice somewhat muted, said, "We're near the top. I can see light coming in from above ... and something's moving around up there. Try not to make too much noise."

Collin came up beneath an overturned aluminum fishing boat. It smelled of seawater and the inside was caked with what could only be remnants of fish guts. DiMaggio and Bubba joined him and both scrunched up their noses.

"What's that noise out there?" Bubba asked.

"Let's go see." With Collin in the lead, they crawled downward and sideways, between several old-style school desks, and reached the surface. Collin found he was wrong when he'd thought the spaceship was filled to the max. There was a lot more stuff jammed in now than there was before. Mountains and mountains more stuff! But that wasn't what captured Collin's attention. Two football fields' distance away was something that could potentially change everything.

It was a small spacecraft of some kind—small only in the sense that it was a fraction of the size of the craft they were trapped in. Cigar-shaped, it was about the size of a naval submarine, but the similarities ended there. It was drab brown and had multiple thrusters around its circumference, midway along its fuselage, and two bigger ones at the tail end of the ship. The other thing keeping Collin's eyes glued to the spaceship was that it was apparently trying to take off.

"That thing's beat to crap," Bubba exclaimed.

The vessel was only able to lift off another mountain of metal by ten feet or so before conking out and dropping back down.

"Let's go … that might be our ticket out of here." Collin moved as quickly as he could while maintaining his balance over the rough terrain.

It wasn't long before the spacecraft ceased trying to get airborne. Good, Collin thought. It would do them little good if it took off and left them behind. Halfway to the vessel, DiMaggio abruptly stopped. Bubba careened into his back and both toppled over.

"What is it?" Collin asked.

DiMaggio got back to his feet and pointed off to the side. Collin was surprised he'd missed it. He could have thrown a rock and hit it.

"The other bus," Bubba said in a near whisper.

No one had talked about it—not one student had mentioned it. Perhaps it was just too unimaginable to go there ... there had been two buses coming back from the game away. This one, nearly identical to the one they had been riding in, held the younger freshmen and JV kids, as well as the four coaches. The three teens stood, deflated. The bus was crushed—flattened to less than half its previous height. Collin scanned the line where the row of windows used to be.

The sound of the spacecraft again attempting to gain altitude brought them back to the job at hand. Collin ushered them forward. "Come on, we're almost there."

They were close enough now to feel the effects of the ship each time it crashed down onto the metal mountain below it. "One thing's for sure," DiMaggio said, "there's an idiot alien driving that ship. Repeatedly crashing down like that can't be good. Asshole's going to wreck the damn thing before we can even steal it."

For some reason that struck Collin as funny and he laughed out loud. The other two chuckled as they all cautiously approached. Collin and Bubba unslung their automatic weapons. Collin flipped the safety off and watched as Bubba did the same. DiMaggio had his Glock out and the three of them hesitated, cringing as the ship clattered down once again, twenty yards ahead. They took cover behind the haunches of a giant statue of a horse and its uniformed rider. Collin was pretty sure it was Civil War era.

The ship sat stationary again, heat emanating from the now-quiet rear thrusters.

"What do we do now?" Bubba asked. "It's not like we can just knock on the door."

There was no reason to respond. The ship's pilot had ventured outside and was now standing, with his hands on his hips, staring back at the ship. Much as Collin, Bubba and DiMaggio were doing.

"Is that your wolf man, Frost?" DiMaggio whispered.

Bubba looked at Collin with a furrowed brow.

"I saw this guy when we were crawling around outside the jetliner. Wasn't sure then if I was seeing things."

"You definitely weren't seeing things."

They continued to watch the furry creature as he now strutted around the outside of the vessel. He wore no clothes and the likeness to a wolf man was less so, now that Collin saw him standing in the dim green light from above.

"We got to do this," Bubba said.

Collin's nod was subtle. He didn't like it. But one thing was clear: these weren't normal times. Their very survival depended on doing things they weren't remotely comfortable with.

Collin stood, aimed his MK5, and fired two rounds at a point near the alien's feet. Startled, the alien crouched down and spun on his heels. He noticed the three humans—each pointing a weapon at him.

Collin rushed forward. "Walk with me, spread out to the sides."

The furry alien stayed perfectly still, his eyes moved between the three—eventually settling on Collin.

"Now what, Frost?" Bubba said.

"Um … I guess we try to communicate with him." Collin gestured with the muzzle of his rifle for the alien to rise up. He did so, slowly—standing up to his full height, several inches below Collin's own.

Taking care not to make any abrupt movements, the creature pointed to something around his neck—some kind of device. The three teens raised their weapons in unison. He shook his head and raised his palms. He tapped at it with a series of quick finger movements and then spoke. "I am no danger to you. I am not your enemy."

Chapter 11

The alien's accent was thick and his voice sounded raspy. "My name is …" He hesitated, as if trying to think of the proper way to say it. "My name is Cine."

The three boys exchanged glances. Collin said, "What are you doing here?"

Cine gestured toward the ship: "I am trying to get this broken-down heap into the air … to get off this collector ship."

Up close, Collin saw that Cine was more cat-like than wolf- or dog-like. His teeth were small and sharp and he had ears, which continually twitched, that stood straight up on the top of his head.

"Looked like all you were doing was crashing the thing," DiMaggio said.

"Is it your ship?" Collin asked.

"As much mine as anyone's. What's left of my ship is a hundred feet below us, in multiple pieces. Thanks to the Notares and this collector … what's called a sim rover … I've been marooned here for weeks."

"The Notares?"

"The beings that sent this ship to both your planet and mine."

"And it was you that I saw down below," Collin said, more of a statement than a question.

"Yes, that was me. I was looking for food. Much of my time is spent looking for food."

"Wait … How do you know about the Notares?" Collin asked, suddenly suspicious.

"The Notares began invading my home world several

years ago. We've learned much about those people, humanoids like you, over time."

Collin took a step toward the little ship. "There room in that vessel for all of us?"

The cat-like man scratched at his chin. "Yes. There's more than enough room. But, as you saw, it's not operational. It's never getting us out into space."

"So you're giving up?"

"This isn't the first time I've tried to put that ship into the air," Cine said. "It's time to give up. Don't put your hopes on that ancient wreck."

Bubba stared down at the furry man. "Just because you failed doesn't mean we will."

"And why is that?" Cine asked back, looking resigned in defeat.

Bubba looked at DiMaggio, then at Collin, and then back to Cine. "Because we're Texans … because we're Lone Stars."

Maybe because he was only the kicker—had limited time on the field—but in all the time he'd played on the team, he'd never gotten pulled into the whole rah-rah team-spirit thing. It wasn't because the Middleton High School Lone Stars were a sub-par team; they almost always won. But right now, listening to Bubba's deep baritone—the pride in his voice—Collin finally got it.

"Show us the ship," Collin said.

Cine looked like he was going to resist. Bubba stood up a bit taller and looked even meaner than normal.

"Follow me," Cine said, taking the lead toward the battered old ship.

DiMaggio leaned in close to Collin as they walked. "Is it me or does Cine speak better English than any of us do?"

"Yeah, kinda weird … huh? Keep an eye on him. I'm guessing he's a lot more dangerous than he acts," Collin added.

As they came around the far side of the space vessel, Collin had to cringe. As bad as the rest of the ship looked, this side looked downright terrible. It was dented, with several large scorch marks; Collin began having serious doubts the ship could ever get airborne.

Midway back from the bow of the ship, Cine used a recessed handle to open a seven- or eight-foot-high hatch. Before he could move inside, Collin yelled, "Hold it right there."

Cine hesitated, looked inside the dark confines of the ship, then back at the three approaching teenagers. Collin was the first to reach the hatch, brush past Cine and walk inside. There, close to the hatch, was an assortment of things lying on the deck—a toolbox of some sort, coveralls, and a weapon. About the size of his MK5, Collin guessed this one was a whole lot more advanced.

"An energy weapon?" Collin asked, picking up the gun and appraising its alien technology.

Cine reached for the weapon. "That's mine … I'll need it."

Bubba placed the muzzle of his MK48 against Cine's temple.

"Sorry. We'll keep it for now," Collin said, passing it over to DiMaggio. "Why don't you show us the ship?"

"And I thought the outside was bad," Bubba said. "What's that smell?"

Collin had to agree, the interior of the vessel was pretty horrific. Just as battered as the outside, there were also dark, rust-colored stains splashed onto the bulkheads and across much of the deck. He could only surmise it was dried blood.

Seeing Collin's expression, Cine said, "From what I've determined from the ship's log, few here survived their last attack."

Collin took in the compartment, which spanned about forty feet in width, from one side of the ship to the other, and about a quarter that footage in length. "What is this area?"

"It's an airlock. You understand what that is?"

"Yeah, I know what an airlock is."

Cine moved forward and, with a soft clang, the hatchway split apart into four segments, disappearing into the bulkhead. They entered a grimy, dimly lit corridor. "To the left are crew berths. All are identical."

As they moved forward, toward the bow, Collin noted several smaller corridors off to the left, each with numerous hatchways spaced every ten feet or so. He figured there were close to fifty individual quarters located here. Cine picked up his pace and soon they left the crew compartment and entered what looked like a galley, off to their right, and a wide-open mess area opposite it. There was a stairway off to right, just past the galley. Cine did a U-turn into the little stairwell and led the trio up to a second level.

"Hold up, Cine." Collin took in what must have been some of the ship's operational stations. Chairs, more like metal stools, were positioned in front of consoles. "What is this area?"

"I don't know. Probably environmental or geological diagnostics were done here. This is ... was ... a survey ship ... for mining, that sort of thing." He continued on toward the bow. Again, he seemed to be in a hurry.

"Hold up there, Cine."

Collin was practically jogging to keep up. "What the hell ... slow down!"

Cine didn't slow down—in fact, he bolted straight ahead for the next hatch. Like the others, the hatch separated into four segments and opened as he approached. Now sprinting after him, Collin saw Cine dive into the compartment. Barely having time to sling his MK5, he dove in right after him. He landed hard on the deck and just missed catching a grip on Cine's right foot.

It occurred to Collin that the question he hadn't asked Cine was if he was alone—if there were others on board the ship? Now he knew the answer to that question. Sprawled on the hard metal deck, what must have been the bridge, Collin looked up to see two more furry, cat-like men pointing weapons at his head.

"I'll take your weapons," Cine said.

Collin glanced back and saw that the hatch was closed. Bubba and DiMaggio wouldn't be able to help him. Slowly, Collin unslung his rifle and handed it over to Cine.

"That, too," he said, gesturing toward the Beretta holstered on Collin's hip. "Very slowly."

Collin did as told and handed that one over as well.

"You can call him Orman, our leader, and the other one is Pack."

Both of the cat-like men fingered the devices around their necks as Cine had done earlier.

"Another from the blue planet?" the biggest of the three aliens, Orman, asked Cine.

"He is their leader," Cine answered.

"I'm not the leader of anything. But I suggest you lower your weapons. That is, if you ever want to leave this ship. Cine will tell you, you're outnumbered and the people I'm with are not the type you want to make your enemy."

Orman seemed to consider this. "You and the others … you are not full grown. How is it you command your own spacecraft?"

Collin was about to correct the alien but then realized what he was alluding to: the jetliner. As far as they were concerned the ship was more than a vessel transporting people from Chicago to Los Angeles. They had no way of knowing if it could leave Earth's orbit or not. "On my planet, people my age have much responsibility. As you saw, Cine, our spacecraft was sucked up into this … what did you call it, a sim rover? We're in the same situation as you are. It makes sense that we all work together to get out of here."

"We will not be your captives," Orman said.

Collin determined two things in that instant: First, the three of them weren't the cleverest bunch. They had full leverage right now and were seemingly ready to give that away. Second, they had about them the stink of desperation. It was a term Collin's father used when he talked about people giving up … on a situation … on life.

"We … I'm not interested in keeping anyone captive. What I do want is to get my people secured on board this craft before that aperture opens up to space again. Help me do that and I'll help you get this ship functional again."

They looked at each other.

"You know how to repair this type of spacecraft?" Cine asked skeptically.

Hearing his uncertainty, Collin took a long appraising look around the small, cramped, bridge. There was a windshield, or viewing window, at the front of the compartment that looked out upon the endless expanse of the green-lit mountains of metal beyond. Inside, there were three curved consoles arranged in a U shape. Certainly more advanced than anything Collin had ever seen before, yet, compared to the cockpit of the 777, its high-tech functionality still seemed pretty basic. Where the jetliner cockpit had a myriad of switches and dials, this cockpit or bridge was all about tiny, colorful display screens. There weren't any switches, per se, but there seemed to be a method for interfacing each display that Collin would need to figure out.

Collin turned to Bubba. He knew his dad owned an auto repair shop and that he, Collin himself, was a natural with math and the sciences: physics, chemistry. If he hadn't been abducted into space, he was in line to begin a full scholarship to MIT, beginning fall semester.

The three cat-men creatures tickled the devices around their necks and began speaking in a language that sounded more like growling and purring than typical speech.

They seemed to have come to some kind of agreement. Again, with the tickling of the neck device, Orman said, "We will trust you. You will lead us out of this sim rover. After that, we will need to talk more."

Again, he's spieling this leadership crap, Collin thought. He'd never been the leader of anyone. Even the thought of it made him nervous. But, in all truth, hadn't he been leading ever since they'd been abducted? Wasn't he already taking charge? His mind went to Darren, who was comfortable in that position ... in fact he strived to always be in command. But the thought of handing the reins over to him, let Darren even try to get them out of this predicament, was ludicrous.

Collin nodded. "Let's work together ... but we'll need to work fast."

Chapter 12

Cine opened the hatch, startling DiMaggio and Bubba. Both looked up in surprise. Collin, seated at a bridge console with Orman, broke off their conversation to signal them to come in.

"Frost! You all right?" Bubba asked, looking ready to kill someone. The cat-like man looked at him warily and then at Collin.

"It's okay. We're going to work together. Truth is … our chances of survival depend on us being able to work together."

Bubba and DiMaggio looked skeptical. "Why do we need them? How do we know they won't try to F- with us later?" DiMaggio asked, his eyes never leaving Cine.

"We're going to have to trust them … just as they're doing with us right now."

Collin changed the subject. "Bubba, I was wondering if you could help us figure a way to get this ship operational. You know, since your father owns an interstellar spacecraft repair depot."

Bubba smiled at that and was about to say something when, seeing Collin's serious expression, he caught himself. "Um … I guess I could try. I am … better with the more mechanical aspects."

"That's fine. It'll be a learning experience for all of us. Orman, here, is conveying his fairly good knowledge of this spaceship. We're starting with bridge operations. Next, we'll move on to Engineering … it's there he believes there's a problem."

Bubba took a seat next to Collin.

"And what do you want me to do, Collin?" DiMaggio asked.

"I want you to take Cine with you and bring everyone back here. We need to get everyone on board as quickly as possible."

"You serious? Darren's not going to—"

Collin cut him off, holding up a hand. "Do whatever you have to do to get him and everyone else back here within the next hour or two. Do whatever you have to ... use your imagination. Hell, lie to him if you have to," Collin said with a crooked smile.

★ ★ ★

Over the next two hours Collin learned as much about the spacecraft as possible. There were times, Collin guessed, when Orman was becoming suspicious of his lack of knowledge concerning even the basics associated with space travel. It was only Collin's rudimentary understanding of physics, and what he'd learned reading Discovery magazine and watching Nova, that he was able to maintain any semblance of believability. What kept getting in the way for him was the simple fact that, at current levels of human understanding, space travel between interstellar bodies wasn't even remotely possible. According to Einstein's special theory of relativity, objects will always gain mass as they accelerate to greater and greater speeds. To get an object, like a spaceship, to move faster, you'd need to give the vessel some sort of monumental push. A spacecraft with more mass would need an even bigger push ... say, than a smaller ship with less mass. In any event, if an object did reach the speed of light, it would have an infinite amount of mass and would need an infinite amount of push, or acceleration, to keep it trucking along. There was no amount of thrust—no rocket engine, no matter how powerful—that could accomplish this feat. In fact, as far as modern Earth science was concerned, nothing could exceed the speed of light.

What Collin was inadvertently discovering was that space travel was made possible not so much by bending the rules of physics, but by compartmentalizing those rules. When Einstein was working out the fundamentals of his principles behind the relativity of time, he wasn't keyed into other, perhaps even more important, rules of physics associated with string theory and quantum entanglement. Everything changed when one type of mass was no longer the same mass we had come to understand. What we as humans in the twenty-first century believed to be hard physical laws, in reality were only one subset of a much greater theory. Just as science has observed the wave-particle duality aspects of light, what Collin was coming to terms with was that mass had the same dual attributes, under certain re-creatable situations.

Collin felt as though his head was going to explode. The more Orman spoke, the more Collin wanted to interrupt and have him go back and provide the basic principles behind the science—the barebones physics of it all. But he didn't, and eventually he was able to piece enough of it together for a novice's understanding of things. As the conversation moved to the ship's engines, which Orman referred to as drives, Collin started to feel somewhat better. Sure, he was talking of things such as dark-matter containment pods and something called the special manifold construct … which apparently let the spaceship, and all space-faring vessels, travel within some kind of bubble or shield, where the rules of physics were not only taken advantage of, but used against one another to create an entirely new form of physics.

For hours, Orman was incredibly patient and it now

occurred to Collin that he was probably well aware of the teen's ignorance of even the basics of space travel—the fundamental science behind it all. *So why is he still helping? Why continue the ruse?* The only thing Collin could come up with was the simple fact that, after several weeks of being stranded in this junk-metal hell, they'd made zero progress getting out of here. For some time, Cine had watched them back at the jetliner from a distance; maybe he had seen something in the Earth beings? Collin didn't really know and, at this point, figured it didn't much matter.

"Can you show me the engines … the drives?"

"There's only one drive." Orman stood. "Follow me."

Collin got up and saw Bubba getting to his feet as well. He'd totally forgotten about him being there. He'd been as quiet as a mouse, listening to them for hours without a single interruption.

Once Orman exited the bridge, Bubba pulled Collin in close. "Man … I had no idea you were that smart. You're like some kind of genius or something."

Collin thought Bubba was pulling his chain: rubbing in the fact that he was clueless about much of what the furry alien had spoken about. But he then realized Bubba was serious and replied, "Let's just hope they think I'm as smart as you do."

Engineering spanned two levels and was reachable from both the upper and lower decks. Orman took them through the upper deck's compartments, which were in somewhat better shape than the lower deck. The three of them entered Engineering, in the stern of the ship. This part of the craft was outright tidy compared to the rest. About the size of a modern-day Starbucks, both the compartment and sub-compartments had floor-to-ceiling technology.

Collin spun around, taking it all in. If he was out of his

element on the bridge, he was even more so here. Orman began speaking again:

"The primary power plant for this vessel is, of course, here." He gestured with a small clawed finger to a barrel-shaped section at the farthest back area of Engineering. "Like all antimatter drives, it's always in a ready state. As you can see," he stood up tall and pointed to a series of waving and fluctuating optical meters high above, "our output power levels for the anti-matter reactor are well within optimal range."

For the first time Bubba said something. "Sounds like a transmission problem to me."

Both Orman and Collin turned around to face him.

"Well, it's a drivetrain problem … If it's not the engine, which clearly it's not, it's got to be another aspect of the drivetrain. You don't have to be a rocket scientist to figure that out."

Collin was ready to signal Bubba to put a sock in it, but saw Orman actually taking an interest in what the big guy was saying.

"Show me how the anti-matter reactor connects to …" Bubba hesitated, "to the rest of the propulsion system."

Orman stared at Bubba for several beats and then walked to the other end of Engineering. Bubba followed him and looked at the complex assortment of rounded-looking canisters, tubes, lines of varying sizes, and more small display screens—which were showing fluctuating readouts of something incomprehensible to Collin.

"Can you walk me through what each of these readouts is telling us?" Bubba asked.

"I could try," Orman said. "Let's start with this one."

Collin felt a tap on his shoulder. He turned to see DiMaggio standing there. He didn't look happy.

"You're back. Everyone come back with you?" Collin asked.

"There was some trouble. You better come see."

Chapter 13

Collin and DiMaggio exited the ship and found their fellow Middleton High School teammates already assembled before them. They looked tired and, worse, dejected. All eyes fell on Collin as he moved into the center of the group. Then Collin spotted Humphrey and Darren. Both looked as if they'd been dragged behind a wagon.

"What happened to—"

"Shut up! Just shut the hell up, Sticks!" Humphrey said between clenched teeth. His face was so badly scratched that he was barely recognizable. Smeared blood was caked around his eyebrows and ears. His lower lip was swollen and cracked.

"We don't take orders from you or that freaky-looking alien either, for that matter. What were you thinking, sending them back for us like we're little children?" Darren added.

Cine was standing at the back of the group, looking no worse for wear.

Darren continued, "You do realize we've spent hours carting those stinking, disgusting, dead bodies out of the railcars … right? We're supposed to just drop what we're doing and come running when you call?"

"What happened between you and … you and Cine?" Collin asked.

"Let's just say he got a little too close to our food supplies."

"You attacked him?"

"Hey, we don't know who this freak is! All we know is he's an alien and trying to take what wasn't his."

"Well, at least you made it here. This ship is the safest place for us. There's breathable air, in case the aperture opens up, and we might be able to get it flying again," Collin explained.

"That?" Humphrey spat. "That's a ship? Because I was under the impression it was a big turd … a gargantuan big piece of shi—"

Collin cut him off. "Do you have any better ideas, Humph? You want to go back to the railcars, be my guest." Collin turned to the rest of the group and spoke louder now, "Any of you want to return to the railcars or the jetliner, be my guest. Maybe you're thinking if you just wait long enough you'll be rescued … somehow … by someone. Good luck with that. But if you're going to go, go now."

Collin continued to stare at the grimy group of teenagers. His frustration quickly turned to regret. These were kids, like him, and they'd pretty much lost everything important to them. And they were all scared and confused and probably at an emotional breaking point. Collin saw Lydia standing next to Tink at the outer fringe of the group. Both looked small and terrified. It occurred to him that what they had all gone through, clearing out the railcars, must have been one of the worst experiences imaginable. They didn't need a lecture right now … they needed a shot in the arm. They needed hope.

"This ship, this big turd-looking ship, looks almost as bad on the inside," Collin said. "With that said, there's individual cabins for each of you."

The expressions on the teens' faces lightened some. Collin even saw a few smiles. "You've met Cine. Um … we should be nice to him and his two friends. They found this ship first and we'll need their help if we're going to survive." Collin realized this was the longest speech he'd ever given in his life and suddenly felt embarrassed.

Bubba came out of the ship and walked over to Collin. "We want to try it again."

"You figure something out? Got it working?"

"I don't know **anything** about spaceships, man. But I do know simple mechanics. I think these guys have been trying to use a kind of burst mode … maybe something that's used in open space. But takeoffs and landings in an atmosphere would probably be different. I don't think it's an engineering problem, after all. I don't think they were accessing the right controls from the bridge." Bubba shrugged his shoulders.

Collin looked at Bubba's large black face. His mind flashed again to the bus ride and the obnoxious bully who'd taken delight in punching his arm. Then, there was the frightened boy-man who'd actually peed his pants in terror at being abducted. *Talk about stepping up*, Collin thought. Bubba's transformation was certainly a welcome and unexpected surprise.

"You going to just stare at me, or what?"

"I'll join you in the bridge in a minute. I need to get everyone who wants to come on board." Bubba rushed back toward the ship. Cine followed him inside.

DiMaggio said under his breath, "There's something else."

"You said to lie if I have to. I told Darren that you were waiting for him to come take charge. That he was the one everyone wanted to follow. So … he's here to take command. Sorry, I didn't know what else to do … you know, to get everyone back here."

Collin smiled and said, "That was actually a good idea. No worries." He approached Darren and Humphrey, who were now talking to several other teammates. Undoubtedly, he was conjuring up some kind of plan or scheme.

"Darren, I'd like to bring you up to speed on what's happening here with the ship. Get your thoughts on how to proceed."

Darren kept talking for several more moments before

looking over to Collin. "Looks like you've got everything already in hand. You don't need my help."

Collin looked at his smug face and then at the faces of Clifford Bosh, Owen Platt and Garry Hurst. All were loyal compatriots of Darren and Humphrey. Collin realized he'd need to take a different tack.

"We won't make it without your help. All your help. It's not a fluke the Lone Stars are undefeated for two years. You're a good quarterback, Darren … but that's not why we've won so many games."

"Oh yeah? Why else?" he asked, looking ready to throw a punch.

"You inspire. When you're not being an ass hole, you're a great leader."

"Yeah, well, I already know that," he said with a smirk. The other boys chuckled.

"Here's the thing, though. You're not going to lead us, moving forward. I am. I'm smarter than you are and I'm the best chance we have to get off this collector ship and to eventually make our way back home."

Humphrey huffed and shook his head. "Ego a bit much, dude?"

"It's not ego … it's just the way it is. So what I'm offering, what I'm hoping you'll agree to, Darren, is for you to continue to lead … but with me. We lead together."

"With you being the boss man?"

"Yeah, I guess."

All the teens, including Humphrey and DiMaggio, looked to Darren for his response. "I'll think about it."

Collin nodded but didn't say anything more. He and DiMaggio exchanged glances and the two headed for the ship. Collin abruptly stopped and turned toward the crowd. "Anyone coming with us, now's the time to decide. We're going to try to lift off in a few minutes." Collin and DiMaggio entered the battered spaceship and headed for the bridge.

Bubba was seated next to Orman at the center console. Collin sat down on Orman's right. "So, where are we at?"

Bubba said, "Seems none of us have piloted a spacecraft before." Collin looked at Orman.

"I'm a musician. All three of us are musicians from the planet Dacci. When we were sucked up into this collector ship, our vessel was transporting us, and others, to perform on a planet near our own."

That explains a lot, Collin thought. Sure, they knew more than he and Bubba about advanced technologies, but not enough to pilot this ship.

Collin got up and went to the forward observation window. He looked down and to the right. He saw the last of the group moving toward the hatch.

"Give it a second for the hatch to close. Okay ... let's see if you can get us off the ground, Bubba."

"Me?"

"What's the worst that can happen? Give it a try," DiMaggio said, standing behind him.

Bubba looked over to Orman and together they moved their hands over two different sections of the panel. Apparently, the pilot interface was just a matter of hovering one's fingers over certain areas and moving them either up or down.

Immediately, Collin felt the vibration of the drive coming alive, toward the stern of the ship. "That's a positive sign, right?" he asked.

Bubba shrugged.

"We got this far before," Orman said.

They manipulated the panel controls with fingertips and the ship rocked and shook and then, slowly, lifted into the air.

Collin watched Orman. He was ever so slightly nodding

his head. "Drives are sustaining."

Getting to his feet, Collin felt exhilarated to the point he hauled off and slugged Bubba in the upper arm. "You are the man, Bubba!"

The big defensive tackle looked ready to jam Collin into the closest bulkhead. Then he grinned, "I am ... aren't I?"

"What are those?" DiMaggio asked, pointing to a large display beneath the forward observation window. "They're moving toward us, aren't they?"

Orman's oblong-shaped eyes went wide. "Yes. They're spider droids, deployed by the sim rover. I think we're in trouble."

Chapter 14

Collin's attention was split between Bubba's not so smooth attempt to keep the ship up in the air and the three approaching droids.

"Where did they come from?" Collin asked.

"They were there the whole time. When they stop moving about they blend in with everything else. We've seen them before ... especially when we attempted to take off," Orman said.

The three mechanical spider-like droids made their way over the acres and acres of collected metal with almost graceful agility. Collin walked over to the forward observation window to get a better look. They were enormous—easily two hundred feet tall—with six spike-like thin legs that constantly moved. One of the spider droids halted and used two of its legs in unison, like claws, to move an old tugboat out of its way. Collin let out a breath; not only were those things agile, they were incredibly strong.

The ship dipped and Collin felt his stomach rise into his throat.

"Sorry, my bad," Bubba said. "I don't have the best dexterity."

"Let me try." Collin sat down next to Bubba and watched him work the controls for a while. He glanced over to Orman. "Isn't there some kind of computer assist or AI that does this sort of thing?"

"Of course there is. It's not operational. I think that's the reason this ship was abandoned. Flying a vessel like this manually is uncommon ... would certainly require special training."

"Wait a minute, I think I'm getting the hang of it," said Collin. Bubba had tried hovering his fingers splayed apart over the motion controls, but the controls seemed to respond better when his fingers kept in contact with each other. "Look, you control the pitch, yaw and roll aspects by tilting your hand around and side to side, like this ... also by tilting your hand either forward or back."

"And going straight up and down?" DiMaggio asked.

"Bubba had that figured out. You raise and lower your palm. What I'm not yet figuring out is its forward acceleration."

"Two of the spider things are approaching. I guess you have less than a minute before they'll reach us," Bubba said.

"Oh, crap ... it's right here," Collin said, using his other hand on the motion detector, directly to the left of the other one. The ship lurched forward with such acceleration it threw everyone but Collin to the deck. He'd been somewhat prepared for it. "Sorry—thing's pretty sensitive."

Orman reached over and activated something on the console. "G-force dampeners. Something else the AI would have taken care of, if it was operational."

Collin was smiling now as he confidently took better control of the ship. He brought her even with the top of the closest spider droid. They could now see its oblong central body, where all the legs joined. With amazing speed the spider droid reached up two of its spiky legs and grabbed at the ship. Collin quickly brought his right palm up higher from the motion pad and they all watched as the two spiked legs missed pinning the ship's bow by mere feet.

"That was close," Bubba said.

But everyone's relief was short-lived. All three spider droids were rapidly rising into the air.

"You've got to be kidding ... those fuckers can fly!" DiMaggio said, exasperated.

Collin moved both hands to accelerate the ship while changing their forward direction.

"They're anticipating … see … they're now coming at us from the sides as well as from the front," Bubba shouted.

"I can see that," Collin snapped back. He brought the ship lower, did a quick turn to port and flew between the droid's legs. Reflexively, two spiky legs shot forward, one making contact with the ship's hull. The sound was nearly deafening. Collin struggled to compensate for the sharp glancing blow to their stern.

"Go back up! Up! Damn it, go higher!" Bubba yelled.

"Everyone just shut up!" Collin snapped back. He brought the ship back up but wasn't fast enough to avoid the droid approaching them from the ship's starboard side. With almost simplistic ease, the droid pinned the ship between two outstretched legs. A moment later, a second droid joined in and its two spiked legs held the ship firmly in its grasp.

"Now we're really screwed," DiMaggio said.

Collin brought his hands away from the controls and sat back in his seat. "There's nothing I can do."

No one said anything as they watched the two droids carry the ship to another area.

"Where are they taking us?" DiMaggio asked.

"There's a compactor. It's huge and I suspect it's where the droids will deposit us," Orman replied.

Collin bit his lip and tried to think of something, anything, they could try. "I don't suppose this ship has any kind of weaponry?"

Orman shook his head. "I told you, this is a mining vessel." But then he sat forward. "Ships like this do have a high-powered laser gun mounted to their underbelly. It's used to open up fissures within a planet's crust … part of the excavation process."

"How do you work it? Where are the controls?" Collin asked, suddenly very interested.

"I don't know. I don't see anything on the panel, or on the others that—"

"I know where it is!" Collin was up and running from the bridge before anyone could react.

As Collin ran through the narrow corridor, he saw the startled faces of the other teens milling around turn to see what the commotion was about. By the time Collin reached the set of consoles he'd noticed earlier, located mid-ship, he'd dodged three students and knocked over Tink en route. "Sorry, Tink!"

He reached the area Cine had earlier said was used for environmental or geological diagnostics. Collin positioned himself at the console and tried to make heads or tails of the control panel before him. He moved his hands over the various motion pads and, one by one, the different systems came alive. A display activated and Collin saw movement. "What the hell am I looking at?" he asked himself.

"That's right below the ship." It was Orman, who'd crept up behind Collin without making a sound. Looking back, Collin saw a group forming behind him. Lydia stepped forward and was at his side.

"What are you doing, Collin?"

"Um ... not really sure." He now saw that Orman was right. What he was looking at were the moving legs of two droids, in unison, stepping through the junk below. They had slowed their pace and it became instantly apparent why. They'd reached the compactor, a square and substantial-looking container. Collin felt Lydia lean into him, felt the soft material of her mini skirt touch the skin on his arm.

"I'm scared, Collin," she whispered. "Are we going to die?"

"Maybe." He looked up at her and saw fear in her eyes. "But maybe not." He tried to give her a reassuring smile but wasn't sure it worked. He scanned the panel in front of him. "Where the hell is it?"

"There!" came Bubba's baritone. He pointed to an area on the panel that was closest to Collin's chest—right in front of him.

Collin moved his palm over the controls and two more sets of controls came to life. Characters were being displayed that Collin couldn't understand. He turned to see Orman studying them as well. "What does it say?"

"I think it's a measurement … no … it's a charge level. It's asking you how powerful a charge level you want the laser to use."

"Holy crap. Look, Collin, we're being lowered into that thing."

Collin didn't need to look. What he needed to do was figure out how to fire the laser. He moved his palm over the motion pad associated with the weapon and watched as the strange characters changed.

"Am I increasing the charge level or decreasing it?" he yelled.

"I don't know," Orman yelled back.

"Damn it!" Collin swept his palm again until the characters stopped changing. *Had he turned it up to max, or just turned the damn thing off?* He'd have to chance it. *Now, what do I do to fire?* Collin scoured the panel, his eyes moving from one section to the next. His gaze caught sight of the display and their furthering descent toward the compactor. Four massive block walls then separated, like the mouth of a hungry beast ready to devour its quarry.

A big black hand reached over Collin's shoulder and slapped at a section on the console that was high and to the right of Collin's own right hand. The display flashed white and then blue as the ship shook. The noise erupting was so loud Collin and those around him had to cover their ears.

The display cleared, revealing a black, smoldering orifice. Small at first with cracks and tears all around its circumference, the opening steadily began to expand—literally rip and tear outward. Within seconds the opening was now so large it even eclipsed the size of their ship.

"Look!"

Open-mouthed, Collin watched as debris started to fall through the vast opening. "We blasted a hole right through the compactor ... right through the collector ship's hull!" He watched the small display and saw the droids' legs straining—actually shaking against the forces of the now-breached depressurizing fuselage. One of the droids toppled into the blackness.

"We need to get back to the bridge," Collin said, getting up from the stool. He made quick eye contact with Lydia and made another attempt at a smile.

Bubba, DiMaggio and Orman were right on his heels as he entered the bridge. He sat down just in time to look up and see they were falling—no, being pulled—into the dark opening. He yelled, "Hold on!"

Chapter 15

"You did it!" It was Darren's voice and he sounded truly amazed. "You got us out of there."

Collin glanced back, seeing virtually all on board standing in a semi-circle outside the entrance to the bridge.

"Don't start celebrating just yet, Sticks," Humphrey said. He'd wedged himself into the bridge and was pointing to the observation window. The collector ship, which was even bigger than Collin thought, was starting to distort.

Orman also moved into the bridge area and went to Collin's side. "It's imploding! We need to get as far away from that vessel as possible."

Collin nodded, seeing his point. He looked down at the console and, for a moment, forgot everything he'd learned mere moments before.

Lydia was back at his side and he felt her hand on his shoulder. "You can do this, Collin." He looked up to see she was smiling and gently nodding her head.

"Two hands, Frost," Bubba said, moving into the seat at his left.

Collin brought his hands up and over the motion controls and began maneuvering the ship away from the sim rover.

"We need to go faster ... a lot faster," Orman said, his eyes locked on the display.

Collin noticed it too. The sim rover was starting to vent fiery explosions, which were quickly dissipating in the vacuum—the total lack of oxygen—of space.

"It's going to blow ... like a mother fu—"

The last word never left Humphrey's lips. Collin jerked his palm forward, over the motion detection pad, and the ship abruptly lurched forward just as the sim rover exploded into a magnificent fireball. Lydia fell into Collin's lap with a scream while, with the exception of Bubba, who was already seated, the others ended up on their backsides or sprawled awkwardly onto the deck.

Somehow Lydia's arms ended up encircling Collin's neck—her face mere inches from his own. Again, his eyes took in her face: the play of freckles across the bridge of her nose, the expressive lips that were curled up ever so slightly, and her eyes, taking in his own features—his eyes—in the same way. He felt her hands slide from around his neck and come to rest on his cheeks. She kissed him. It was brief and she was up and off his lap before he could do or say anything. Was that a real kiss or just a good job kiss? Collin wondered.

There was cheering and high fives and even Humphrey was throwing air punches and yelling "Yes! Yes! Yes!"

Like Collin, Bubba was leaning back in his seat. They exchanged a quick fist bump before bringing their attention back to the observation window and the total blackness of space. As the sounds of the teens' excited voices left the bridge—other, repetitive sounds began to take their place. First one, then two, then five console panel lights began to flash. The rhythmic sound of alarms soon blended into a constant stream of annoying blaring.

The three cat-like aliens had remained, still standing behind Collin and Bubba. The quiet one, named Pack, leaned in over the console.

"Hull breaches on both decks. We're also not properly filtering oxygen."

Collin's mind flashed back to the sim rover and its hull breach. "Are we in trouble?"

"We've got time … not a lot … but some." The three Daccian cat creatures hurried from the bridge.

DiMaggio took a seat to Collin's right. "Is there any way to turn that alarm off?" Collin waved his hand over the flashing lights and, one by one, the sound volume on each began to lower to a tolerable level.

Collin leaned forward, first taking in the distant stars beyond the observation window, and then, lower, on what was appearing on the group of display screens.

"We're not in Kansas anymore … or Texas, either, for that matter …" Bubba remarked.

"Or even our own solar system," Collin replied. The center display partially showed a single planet. It was primarily purple and deep amber in color, with wispy white streaks—perhaps from surrounding, high-atmospheric, cloud layers.

"What do you say we give it a break for a bit? Explore the ship … maybe get situated?" Collin suggested.

★ ★ ★

Collin descended the stairs, followed by DiMaggio and Bubba. What they discovered on the first deck were kids busy at work cleaning up the area. Tink was in the kitchen, arguing with two of the Lone Stars' defensive tackles—something about doing more work and less clowning around. The mess, or dining area, was already looking better—someone had cleaned the grime off the floors and straightened up the tables and chairs.

Moving toward the stern, the three made a right, toward crew quarters. Ahead, Collin saw most of the doorways were open. They stopped at the first set of opposing hatchways, where two big guys were conversing across the hall from each other. Bubba signaled hello, with a slight chin nod, to a similarly large black kid, Royce White, who was the Lone Stars' starting center.

Collin took a look inside the compartment and was surprised to see it still held a bunch of things—possessions left from its previous occupant. Royce was holding up a three-dimensional, almost holographic-looking, image of an alien—actually two aliens. One was, Collin surmised, an infant, sitting on the other's lap. Just like any mother and child portrait.

"I can't decide who's uglier, the mother or the kid …" Royce said, holding up the image for Collin, Bubba and DiMaggio to see. "I was just telling Panichello that he should keep it since this one looks just like his own mother."

Everyone laughed, except Panichello. "Bite me," he said, turning into his own quarters.

"Compartments are pretty nice," Collin said, taking in the bed, a small workspace that held a counter-like desk and what he assumed was a toilet, behind half a bulkhead wall.

"Is that the can?" DiMaggio asked Royce.

"I hope so or I just dropped a deuce into something I shouldn't have."

There were more chuckles. Collin continued down the corridor, waving or nodding to each cubicle's inhabitant. He noticed friends took compartment cubicles next to their friends. The cheerleaders were all bunched together in one section of six compartments next door to each other. He looked for Lydia but didn't see her in any of them.

Collin made a left and found the corridor for quarters lining the starboard side of the ship. Quarters here looked to be inhabited as well. He found Humphrey, Clifford Bosh, Owen Platt and Garry Hurst had selected compartments clustered next to each other. Continuing on, he passed another compartment. Inside, Darren was sitting on a bed in deep discussion with Lydia sitting next to him—her hand resting on his knee. Collin waved as he passed. Darren scowled and used the toe of his shoe to swing the hatch closed.

The next few compartment hatchways were wide open. Apparently no one had laid claim to these.

"I guess I'll take this one," Collin said, looking inside the small area. For the first time he noticed each had a small porthole window that looked out to the black space beyond. Bubba and DiMaggio took the next two compartments down the line from Collin's.

Collin sat on the bed and looked around the sparse space. Strange … no personal items in here, he thought. He doubted anyone had lived here when … whatever … had happened to the ship.

He heard a noise and looked back to the open hatchway. Orman stood there, looking agitated.

"What is it, Orman?"

"Looks like we'll be able to patch the hull breaches. Cine and Pack are working on the last of them now."

"So, is there some other problem?" Collin asked, unsure what Orman wanted.

"There's an incoming hail. A ship is approaching."

Collin just stared at Orman. *And this is the last thing on your list to inform me about?* he thought. He got off the bed, squeezed by Orman, and yelled down the corridor: "Bubba, DiMaggio … we've got company!"

He didn't wait for the others as he made his way out of the crew quarters, past the mess and kitchen, and back up the stairs. When he entered the bridge, it was empty. Empty except for a video image of a humanoid face on the center display, staring back at him.

Chapter 16

Collin looked for a way to open up a line of communication. The man tilted his head and furrowed his brow. Collin turned toward Orman and shrugged his shoulders.

"I already opened the channel. You can speak freely to him," Orman said.

Collin flushed, feeling stupid. He sat down and looked at the unkempt, unshaven man on the display. "Um … hello?"

Again the man's brow furrowed. He began speaking, though it took several beats for Collin to hear actual words coming from his mouth—and then they were totally out of sync.

"It takes a second for the translation to catch up. The longer you talk the more it becomes in sync," Orman said, looking exasperated at Collin's total lack of understanding modern technology.

"I am Capitano Dante Primo, Duca of the Brotherhood house of Torre, I am Captain of the *Tyrant*. I wish to speak to the commander of that vessel, boy."

Collin exchanged a quick glance with Bubba and DiMaggio. Bubba said, "That's a mouthful … tell him he can suc—"

"I'm the commander," Collin said, putting his attention back on the display.

Captain Primo looked somewhat bemused by that. "Okay … and who are you?"

"Collin Frost … I'm Commander Collin Frost." Collin purposely didn't look over to Bubba or DiMaggio; so far, they hadn't snickered or made any snide comments when he named himself commander.

"Fine. Commander Frost. I'd like to commend you on your escape from that collector ship. Can't say I've ever heard of that occurring before." Bubba began to fiddle with the console when a second display, to the left of the captain, suddenly came alive: the image of a sleek-looking spacecraft appeared. Without any nearby object around to compare its size to in open space, it was difficult to guesstimate how large a ship it actually was.

"Thank you, Captain. It was a close call."

The captain slowly nodded as if considering his next words. "That's a ... um ... mining or excavating vessel, if I'm not mistaken ... yes?" he asked.

"That's right."

"No weapons systems. So how did you—"

"Excavation laser. Turned it up to the max setting and fired away."

Primo laughed out loud and Collin heard others laughing behind him, joining in. "You have a name for that ship, Commander?"

This time Collin let his eyes quickly dart to DiMaggio before answering. "Best we can come up with is the *Turd*." He laughed again as he rubbed his forehead, trying to get serious.

"Look," said Primo, "I don't know what you're doing way out here ... surprisingly close to entering Her Majesty's outer border."

"We're not from here. We're from planet Earth. We don't know anything about a border ... or Her Majesty, either, for that matter."

Primo looked like he'd swallowed something unsavory. "That collector ship you destroyed came through a Rolm portal about eight hours ago. It was one of her ships. Our sensor readings told us it was coming from more than twenty-eight light years' distance away … from what we call frontier space."

Collin didn't know what to say to that.

"Listen, kid, you've picked a pretty nasty place to be cruising around in."

"Why's that?" Collin asked.

"There are two kinds of ships in this quadrant … those that are aligned with Her Majesty and those that oppose her."

"Who is …"

"Her Majesty? She's a goddess," he snickered. "At least, that's what her faithful minions would tell you. This is a vast solar system, with four suns and no less than one hundred surrounding planets. She is the undisputed ruler of all space within this system and she, and her council, do not take kindly to uninvited guests, travelers, interlopers … the consequences being a quick and not so glorious death at the hands of her Kardon Guard."

"Are you … a part of this Kardon Guard?"

The captain's teeth flashed white with a smile. "No, young man … I certainly am not associated with the Kardon Guard. You could say I …" he gestured to the unseen beings around him, "and all those here are on the other side of things … the side that opposes Her Majesty Queen Arabella Valora."

Collin thought her name was beautiful. He wondered if Her Majesty looked anything like her name.

"Where did you say you originated from?" Captain Primo asked.

"Earth. We need to get back there. We need to go home."

"Well … I'm sorry to tell you, but you'll be stuck here for a while." He continued to stare back at Collin for several long seconds. "I'm going to make you an offer. One you should take very seriously. Align with us, our Brotherhood, and perhaps we'll find a place for you and your kind within our fleet."

Collin didn't want anything to do with their space war, one taking place twenty-eight light years from Earth. He didn't know anything about this man's so-called *Brotherhood*, either. Why should he take for granted that Her Majesty, the one with the pretty name, would be any worse to align with than the captain?

"We'll take our chances. Perhaps we'll go back the way we came … what did you call that portal? Rolm something?"

"That's right, it's a Rolm portal. They're interspersed throughout the universe … surprised you haven't heard of them. Your problem will be getting anywhere close to it. The Kardon Guard maintain a small fleet of warships there … you'd be vaporized before you got within a light year's distance of it."

"Well, we'll just have to take our chances then, I guess."

Collin caught Bubba trying to get his attention out of the corner of his eye. Bubba spoke under his breath, "We're being pulled in toward their ship."

"Your compatriot is right, Commander Frost. Our readings tell us your AI is inoperable. I'm not so sure I could pilot a ship without an AI … it would be a challenge. How about we bring this conversation closer, to a one-on-one? We'll assist you with that."

Collin sat back and watched as the perspective on the display changed to include the Brotherhood's ship, the Tyrant, and their own slowly approaching, extremely small in comparison spacecraft. It was evident the Tyrant was four or five times the size of the Turd.

For the first time, Collin was able to make out someone else on the display. Another man was talking in low tones into Primo's ear. Primo then brought his attention back to Collin.

"Seems your physiology isn't as similar to our own as

we'd first thought. We're bringing your vessel into one of our freight bays." He pursed his lips and looked contemplative. "Apparently not only is the gravity on your home planet significantly stronger than our own but your molecular structure is also different … your physiology, too. We certainly wouldn't survive on your Earth planet … but you should be able to survive in our environment. We'll need to make special accommodations for you, though. Stand by … this will only take a few minutes."

The display went dark. Orman checked the board and said, "The connection has been broken."

Collin let his last words sink in: should be able to survive. "Orman, what do you know about this Brotherhood … or any of this?" Collin asked.

"Nothing. We're as unfamiliar to this area of space as apparently you are. You are wise to keep your options open, but you may want to play along … don't do anything to antagonize this Captain Primo. Our survival may depend on it."

Collin thought about Orman's suggestion and nodded. "Agreed. We're not exactly in any position to dictate anything, anyway. We're pretty much at his … damn … everyone's mercy."

The second display began to distort and then it too went totally black.

"They've jammed our video inputs," Orman said. "It's unsurprising they'd want to hide their technology from outsiders."

The ship shook as loud sounds from outside the hull reverberated within the confines of the small bridge. Then everything was still.

"I guess we've arrived," Collin said, getting to his feet. Collin got out of his chair and the captain also descended the stairs.

"What the hell's going on, Sticks?" Humphrey said.

Bubba, directly behind Collin, answered, "It's Commander Frost to you, Humph. We're meeting a few more aliens so we need to keep things cool … you understand?"

This was the first time Bubba had openly sided with Collin against his close teammates. Humphrey looked at Bubba with suspicion.

"Oh … He's a commander now? Give me a break. There's no way I'm calling Sticks Commander."

Humphrey and Darren realized they'd have to walk backward down the stairs to make way for those descending. Darren stopped at the bottom of the steps and held up his palms. "Just stop for a second and tell me what's happening. Can you do that, Frost?"

"I'm not real sure what's happening, Darren. Another ship just arrived and now we've been sucked over to that one. And apparently we dropped into some kind of interstellar war."

"Terrific job, Commander Sticks," Humphrey said. "You're definitely the one to be leading us. Yup, a first rate job there, Commander Sticks."

Collin ignored Humphrey and continued toward the airlock compartment. He thought about whom he wanted with him for the forced meet-and-greet. He entered the airlock and stopped at the mid-ship hatch. "Bubba, DiMaggio and Orman, please come with me. Darren, someone needs to be in charge here while I'm gone."

Darren's nod was subtle, but it was enough to convey his acceptance. "Let us know what's going on, okay?"

"I will, I promise."

Darren slapped Humphrey's chest with an open hand and the two stepped back and closed the inside airlock door. Orman initiated the opening of the outside hatch and the four waited, side by side, to greet Captain Primo.

Chapter 17

When the outer hatch opened, Collin saw eight armed, uniformed men waiting for them, pointing energy weapons of some kind in their direction. The ninth man, the one Collin recognized as Captain Primo, stood off to the right of the hatch and was inspecting the hull of the *Turd*. He rapped on its surface with his bare knuckles.

"Exotic dense metals … no wonder Her Majesty sent a collector ship into the frontier. Your little turd of a ship may not look like much, but its composition would be highly coveted in these parts." Primo looked over to Collin. "You see, it's the molecular structure of things, of everything from where you're from, beyond doubt also affected by the eons of time, since the environmental gravitational forces are far greater there."

Collin noticed Captain Primo was as tall as he was, but the similarities ended there. He was far more muscular and moved with a confidence Collin couldn't imagine ever having. Dressed in the same black trousers and dark maroon jacket the others wore, he alone wore a gold sash running diagonally across his chest. There was something cool about the way these guys dressed.

"Welcome to Notares space. Commander Frost, I presume?" he asked, holding out his hand, like someone from Earth would do. "Is it customary for your people to shake hands on Earth?" Primo asked.

"Yes, it is." Collin stepped forward, leaving the airlock of the *Turd*, and entered the freight bay of the *Tyrant*. With his right hand outstretched, Collin took Primo's hand in his own. Suddenly and for no apparent reason the captain went down on his knees and tried using his left hand to pry free the hand held in Collin's grasp. His face was locked in a painful grimace—his rapid breathing coming in short, agonizing breaths.

Two soldiers rushed forward, placing the muzzles of their weapons pointblank toward Collin's head. One of the men said, "Release him ... do it now!"

Collin did as told and raised his hands. The mere action of moving his hands upward caused him to rise up off the deck several inches.

"I'm sorry. I'm very sorry, Captain Primo," Collin said, a look of real concern on his face. "I don't know ..."

"It's all right, nothing's broken," Primo answered, standing upright again. "I should have known better. We already knew your physiology was different." He rubbed his one hand with the other. "Mother of Dawn, that hurt!" Almost smiling now, Primo appraised the others in Frost's group. "Why don't you introduce me to your team?"

Self-consciously, Collin looked to his friend: "This is Paul DiMaggio."

DiMaggio put out a hand and then changed it to a fist. "We sometimes do what is called a fist-bump on Earth." He turned to Bubba and the two exchanged a quick bump. Slowly he turned back to the captain and held out a fist. Primo raised his eyebrows and carefully gave DiMaggio's fist a solid bump of his own. He seemed to like that, turning to one of his own men and repeating the fist-bump process with him.

Collin noticed Primo had a small circular device, about an inch in diameter, high up on his jacket, near his collar. He suspected it was a translation device of some sort. There was no lag or delay hearing him speak their language, although the movements of his mouth did not synchronize with the words he heard.

"Again, who are your team members?"

"This is John Washington, we call him Bubba. Over there is Orman."

Primo took in Bubba's sheer girth and shook his head. "I wouldn't want to mess with you, young man. You seem to have great physical prowess." He gave Bubba a more gentle fist-bump. Collin was sure it was to save himself from more pain. The captain turned toward Orman. Orman didn't extend out a hand or fist, but nodded in the captain's direction.

"I'm sorry for what happens next. We cannot have you moving about this vessel in your current physiological state."

It was then Collin noticed the hovering cart. Apparently defying the rules of gravity, the cart hovered several feet off the deck and was maneuvering over to where Primo was standing. There were twenty or thirty circular bands, like bracelets, positioned in two rows on the cart's top surface.

"These are what we call minimizers. For as long as I've been in command here, or any other place, for that matter, I don't remember having to use these."

"What exactly are they?" Collin asked, looking suspiciously at the devices.

"They will normalize your movements. I'm sure you've noticed by now that you are having a hard time keeping your feet securely on the deck. And you've already seen firsthand what your body strength can accomplish here. Wearing these is just as much a protection for you as it is for us."

One of the armed soldiers placed his weapon on the second shelf of the cart, picked up one of the bracelets, and approached Orman. With the flick of a small switch, the minimizer bracelet opened. Collin watched as the soldier knelt on one knee and, still holding on to the bracelet, reached for Orman's furry leg.

The feline-like creature's reactions took everyone by

surprise. With one swipe of his clawed hand, the soldier's hand was cleanly removed at the wrist. Blood spurted into the air from the man's stump in quick, rhythmic jets that covered the bulkheads and everyone around him in red.

Total chaos followed. Three energy pulses burned into Orman's upper torso. When he didn't immediately go down, five more followed. Collin stood transfixed, his mouth agape. Bubba, on the other hand, was already moving. Collin had seen the big guy move like that a hundred, maybe a thousand, times before—where he'd come up from his three-point stance and rocket forward just as the ball was snapped. Two hundred and fifty pounds of sheer brute force that typically devastated the opposing lineman—no matter how big he was. Bubba was almost always the bigger, and certainly the stronger, player.

The first unfortunate soldier to come into contact with him never knew what hit him. As Bubba's thick left forearm came up, another automatic movement gleaned from countless practice hours on the field, the soldier was hit across his chest, elevated up and off the deck several feet, and plummeted hard against the bulkhead fifteen feet behind him. His body stayed where it hit, within the same identical-shaped indentation.

DiMaggio gave Collin a shove, saving him from a soldier's weapon fire. DiMaggio moved like lightning, and was upon that same soldier in the blink of an eye. Finally Collin joined the fight as well, but his target was Primo. Fists clenched, Collin headed for the captain who, at this point, hadn't made any aggressive movements.

"Stop!"

It was too late. Collin's forward momentum jammed his shoulder directly into Primo. The impact struck the captain in his midsection and threw him ten feet away, skittering across the deck. Still conscious, he yelled again, "Everyone stop!"

As fists poised in the air, energy rifles raised and ready to fire, everyone stopped where they stood. Primo held his injured ribs and spit blood. "No one move."

He slowly, painfully, got to his feet. Collin watched him grimace and, as he assessed the injured around him, Collin did the same. Both the soldier who'd lost his hand and Orman were dead. The smell of burnt fur still permeated the air. The soldier still buried within the back bulkhead was obviously dead, and four more lay unconscious on the deck. Bubba had multiple burn marks across his chest and upper thighs. Collin realized that he too had been shot, once in the upper arm and once on the back. The wounds stung but didn't seem to be life-threatening.

The four still-standing soldiers maintained their weapons' aim on Collin, DiMaggio and Bubba.

As Captain Primo approached, Collin braced himself for whatever would be coming next. The man stood up as tall as his injuries would allow and was now face to face with Collin. Through bloodied teeth, the captain smiled.

"You may be young ... but you are warriors just the same."

Chapter 18

Sitting in the *Tyrant*'s infirmary, Collin tensed as a medical technician, *or maybe a doctor?* swabbed at the burn marks on his back.

"Just sit still … this is the last of them," the older man with a white beard said. He sounded grumpy, almost angry, but his eyes betrayed humor and kindness. "Your wounds are superficial, which shouldn't be possible … your physiology is quite remarkable."

Collin felt a slight tingle occurring on both earlobes. Touching his left ear with his fingertips, he felt where the doctor had pierced his earlobe; now a small device was inserted there, no larger than the size of a pinhead. He'd been told that once these were attached, he'd have no trouble understanding what was being said, as well as communicating to others. He'd also be able to remove the devices within a few days—the doctor didn't explain how—but he'd soon be able to easily converse in their common language Maisann.

DiMaggio and Bubba were both being treated by other medical personnel off to his left, while Orman's body lay prone on a table directly across from him.

"Is Orman going to be all right?" Collin asked, surprised he was still alive.

"You can call me Dr. Albergo, and yes, he's fine … just unconscious."

Collin nodded and assessed the black bands now secured around his ankles and wrists. He saw Bubba and DiMaggio doing the same thing. The effect on his overall physiology was profound. He felt drained just lifting an arm.

Seeing his fatigue, Dr. Albergo said, "Your energy will return ... in time. Those are necessary to keep your muscle strength in check."

Collin was about to protest when he heard a familiar voice, "I'm fine ..."

"Well, your ribs need attention; at least two or more are cracked," a woman's voice said from behind a bulkhead.

"I'll come back when time allows ... I promise." Captain Primo stepped from around the corner. He looked like crap. He swiped at a bead of perspiration over his brow as he headed directly for Collin.

"You should be dead, you know. You all should ... especially the furry one over there."

Collin shrugged, which he immediately regretted. Teenagers shrug. Spacecraft captains do or say something cool. Dr. Albergo nodded to the captain and left.

Bubba and DiMaggio, finished with their medical treatments, were now standing on either side of Captain Primo.

"I need to get back to my people, my crew," Collin said.

Primo pulled up a stool and sat down with a grimace. "As I said before, this is not an area of space you want to roam around in without protection."

"We'll manage."

The captain said, "You think? Well, let me tell you a little about the Kardon Guard. When it comes to vessels outside of the monarchy's own ... they shoot first and don't bother asking questions later."

"This Brotherhood of yours ... who are you. What's your deal?"

Primo didn't answer right away. He seemed to be thinking about something else, or perhaps he didn't like the question. "The Brotherhood has been around as long as the monarchy.

Only recently has friction arisen to the point the two ruling bodies had to separate. The balance of power has gone back and forth over the last few years. Where once my ancestors, the knights of the Brotherhood, protected the monarchy against the queen's enemies, we now fight her Kardon Guard on a daily basis."

"Why? What's your ... the Brotherhood's beef with the monarchy about, anyway?"

Primo exhaled, looking tired and reluctant to explain.

"Can't you just resolve your differences, maybe rule together? Maybe you can put your hatred aside and—"

"I never said I hated the queen," Primo said back, irritated. "You're young and naïve, Commander Frost. There are far too many things you are unaware of that I don't have the time or inclination to explain. Leave it to say there are fundamental differences between the two of us. The Brotherhood is about the joint-rule of independent planetary states ... the monarchy is all about one rule governing ... the queen's rule."

"You said she was revered, thought of as a goddess? If the people like her, love her, maybe that's good enough."

"Yes, they do love her. But they don't love the often-cruel monarchy's Council of Elders and they certainly don't love the lack of personal freedom and independence that's now placed on all who live within Notares space. It's a dichotomy, but that's simply life here."

Collin didn't see how any of this concerned him, or his people back on the Turd. What he really needed was to get home—to whatever was left of Earth in the aftermath of that sim rover collector ship's assault on the planet.

"Captain Primo, we just want to get back home. Can you help us do that?"

"Yes, that I can do. But the price for that will be one year of service to the Brotherhood."

"Are you crazy? We're not giving you a whole year of our lives … that's totally ludicrous!"

"You need to settle down, and I mean right now!" The captain's steady gaze did not falter from Collin's face.

Collin's lips hardened into a tight, straight line. In a lowered tone he said, "Service? What kind of service?"

"Brotherhood forces have taken terrible losses in recent years. We've sustained devastating military setbacks. Our numbers are waning. Simply put, we need able-bodied combatants to go up against the Kardon Guard. Your crew will be properly trained: integrated into our fleets, our armies."

Collin was already shaking his head. "No fricking way. If—and it's a big if—we go along with this year-of-service-thing, we stay together. And how do I know you'll keep your end of the bargain?"

Primo thought about that for a moment, then said, "There's a Rolm portal here in Notares space. It's how you arrived here. With the right equipment installed on your vessel, and a specific input code, you can travel back to the sector of your own home world. Every three months, I'll provide four digits of the sixteen digit code. You'll know the digits are valid, since entering even one incorrect digit results in an error message."

"There's two problems with that," Collin responded. "One, how would I know the code you provide will take us where you say it will … and the final four digits … those could be totally bogus."

Primo raised his eyebrows. "You make good points. The portal interface updates as you enter the digits … the more digits entered, the more specific the interface is to the location where the exiting portal will be. By the end of the twelfth digit entered, you'll have narrowed the field of exit portals down to a dozen or so within the sector of your home world. But understand, if you don't exit through the one closest to

Earth, your trip home will be many months, if not years. So ... there will be a level of mutual trust required for this to work."

Collin thought about that and the simple fact that he ... that they'd ... all be giving up a year of their lives stuck here. What were their odds of even surviving out the year? What did any of them know about interstellar wars? When it came down to it, would they be able to fight ... to kill others in battle as part of the captain's deal? He didn't know the answers but didn't see any alternatives, either.

"The Turd is not a combat vessel ... it's like ... really hard to maneuver."

"That's because the AI's fried. Nobody flies manually unless it's an emergency. A new, highly-advanced AI can be added to your ship."

"Wouldn't it be better just to give us a new ship?"

"First of all, we don't have extra ships just lying around to hand out. Second, that ship of yours is unique ... the hull's dense molecular structure would be nearly impervious to Kardon Guard weapons." Primo continued to stare at Collin and then at Bubba and DiMaggio. "I propose we retrofit your ship ... it will take us a least four weeks at Nero Station ... maybe as many as six."

"What would you do to it?" DiMaggio asked.

"Quite a bit. By the time we're done, it'll be three times its present size. New, more powerful, and reactive anti-matter drives will be installed into parallel-mounted side structures; weaponry will be added ... you won't recognize the ship when it's done. It may not be pretty, but it'll be a highly effective combat vessel."

"What do we do in the meantime?" Collin asked.

"You and your crew will need every minute of that time to go through the Brotherhood's combat training ... which will take place there on Nero Station as well. It will be an abbreviated version; our actual new-recruit training program takes well over a year. And your officers will require even more training. Don't expect much sleep in the coming days."

"I haven't talked to the others yet. Without their buy-in, I can't agree."

An overhead light began to strobe, followed by a repeating alarm klaxon. A male voice echoed over a PA system: "Capitano Primo, we've got three Kardon Marauders inbound to our position. Their weapons are charged and they have a lock on us."

"Shields up, I'm on my way." Primo hurried off his stool and headed for the exit. Over his shoulder, he said, "Come with me … looks like your training's already begun."

Collin got to his feet and pulled on his T-shirt. Bubba put a beefy hand on Collin's shoulder. "Dude, are you sure you want to go this route? I'm not liking this … not one bit."

"I haven't agreed to anything yet. In the meantime, maybe we can see what we'll be up against."

The three teens almost lost their balance as the ship suffered a jolt. Distant sounds, like thunder, were now a continuous addition to the alarm klaxon. Collin, Bubba, and DiMaggio hurried after Captain Primo.

Chapter 19

Three armed soldiers were waiting for them as they came out of the infirmary. Primo was running up ahead, in the direction of the bow. Collin, DiMaggio and Bubba hurried after him, with the three soldiers following close behind.

Collin hadn't noticed before, but the *Tyrant* was a magnificent vessel. He recognized how the use of rich colors and tasteful textures could be soothing to the senses … not so much right now, with the ship under attack, but his overall impression, nonetheless, was one of elegance: bulkheads painted a deep red and appointments, such as hatchways, that looked to be made of gold or a lightweight counterpart to gold. There simply couldn't be found a more dramatic counterbalance to the dismal interior on the *Turd*.

Captain Primo no longer tried to hide the pain he felt in his ribs. His right arm was pulled in close—holding on to the left side of his torso. He'd come to a double hatchway of brushed gold metal that opened silently into the side bulkheads as he approached. Once inside, he turned toward the three teenagers.

"Hurry up!" he said, waving them inside.

It was an elevator of sorts. As soon as they'd cleared the opening, the hatch doors closed and the ten-by-twelve-foot car began to move sideways. Collin felt the G-forces increase, to the point he and the others had to look for handholds to keep them standing. Primo didn't seem to notice and continued to stand upright, still holding on to his ribs.

"When you're on the bridge you will stand out of the way and keep quiet. If you have a question, keep it until I, or one of the other officers, have time to address it later."

The car was slowing and soon came to a stop. Another set of double hatchways opened into a compartment bustling with activity.

"Stay in the back of the bridge!" the captain barked, already heading forward, toward the front of what Collin now knew was the bridge.

The three teen boys looked at each other. Wide-eyed, Collin took it all in. The bridge was big—easily twenty yards wide and thirty yards from front to back. Virtually every surface was alive with blinking lights, varying types of readouts, and display screens. Collin watched the men and women sitting at their various stations—each station was encircled by a wrap-around, quasi-transparent screen. At the forward area of the bridge was a large curved display that showed three approaching vessels. A row of ten smaller display screens depicted a myriad of other views, including a logistical view of nearby space and the four spaceships: the three approaching ones and the Brotherhood's. Now the logistical view swapped places with the live feed. Seeing it full-sized, Collin noted there were hundreds of colorful vector lines and numerical readouts, which were constantly refreshing and changing values.

Bubba nudged Collin and gestured toward the center of the bridge. On a slightly raised platform were three padded command chairs. Primo sat down in the middle one and immediately a quasi-transparent screen, albeit much smaller than those used in the surrounding stations, appeared at his chest level. Looking up from his personal display, then back and forth to the forward logistical display, Collin realized the captain was deeply concentrating and making some kind of an assessment. With a wave of his hand, the chest-level display disappeared.

"Tactical … we'll need to use pounders on those birds.

Let's try out the new guns you've been so excited about."

At the Tactical station, a round cubicle affair and nearly identical to all others on the bridge, a chair spun around one hundred and eighty degrees so the bald-headed man in it was facing directly toward Primo.

"Aye, Capitano. Their shields are the older, low-freq caliniums. Pounders should work well, sir. All three warships will be within range within thirty seconds."

"And Jib … hold off on charging weapons until the last second. Let's not give them a heads-up."

"Aye, sir." The tactical station chair spun back around to its normal orientation.

More and more stations became active and chairs began spinning about—changing orientation as the various occupants conversed with others around them. Collin felt a kind of combined electricity—a buzz of excitement, which was almost palpable. At that moment he realized something else … he loved this. More than anything else, he wanted to be a part of it. Looking to Bubba and DiMaggio, he saw in their faces, too, that they were eating the action up.

Primo signaled them, waving a hand in the air for the teens to join him. The three moved through the throngs of bridge crew who were scurrying about. Workstation chairs, too, were constantly turning back and forth. As the three approached the center of the bridge and the raised platform, Captain Primo was on his feet and staring at the forward display.

The three nervously looked at each other. Collin shrugged, as if saying maybe we weren't supposed to come up here. Primo glanced down at them. "Sit. I want you three to see how it's done." He gestured toward the three, padded, ruby-red command chairs. "Hurry up … things are happening quickly."

Collin took the center chair and instantly felt what it was like to be in the command position of a powerful warship. He looked toward DiMaggio and Bubba and then across to the surrounding bridge, with its almost frenzied level of activity.

"All three ships are in range. They're splitting up, sir. In ten seconds we'll be flanked, at both port and starboard," said the officer called Jib, from Tactical.

"Charge guns," Primo ordered, taking a step closer to the display.

"Charged … we have a lock on all three birds."

"Fire guns!"

"Firing guns … cascades burst and targeting propulsion."

The display screen went back to the live feed. The three attacking ships had changed formation and were approaching from three different angles. At this distance Collin could see they were similar-looking to the *Tyrant*, but much smaller.

It started as a rumble, which quickly turned into an ongoing pounding that Collin felt in the seat of his pants. Bursts … no … more like streaks of light were shooting from the *Tyrant* simultaneously, in three directions.

"Incoming!"

The three attacking ships were now firing their own energy weapons. A female at a station perpendicular to Tactical was working her station board—her hands moving in a blur. "Shields holding at eighty percent, Captain."

The first of the three attacking ships was coming apart. A flash of white light erupted from its stern and then it toppled over, end over end, moving out of view.

"Guns acquiring remaining birds."

If anything, the rhythmic pounding of the guns had increased. Collin felt his heart rate increase accordingly. The relentless barrage continued until another one of the attacking ships flashed white. The ensuing explosion brought everyone to a standstill. A quiet hush momentarily stifled all activity.

"Stay on station," Captain Primo commanded. The bridge crew resumed their duties.

Jib said, "We're being hailed by the remaining ship, Captain. She's just discharged her batteries … guns have been retracted."

"On screen, Jib," Primo ordered.

As surprised as Collin was to see this face on the screen before them, Primo looked more surprised.

"Real nice … so now you're gunning for me, too?"

Collin, DiMaggio and Bubba all sat forward in unison. They were looking at a woman's face, so angry her cheeks had flushed a bright pink, her brow was furrowed into deep creases and her lips were pressed into a rigidly firm straight line. It didn't alter the fact that she was stunningly beautiful. With the exception of a few errant strands of yellow, her blonde hair was pulled back into a high ponytail. She wore a uniform similar to that of the Tyrant's crew, only hers was deep blue in color. Although Collin couldn't tell what the markings on her collar were, it seemed obvious she was also an officer of high rank.

"Principessa … you shouldn't be out here. It's a good way to get yourself dead."

"I could say the same to you. This is Her Majesty's space, Dante—"

"No … it's not, Tina. We are clearly within Brotherhood boundaries."

Heads turned and eyes flashed toward the captain. Apparently using a casual, far less formal, nickname was a no-no, Collin thought. She glanced down for a moment at something off screen and seemed to realize he was correct.

Collin thought he saw her lips pull up at the corners for just an instant. The two stared at one another for several long beats before Primo finally spoke: "Perhaps it's best if you return to less hostile surroundings."

She continued to look at Primo. Her expression now showed sadness—and sadness showed equally on Dante Primo's face. The display went black and then changed to a live feed of the opposing small warship. Its engines flared and the ship rapidly moved away.

Primo continued to watch the display. The three boys looked at one another. DiMaggio smiled and raised his eyebrows.

The captain turned back to the three of them.

"Who was that?" Collin asked.

"That, Mr. Frost, was Principessa Constantina Valora … my wife."

Chapter 20

Collin, Bubba, DiMaggio, and Orman were escorted back to the *Turd*. With their minimizer bands removed, they reentered the airlock and waited for the outside hatch to close.

Darren and Humphrey were waiting right outside the inner airlock hatch and they didn't look particularly happy.

"Where the hell have you been?" Humphrey bellowed. "Did you forget none of us have eaten anything for nearly a day and a half?"

"Let's move on over to the mess … I'll update everyone at the same time," Collin said, keeping cool.

That seemed to enrage Darren. He moved in front of Collin and jabbed a pointing finger into his chest, "No … you'll stop and tell me what's going on, right now."

Collin felt Bubba tense behind him. Collin put up a hand to restrain the big guy from intervening. "Darren, you're going to have to trust me on this. Some pretty big decisions need to be made and they will affect all of us. So I'm talking to the group. Get out of my way so we can bring you and everybody else up to speed."

A crowd began to form around them. Royce White, looking mean and hungry, strode up and stopped next to Darren. "Just let them say what they have to say, man."

Collin saw something in Darren's eyes he hadn't seen before. *Desperation.* Even more so than Humphrey, Darren was teetering on the edge.

They continued into the mess where Collin climbed up onto a table. Bubba's deep voice filled the compartment. "Pipe down … let Frost talk."

Collin looked around the mess and took in the facial

expressions of his thirteen football teammates and the six cheerleaders. They look tired, hungry, defeated. He gave thought for another few seconds on how he was going to approach them regarding the new developments.

"Are you going to just stand there all day, Sticks, or are you going to say something?" Collin ignored Humphrey's big mouth, took in a deep breath and smiled.

"I have some good news and some shitty news."

"Tell us the good news, Collin," Lydia said, looking up at him, ever hopeful.

"We can go home … the captain of the ship we're moored next to, the *Tyrant*, has promised us that much."

"And the bad news?" Darren asked.

"It won't be for at least one year."

Expressions quickly turned to exasperation and then to anger. The three inseparable friends, Clifford Bosh, Owen Platt and Garry Hurst, now stood alongside Darren and Humphrey. *Is this the start of some kind of mutiny?* Collin wondered. They looked ready to kill someone—namely him.

"Hey … we're free to go it alone … I'm just reporting what was said. We decide as a group, okay?" Collin proceeded to relay the information back to them, as it was told to him by the captain; that the only viable way back to Earth was through something called a Rolm portal. He spoke about the Brotherhood, the princess and the Kardon Guard, and that they were currently sited in the middle of a two-year-old interstellar war.

"What are we supposed to do for a whole year?" Owen Platt asked.

"One of the conditions the captain demands, in exchange for helping us return home, will be for us to join them in their fight. We'll be put through some sort of basic military training that will take up to six weeks. While that's going on, they'll be retrofitting the Turd into a warship. Both will take place on a space station, something call Nero Station."

"Join their army? No, thank you. And retrofit this piece of crap ship … why even bother?" Humphrey asked, starting to look hostile again.

"Here's how I see things. One, we won't last a week on our own in space. We'll die of hunger or, even more probable, we'll be blasted into bits by the Kardon Guard. Two, don't forget we're just a bunch of teenagers. What do we know about space travel? This turd of a ship is just barely space worthy … no way would it make it back to Earth, even if we did find an accessible portal out there. And three … there's something else … something pretty cool I haven't told you yet."

"Just spit it out, Sticks," Humphrey said dismissively and with disdain.

"Our physiology, and our molecular structure, is different than theirs. Even this turd of a ship is different."

"Oh boy … that's exciting," Humphrey sneered.

Bubba stepped up onto the table next to Collin. "It's true. We're like some kind of supermen here. We got into it when we first entered their ship. One of their soldiers got a little too hands-y with Orman, who then took a swipe back at the soldier and took the guy's hand off, at the wrist. Even while they were firing their plasma weapons at us, I was able to push a guy twenty feet into the air and saw him get half-buried into a bulkhead. Frost took down the captain. After that, we all took multiple plasma shots from their guns … they nearly killed Orman."

"How are you still alive?" Lydia asked.

"Our dense molecular structure," Collin replied. "That, and the gravity field they're used to is far less than Earth's. In the end, they had to put special bands, they call them minimizers, on our arms and legs so we wouldn't accidentally break something, or worse, kill someone."

"Can we all stay together? Or will they separate us?" Lydia asked.

"No, we're not being separated. We told them that was not an option for us … we stay together, no matter what."

Lydia turned to the five other cheerleaders. A few moments later, Tink asked, "Would we be put through their training too? We're girls, not soldiers." The other cheerleaders nodded their heads in agreement.

"I suspect you'd be able to physically do, or achieve, far more than any man there, Tink. I wouldn't expect any special treatment for you gals. Like it or not, we'll all be trained to be warriors," Collin said.

Collin watched as a new look came over Darren's face, then Humphrey's, then the others'. He'd purposely saved that bit of information for last. What red-blooded American teen, male or female for that matter, wouldn't be intrigued by the possibility of having superhero-like strength?

Collin and Bubba stepped down off the table. Discussions had sprung up and Collin simply needed to let them come to some decision among themselves. From the sound of things, raised voices … arguing, it would take a while. He felt his stomach rumble and a wave of nausea creep over him. He, too, needed to eat, but he decided to wait it out in his quarters. But before he even left the mess, the room went still. Darren was now standing on the same table Collin and Bubba had earlier.

"So it's agreed. We're going along with this, right?" Darren asked, looking around the mess compartment.

Heads nodded, but nobody looked overly excited about the prospect. Darren pointed an outstretched finger at Collin. "We find out this is bullshit, that they're tricking us … I'm going to wreck you, Sticks."

Collin also saw baleful expressions on Humphrey, Bosh, Platt and Hurst. His fault or not, he'd be contending with all six of them, if things didn't play out pretty much as he'd described.

Collin wasn't going to leave it at that. "Make threats all you want, but remember one thing ... we're in this together. We are all we have, and only by banding together will we survive—come through this alive and make it back home. No matter what occurs over the next few weeks, I suggest we don't let them forget who they're dealing with."

Bubba put his hands on his hips and stared back at his teammates: "Mess with us ... any one of us ... and you've messed with the wrong team! Tell me who've they messed with?"

The response was a weak scattering of voices, "The Lone Stars."

"Louder," Bubba said. "Who?"

More chimed in, "The Lone Stars."

"I still didn't hear you! Who?"

Now everyone yelled back, even Darren and Humphrey, along with Bosh, Platt and Hurst, in response, "THE LONE STARS!"

Chapter 21

They were told they could bring one bag or satchel each. Collin had his leather rucksack slung over one shoulder. Inside were his Beretta, extra mag, small flashlight and several other odds and ends. One by one the students walked off the Turd, into the freight bay of the Tyrant.

This time they were greeted by far more soldiers, and bigger weapons were trained on them. No more than a few seconds passed before each teenager was fitted with four minimizer bands. None of the Daccian, catlike beings resisted having the bands placed on their wrists this time. But the three had decided not to fight for the Brotherhood. Instead, they had agreed to a house arrest-type situation where they would not be permitted to leave their suite of compartments for the extent of one year. They did not seem overly concerned with these restrictions and had gone along with them without any argument.

As the fourth minimizer was firmly secured around Collin's right ankle, he felt the same draw on his energy he'd experienced before. Added to that, his lack of sufficient nutrients in a long while was draining, and he was finding it hard to keep his eyes open.

They were moved to what looked like a ship's hold. The space was tight and the temperature had to be in the forties or fifties, chilly but bearable.

A young officer in a dark red coat entered the hold. "I am Lieutenant Maugeri. Please forgive these accommodations. The *Tyrant* is currently en route to Nero Station. We will arrive there within thirty minutes."

★ ★ ★

They had arrived at Nero Station. As quickly as they'd been ushered into the *Tyrant*'s hold, they were ushered right back out again. They were led through some kind of tubular concourse that connected the *Tyrant* to the space station. A series of small portholes offered a view of Nero Station beyond. Everyone in the group moved to the portholes and looked out.

"Holy crap … Look at this thing …" someone said. Collin wasn't sure who.

Gleaming, everything stark white—it was probably the biggest non-natural *thing* Collin had ever seen. Evidently they were standing within a small connecting tube that was part of another major spoke of what was, in a sense, a ginormous wheel. There were twelve such spokes, each of which was probably miles in length. The spokes connected to a substantial outer ring. The center hub, which everything connected to, was thick and cylindrical. Like twinkling stars, a thousand little porthole lights glimmered—contrasting against the blackness of space beyond. Collin noticed another spacecraft was slowly moving in toward one of the other spokes—farther out from where the *Tyrant* was currently secured. Then he noticed there were other spaceships, of different shapes and sizes, around the distant periphery of Nero Station.

Lieutenant Maugeri said, "Let's move it along."

They continued down the concourse tube. Collin was somewhere in the middle of the pack. They were being ushered down a long, softly lit corridor. In time they emerged into an open, congested, atrium. Collin guessed this was a transport arrival level that circled around the station's hub;

an area where those disembarking from their moored vessels would eventually converge. It was a colossal-sized space, with spectacular views of the surrounding station's outer ring via wide observation windows. Everything was ridiculously clean. And, like Captain Primo's *Tyrant* ship, the bulkheads were in rich colors of reds and gold.

They were herded off to a wide, central column. An elevator arrived and they moved inside. Before Collin knew it, the doors reopened and they were walking along a different corridor.

The listless teens didn't really talk—they simply continued on their semi-imposed march, like an incoherent herd of sheep. That is, until the aroma of something tantalizing, something incredible, reached their nostrils. Heads came up, expressions showed interest, paces increased.

Up ahead, Collin saw Dr. Albergo and Captain Primo. The captain raised a palm to halt the oncoming procession. He looked down the line until he found Collin and gestured for him to come forward to the front of the line.

"I'm glad you've decided to join us ... join the Brotherhood," Captain Primo said.

"It was a group decision. Truth was, there wasn't really much of a choice, was there?"

"Soon, you will all be fed. But first, Dr. Albergo will be administering the same basic procedure you went through earlier—the installation of Com-dots on earlobes. It is imperative that our commands and directives are fully understood, going forward."

Collin didn't say anything in response to that, but understood Primo's reasoning. He turned to the line behind him. "Um ... before we can go in and eat, everyone will have Com-dots ... these things," he explained, pointing to his own earlobes, "placed on their ears. It doesn't hurt much. It allows us to hear what they're saying and for them to understand us. They will flake off eventually, but by that time we'll be able to converse back and forth ... at least, that's what they told me."

At the front of the line stood David Burk, but everyone just called him Brick—as in dumb as a brick. His life was all about football, being an offensive lineman, and since he'd rarely passed any of his non-elective classes, he'd spent most of his free time being tutored. It was good he was at the front of the line ... Brick wasn't a rabble-rouser ... not one to cause problems.

"Brick, they're going to put something on your ears. It won't hurt. See? I've got them too."

"Yeah, okay. We eating soon?" he asked, his eyes locked on the mess entrance less than ten feet ahead.

Collin nodded to the doctor and watched as Brick's two lobes were pierced with Com-dots. Brick smiled back at Collin and was quickly hustled into the mess.

One by one, they all capitulated to the procedure. Before moving into the mess, each teen looked first at the captain, who nodded a silent welcome. As the last of them disappeared around the corner, Collin felt like if he didn't eat something soon he was going to pass put.

"Thank you, Mr. Frost, for your assistance here. Please, go eat."

Collin headed for the entrance.

"Mr. Frost ..."

Collin looked back over his shoulder.

124

"It does get easier," said Captain Primo. There was humor in his eyes and something else—*sympathy?*

The mess hall was ginormous. There were enough tables to seat hundreds, but the students sat together in one small section. Most had already gotten their food and were digging into their plates. If the aroma was any indication, this meal should be a feast to remember, Collin thought.

Bubba and DiMaggio waited for Collin and together they moved to the cafeteria-style counter. Where he'd expected to see large metal pans filled, brimming with hot meats and vegetables, there were only display screens. Both Bubba and DiMaggio smiled.

"Took us by surprise as well," DiMaggio said. "You just touch the selector button for the items you want added to your tray."

DiMaggio and Bubba quickly moved down the line, selecting various food items. Both were making comments and jokes about their own selections. Although most items were completely foreign-looking to Earth cuisine, Collin felt there were enough similarities to some foods, like a burrito-type thing covered in gravy, that he felt the odds of them being edible were higher.

By the time Bubba reached the end of the counter, a tray of steaming hot food was coming out on a conveyor belt, from some kind of oven-sized appliance. Collin waited for his tray to emerge, grabbed it up, and moved over to another counter where he collected eating utensils—a spork-type thing and a knife. As he approached the tables, a hand shot up waving three tables away. Setting down his tray, he realized it wasn't Bubba and DiMaggio who'd signaled him. Lydia smiled up at him and she scooted over to her left, closer to Tink. "There's room … here, sit next to me."

As happy as Collin was to be seated next to Lydia, all he could think about was the food in front of him. Without wasting another second, he attacked what was on his tray. Prepared for it to taste like crap, he was happy to discover the food was good. No, the food was outstanding! He took heaping sporkfulls of something that looked liked cooked carrots but was purple—then something that looked similar to mashed potatoes but was green, and then the burrito thing which, strangely enough, tasted pretty much like a burrito.

Collin was three quarters through his meal before he realized the others at the table were watching him. As he scanned their faces, he saw they were waiting for something.

"What? Why are you all looking at me? You didn't like your food?"

Seeing their now empty plates, he knew that wasn't it.

Lydia leaned in closer. "What's going to happen now? Where are they going to take us?"

Before Collin could say anything, Tink asked, "Will the boys be separated from the girls?"

Another girl, Karen Muller, pushed her tray forward and said, "I need to tinkle … where can I do that?"

Collin raised both hands, as if in surrender. "I'm just as new here as you are. I can try to find out …" He half-stood, looking over the heads of those around him. He hadn't noticed earlier, but soldiers had taken up positions all around the mess hall. Before he could turn toward the entrance, a loud, angry sounding voice began barking orders.

"Stand up. Up! All of you … stand up and pick up your trays!"

The man's voice was deep and gravelly sounding—like he'd smoked several packs a day since he was ten. With a quick glance over his shoulder, Collin saw that the voice fit the person.

"I am Chief-in-Command Bragg and from this moment on I will be your boss. Get used to hearing this sweet, melodic voice of mine; you'll be hearing it a lot."

The soldier was middle-aged, with salt-and-pepper gray hair. Short in stature, he was built like a fireplug. His uniform fit tight across his chest. Beneath the maroon fabric, his muscles were big and defined—he was not someone you'd want to piss off.

"You will deposit your trays here, in this bin. You will not talk … you will not eyeball me … you will quickly walk to the corridor behind me and form two lines: one for females, one for males. Do it now!"

There was no hesitation from anyone and as Collin stood he saw the anxiety on all of their faces. The only sound came from trays being placed into a large bin to the left of Bragg. Collin hurried by him, taking in as much as he could from his peripheral vision. As if sensing Collin's appraisal, Bragg's attention shot toward Collin.

"Move it, little babies … double-time!"

Chapter 22

The line of six girls had been led away to, Collin guessed, barracks similar to the guys. Standing at attention now, just moments earlier they'd been ushered into a circular compartment about the size of your typical high school gymnasium. It had rows of what looked like pods, on either side of an open aisle. Colorful flags draped from high above, along the ceiling periphery of the compartment. Undecipherable characters, which were probably names or slogans, Collin thought, were hung beneath each flag. In the open spaces of the bulkheads, between each flag, were various items, including broad swords—crossed at their midpoints; a metal breastplate and helmet that would fit perfectly in Earth's own Middle Ages; and an assortment of other barbaric-looking weapons, which Collin had no reference of, or comparison to, nor a clue to their usage.

The fourteen boys were split into two rows of seven, facing across from each other, on both sides of the aisle. Directly across from Collin, standing at attention, was Humphrey. His eyes were currently boring into Collin's with hatred, as if he'd personally been responsible for everything, from their initial abduction into the collector ship, to ending up here—in these barracks.

Collin continued to stare straight ahead, because the last kid who had let his eyes follow the movements of the now-pacing Chief-in-Command Officer Bragg was ordered to do fifty pushups. Collin figured pushups were the universal punishment for any quasi-intelligent being with two arms and legs.

"Over the next six weeks you should expect three things:

pain, hunger, and exhaustion. Because our timetable has been accelerated, you will feel more pain, hunger, and exhaustion than the recruits who came before you." Bragg stopped his pacing and, with hands on hips, surveyed the two lines. "I've been told you all are different. That you have strengths … perhaps capabilities our native-born boys don't have. Well, let me tell you something. As far as I'm concerned, you're no different. I will break each and every one of you. I will have you all crying for your mommies in your pods at night. I will break you … I will break you … I will break you."

Bragg stopped in front of Bubba and moved in close to him. Nearly looking straight up into Bubba's face, Bragg spoke in a lowered tone: "You will address me as Chief. Is that understood?"

The response was a mix of yesses, okays, and yes sirs … Bragg spun around with anger. "Yes, Chief. Not *yeah* … not *uh huh*, not *sure* … only Yes, Chief."

"Yes, Chief!" came the immediate response.

"Better. Now you will strip down naked. You will pick up your smelly, disgusting clothes and deposit them over there, in that bin. You will then proceed into the lavatories and take a two-minute shower. You will wash your balls, your ass, and your pits. If I smell anything other than soap on any one of you, you will face a most unpleasant regimen of exercise. Now move it!"

Their only saving grace, Collin thought as he disrobed, was that the girls were segregated elsewhere into their own barracks. To call Collin skinny was an understatement. His Sticks nickname was no accident, and standing there naked, in front of the others, was humiliating. Humphrey made no effort to hide his smile as he took in Collin's bony elbows and protruding kneecaps.

The showers were open, a line of twenty shower heads, six

feet up, were spaced evenly on the bulkhead wall. Water came on as soon as Collin stepped up to the shower area. Thirty seconds into it, he realized the tepid water temperature was as warm as it was going to get. He concentrated on getting his body soaped and rinsed as quickly as possible and then stepped away from the bulkhead. He looked for a towel— something to dry off with. Nothing. The allotted two minutes was ticking away so Collin and several others left the head, still dripping wet.

Bragg was still standing where they'd left him, two minutes and thirty seconds earlier. Collin returned to his previous position and stood at attention. One by one the other boys returned; by the time the last of them ran to his space on the line, Collin estimated close to five minutes had elapsed.

"Some of you were only thirty seconds late. Others were closer to three minutes. So you will all be penalized: two hundred pushups. What are you waiting for? Down on the deck!"

Collin did as told and began doing pushups.

"Start over, one of you is doing them incorrectly," Bragg ordered.

Another minute transpired before Bragg said, "Start over, one of you is doing them incorrectly."

Thirty seconds later he said, "Start over, one of you is still doing them incorrectly."

"All the way down, Bubba," Darren said in a barely audible snarl.

"Start over … no talking allowed," Bragg said.

Collin was keeping a running tally in his head and he'd already completed one hundred and twenty-five pushups. One thing about being skinny—he could do these all day. Royce White, on the other hand, was struggling. While his two hundred and seventy pound girth worked well for a starting center, it made doing certain other things problematic. His ample belly was now barely leaving the deck—only his chest was moving up and down. Collin waited for Bragg to issue the command to start over again, but it didn't come.

Collin was the first to reach two hundred, quickly followed by Humphrey, and then Darren and DiMaggio. By the time Royce struggled to his feet, Bragg was standing directly in front of him.

"Pitiful," Bragg said, turning toward the rest of them. "By now you've noticed the flags above your heads. We call them the Flags of the Term. Why? Because only after a full-year term will a new flag be added. Take a close look at these flags. They represent far more than the fabric they're made of. They represent commitment, honor, allegiance, and sacrifice. They represent the very best of the best. *Chains*, which have endured the Brotherhood's basic training over a one-year term." Bragg gestured with his hand to the teens around him, "You all are a Chain … the dismal group of individuals that you are, the fourteen of you, along with the six females, are a Chain. Understand, you are the most vulnerable at your weakest link. With that said, you are the most powerful at your strongest link. You are a Chain … the sooner you come to understand that, the sooner you will begin to prevail here, and in life. Each flag above you represents a graduating Chain … a Chain that consistently scored higher than other Chains within a full-year term. We are at the one-year starting mark now, but I do not expect to see your flag added to the ones above."

Bragg began pacing up and down the aisle. "We measure you by the accumulation of your *tributes*. Tributes are awarded individually, and also for the Chain unit as a whole. I want you to understand these flags, the Chains that prevailed above all others, exhibited the highest level of commitment, honor, allegiance, and sacrifice ... their accumulation of tributes were merely the by-product of those attributes. Unfortunately, you come to us ... into this basic training ... already disgraced. The mere fact that you left your home planet, while under attack, shrouds your reputation. By default you are the lowest of the low. You are nothing more than a bunch of renegades."

Collin wanted to confront the barrel-chested Chief Command Officer. It wasn't like he, or the others, had a choice when they were abducted into the collector ship. He was making them out to be cowards, instead of the victims of bazaar circumstances.

"You will notice words beneath each flag. They correspond to the name of the Chain, the flag that hangs above it. You will select a name for your Chain today. You will select a flag today. You will select a Chain leader."

A second Brotherhood crewmember, who didn't look much older than any of the teens with perhaps the exception of Bubba, entered the barracks, pushing a flatbed hover cart.

Bragg waited for the cart to be delivered where he stood. "This is Mr. Palermo, a recent graduate from basic training. He holds the position of squire. You will show him the same respect you'd show anyone else above your station here. These ... these are your undergarments and uniforms. They will adjust to your bodies' measurements ... simply press and hold the small white square at the backs of the waistbands and collars. Periodically, you will need to readjust your uniforms as your physiques change. You will each take three sets of uniforms. You will wear fresh undergarments every day. Every evening you will place your soiled garments into the bin over there ... you will find cleaned uniforms on your pod bunks every evening, before sack time. When I give the word, go, get your uniforms and undergarments, take them to a pod, get dressed, and pack the others into your pod drawer, below your bunks. When you hear me say dismissed, and not before then, you can go . . . Dismissed."

In a dash everyone converged on the cart. The young Brotherhood guy held up a hand to halt their onslaught. Starting with Humphrey, he handed each a stack of clothes. Collin waited for his turn to be handed his own bundle, then headed to where he'd seen Bubba and DiMaggio go earlier. He found their pods along the far back bulkhead. Collin, taking the pod that was in between theirs, entered the small, egg-shaped enclosure. Inside it was just wide enough to contain a bunk and a desk; he started dressing immediately in the new clothes. The walls of the pods extended to chest-level and he saw that Bubba to his right and DiMaggio to his left were both nearly dressed. It took Collin several seconds to understand how the various garments worked. The undergarments, similar to boxers and undershirts, were huge, but once he got the hang of pressing their little white squares to refit things, like some kind of *smart fabric*, he was surprised how perfectly everything conformed to his body. The uniform's trousers and jacket were dark red and seemed a bit fancy for basic training. He found the locker beneath his bunk. Within it, he found socks and a pair of athletic shoes. Like the garments, they too had white squares attached that enabled a better fit. Dressed, he hurried from the pod, and returned to the same place he'd previously stood.

Bragg was still standing in the same spot. With the boys now back in line, Bragg took a few steps. He stopped and signaled high in the air to someone. Moments later, the girls arrived.

Bragg separated his hands apart in front of his chest: "Spread out from one another ... let's make room for the others."

The six girls moved into various open spots and stood at

attention. Hair wet and looking apprehensive, the girls said nothing, keeping their eyes forward. Collin found Lydia on the opposite line, two spaces from Humphrey. Although her uniform was identical to his own, it didn't fit the same—in fact, if possible, she looked more enticing to him than ever. She must have sensed his gaze because her eyes flicked in his direction. It was then Collin realized Bragg was standing directly in front of him, his face mere inches from his own.

"Is this going to be a problem, recruit? Maybe this is a good time to explain the no-fraternization policy to you and everyone else here. Simply put, there will be none. Got that?"

The response came in unison, "Yes, Chief!"

"Soon, two other recruit Chains, young men and women, will be joining us … shipped in from another Brotherhood star-base. Make no mistake: their arrival only increases the difficulty you will have in adding your flag to those above us. Added to that, these recruits already have two weeks of basic training under their belts.

"Moving forward, your days will be broken up—between morning physical training exercises and afternoon classroom work. Again, you are all at a major disadvantage … you have virtually no knowledge of Notares space, our history … our culture. Now … perhaps some of you may have noticed, each pod has a headband-type device hanging on your enclosure walls, near your bunks. We call these mind-bands. Starting tonight, and every night thereafter, you will slip the bands over your heads before lights out. While you sleep, you'll be immersed in a variety of SLPs—subliminal learning programs. Not perfect, but they should catch you up, at least partially. The good news is, every morning when you wake up, you'll be a whole lot more knowledgeable."

Collin was contemplating what the chief was saying, not really liking the idea of being brainwashed every night while he slept, when he noticed that several young Brotherhood crewmembers were pulling bulkhead walls into new positions. Once these movable bulkheads slid into place, their barracks area would be less than one-third its previous size.

"Earlier, I told you to accomplish three things today," Bragg continued. "Who can repeat them back to me for the benefit of the female recruits?"

Collin watched as Humphrey searched his memory. Collin said, "We will select a name for our Chain today. We will select a flag today. We will select a Chain leader."

"That is correct. You are all dismissed."

Chapter 23

Collin left the line, thinking the chief was giving them far more credit than he probably should have. Until now, getting any kind of united teamwork consensus from this group had proved to be nearly impossible.

As the last of the bulkhead walls were moved into place, Collin noticed the brisk movements of dark blue uniforms nearby. Another Chain. Other young males and females were taking up residence in their new barracks.

"Collin!"

He turned to see DiMaggio waving him over. He and Bubba had assembled a small group over by their pods.

"Come on … Darren's already getting his peeps together." Not surprisingly, Humphrey, Clifford Bosh, Owen Platt and Garry Hurst were over there, jumping around like a bunch of idiots. "Look at him. Darren's acting like a politician or something," DiMaggio said.

Collin, in a glance, noticed that Darren had indeed assembled a group of his buddies together, where they'd set up a camp of sorts in their pods, on the other side of the barracks. When it came down to it, he knew Darren's popularity would probably trump good sense. DiMaggio was right; he was like a politician—grandstanding was second nature to him, and by the growing size of his team, there would be no chance …

"Hey, Frost … are you just going to watch them or get busy over here with us?" Bubba asked.

With a jolt, Collin realized several more people had joined his group. Tink, all smiles, moved in closer to DiMaggio and they fist-bumped. Then, surprisingly, Royce White, the gargantuan-sized center was there, along with three others:

David *the Brick* Burk; cheerleader Karen Muller; and fullback, Brian Owens—putting their team number at eight. Darren's group was already at nine, with the addition of Heather Primm, Doug Summerfield, Dan St. Ama, and Melody Sawyer.

Collin saw Humphrey look over their way, give a cocky smile, and flip him the bird.

There were still three undecided teens, huddling together, between the two groups: Gregg Panichello, Dana Stoker, and Lydia Bennett. They were arguing. *That doesn't bode well*, Collin thought. They needed two to tie, three to win. Collin's heart sank as the three students suddenly stopped bickering and moved in the direction of Darren's group.

"Crap!" DiMaggio said.

Suddenly Lydia stopped in her tracks. She turned and looked over her shoulder. She pursed her lips, smiled, and ran back, joining Collin's group. Collin's mind was reeling. What had just happened here? Their eyes locked for a brief moment before Bubba said, "Cool that you joined us, Lydia … but we're still two people shy."

Cheers erupted from Darren's group. Next came an endless barrage of slurs and taunts.

"Ignore them," Tink said. "It doesn't matter."

But Collin knew it did matter. Their very survival, after basic training ended in six weeks, could very well depend on who would be leading.

"Sorry, man, you're the one who should be leading us," DiMaggio said.

Lydia said, "Collin, we all know none of us would have survived the collector ship without your leadership. This shouldn't be a popularity contest … you're the best man for the job."

Collin felt his face flush. Trying to think of something witty to say, he was saved by the sound of some kind of commotion coming from the entrance to the barracks.

Darren's group had settled down enough to also check what was happening. The chief was back and so was his junior helper. Hushed voices made it impossible to understand what was going on. It was only when three more uniformed recruits entered the barracks that Collin began to put things together. For several minutes the chief talked to the recruits. He saw him point to the flags and to the pods. It became apparent the chief was giving them the same speech he'd given to Collin and the others earlier. He heard the chief say, "Dismissed."

The three recruits moved into the cluster of pods and stopped between Darren and Collin's groups. They turned toward one group first, and then the other.

Both DiMaggio and Bubba were hooping and hollering and punching fists into the air.

"Good to see you guys again," Collin said as they approached.

Moving cat-like, Cine, Orman and Pack quietly joined their group. Orman said, "We changed our mind when we saw the cages we'd be living in over the next year. And we don't like that other human who wants to be leader," he added, pointing to Darren.

"You know they don't count, don't you?" Darren yelled over, as he and his group approached.

"Like hell they don't," DiMaggio said.

"They're not even human," Humphrey said, exasperated.

Tink, by far the smallest of any of them, stepped forward, getting into Humphrey's space. "Well, neither was that wildebeest you call your mother ... but hey ... they still let you into high school, didn't they?"

That insult made everyone laugh out loud, including those on Darren's team.

"Ha ha, very funny, Tink," Humphrey said. He was trying

way too hard to sound angry, but he wasn't … in fact, he was looking at Tink with more than a little interest.

"Okay, great new leader, what's next?" Darren asked, as the two groups merged into one.

"Um … we have two more directives to handle. Any suggestions, Darren?"

All eyes moved from Collin to Darren. He grinned, "Oh gee, that's a tough one … I think we all know what both of them will be."

Bubba said, "Yeah, we're still the Lone Stars … no way that's going to change."

"And we'll stick with the flag for our great state of Texas?" Collin asked.

Nods came from all around.

"Lights out in two minutes!" came the booming voice of Chief-in-Command Bragg. The lights dimmed to half their brightness. The group dispersed as everyone moved off toward their respective pods. Bubba, DiMaggio and Collin were the only ones left. DiMaggio put a fist out, and Collin and Bubba bumped it simultaneously. Then the three moved off toward their own pods.

As Collin entered his pod, something on his desk pulled at his attention. There was a blinking icon on his terminal. Not seeing a mouse or keyboard, he touched the screen. The screen changed to a picture—some kind of coat-of-arms, on a field of dark red—and a shield, with two broad swords crossed in the middle. Above that was a knight's helmet. Surrounding the emblem was an intricate latticework of small, braided chains. Across the shield was a collection of strange characters that somehow he could read. It said Brotherhood. Below that, in smaller text: Commitment, Honor, Allegiance, and Sacrifice.

Apparently the Com-dots did more than merely help

with audible translations. He was about to turn away when a message began to scroll across the screen.

Congratulations, Mr. Frost. As your Chain's chosen leader, you will be responsible for the success or failure of each individual charge within your Chain. Tomorrow, you will meet the recruits on the other two Chains: your competition. Please note, there has been an alteration to our agreement. At the successful completion of the six-week basic training, the Chain that has acquired the most tributes will have their Chain's flag prominently displayed, hanging up with the other Flags of the Term. That part of our agreement has not changed. But with the expense involved with retrofitting it, and the scarcity of Brotherhood warships, the vessel you arrived in … the one you refer to as the Turd … will be added to the winning team's bounty. Undoubtedly, this may affect your Chain's ultimate goal of returning to your home planet at the agreed-upon one-year term. The stakes have been increased, Mr. Frost. It will be interesting to see if you and your Chain can rise to the challenge.

Capitano di vascello, Dante Primo, Duca of the Brotherhood house of Torre

Collin reread the message twice more and each time found himself getting more and more angry. If changing their original agreement was this easy, how many other *adjustments* could they expect? Was the promise to be returned back to Earth bullshit? He continued to stare vacantly at the screen for several more minutes before it suddenly went black. He didn't notice at first that the overhead lights had gone out as well. The barracks were now dark, but not to the extent that he couldn't see his way over to his bunk. He undressed down to his shorts and T-shirt, and crawled beneath the bedcovers. Only then did he remember the mind-band. Looking up, over to the left, he saw it hanging on the pod's wall. It was just within reach; he pulled it down from its hook and looked at it in the dim light. It felt strange in his fingers—made from some material or fabric he'd certainly never seen back on Earth. It was pliable and stretched like elastic, but it held a coolness of temperature, almost like metal. He debated once more if he really wanted to place the thing over his head. But Collin didn't see an alternative if he wanted to stay competitive against the other recruits, the other Chains. He slipped the band over his head and waited for something to happen. Nothing. He felt nothing and experienced nothing out of the ordinary. He let his eyes close and within seconds was fast asleep.

Chapter 24

It was the Brotherhood's equivalent of a bugle call. The instrument was totally unfamiliar and the song or melody was just as unfamiliar. But it had the same effect. Collin shot up in bed still wearing his mind-band.

Bragg's voice filled the barracks from high above. "Get up, remove your mind-bands, and make your beds exactly as they were before you slept in them. Boys, bring a change of clothes to the boy's head; girls, do the same into the girl's head. Crap, shower, and shave. Get dressed and line up in the same formation as yesterday. You have five minutes. Go!"

★ ★ ★

Showered and dressed, Collin took his position in the line and waited for the others to do the same. Only three had arrived before him. He figured he was less than a minute late. He let his eyes rise to the flags overhead, where he again observed some of the odd-looking objects—weapons mounted to the bulkhead. He was now perfectly aware of what they were and what they were used for. One was a knight's *cleave-sheer*—used to remove an opposing knight's head from his neck in battle; another—a spiky, lethal-looking object called a throw-cutter, was used a thousand years earlier as a means to bring down both man and beast—they didn't have horses, per se, but something similar, called a Jarrob.

Thanks to the mind-band, the SLPs, Collin knew a whole lot more this morning than he had last night. What he really wanted to know was what the Brotherhood was all about. And what was their beef with the ruling monarch, and who was the Kardon Guard?

The first thing that came to his mind was disgrace. He not only knew the course of events that transpired from an objective perspective, but he also *felt*, from a subjective point of view, the shame the Brotherhood was currently burdened with since their fall from grace. For a thousand years the Brotherhood had stood at the monarchy's side. Together, both were powerful. The monarchy ruled over all Notares, a vast star system made up of four suns, with close to one hundred planets within its system. Beloved by the masses, a presiding king or queen had ruled with fairness and compassion for a millennium. The many billions who lived within the bounds of Notares lacked for little. There were no poor, nor hungry. Disease was all but eradicated and the standard of living for its citizenry was close to the monarchy's own.

But the Notares star system was not without enemies. Having little in the way of natural resources, especially certain minerals, elements, and rare metals, early on the monarchy had needed help from their charges to acquire what their own planetary system lacked. So for their own survival, their own advancement, they'd become interstellar raiders. A consortium of the best of the best young men and women—warrior knights—had been called up from the far reaches of the monarchy's realm. For hundreds of years, the Brotherhood maintained the honorable role of defender of the realm.

So what went wrong? Collin searched his mind and then the answer became apparent. While the Brotherhood was a large, independent, often secretive organization—outside direct control of the aristocracy—the small Kardon Guard was quite different. Intended to be the king or queen's personal militia, they were a kind of castle guard.

In years past, the animosity between the two groups had always been attributed to a healthy competitiveness between the two necessary, and highly regarded, military factions. Four years ago things changed. With the death of the Kardon Guard's commanding officer, Commandant Montae, a new officer was quickly promoted into the vacated position. The newly appointed Commandant, named Nari, was ambitious, to say the least. There had been rumors that his relationship with the queen had grown into something more than professional, that he even had designs on marrying the queen. But that would first require his induction into the aristocracy—something the Council of Elders would need to pass judgment on. Three years ago Nari began a campaign to increase the duties of the Kardon Guard. Where once the Brotherhood maintained Notares' only fleet of advanced warships, the Kardon Guard determined to acquire their own ships, their own military budget. As the relationship between Queen Arabella Valora and Commandant Nari became more cemented, and even as they appeared in public together at social and important events of state, Nari was pushing for the merger of his Kardon Guard and the Brotherhood.

It was no surprise to the knights of the Brotherhood that Commandant Nari and his ever growing fleet of warships would only stop reaching when he had total, unhindered domination of Notares space. It was also clear that he would soon have designs on the monarchy itself.

When the order came for the dismantling of the Brotherhood, exactly two years past, a declaration of war against Nari's Kardon Guard, but not against the monarchy, was the inevitable result.

Ignoring the Brotherhood's warnings of Nari's obvious true intentions, Queen Arabella Valora, furious, sided with the Commandant and his Kardon Guard. In a broadcast that reached throughout the realm, the queen denounced the Brotherhood, and condemned anyone who maintained allegiance to what she now called an antiquated sect of old mystics and knights to a sentence of death by decapitation. Collin glanced above to the knight's *cleave-sheer*, hung high up on the bulkhead. At least death would be quick, he figured.

The last of the recruits joined the line and stood at attention. Bragg appeared less than a minute later.

"Eight minutes. What takes one eight full minutes to accomplish a simple morning ritual? You there, the one everyone calls Tink. Do you have bathroom problems, perhaps a bit of constipation?"

Tink shook her head, "No!" she replied vehemently, her face blushing crimson.

"How about you ... the big fellow with the belly; you were last out of the bathroom. Were there long lines? Or, perhaps, your shower head was malfunctioning?"

David *the Brick* Burk shook his head. "I actually am a bit constipated."

That brought laughter from everyone and while the chief tried to keep a straight face, he was doing a poor job of it. "Listen up! You will complete your bathroom routines in five minutes or less. After today, you will start to lose tributes. Since you don't currently have any, you get a one-day pass. Understand that life, from this point on, will not only be about acquiring tributes, but also keeping them. Talk to your leader. Any chance you have of returning to your home world will depend on your accumulating more tributes than the other two Chains."

Eyes locked on Collin. All humor was replaced with apprehension.

The chief was pacing; the briefest of smiles crossed his face. Collin learned the first of many lessons to come: *They like to stir up the pot. They like to manipulate.*

"By now some of you, maybe even most of you,

are cognizant of the fact that you know more about the Brotherhood, the Kardon Guard, and life here, within the realm of the Notares, than you did yesterday. We tripled the SLP downloads in order to get you up-to-speed more quickly. Tonight, we'll do the same. Let me know if any of your little brains exhibit side effects. We're going well beyond the recommended subliminal allocation of information in order to even the playing field.

"In a few moments you will be marched up to deck six. There, you will meet the other two Chains. Let me give you this bit of advice before you embark on today's competitions. They want to win. Their futures, like your own, depend on them winning. Here's some free advice— assess your enemy's strengths, as well as their weaknesses, and make adjustments accordingly. Be strategic. Any questions?"

Darren was the first to raise his hand.

"Mr. Mallon?"

How the chief knew Darren's last name was beyond Collin's understanding. It was then he realized the second important lesson since being there: the mind-bands worked both ways … not only did they deliver information into the mind—they collected from it as well.

"What is it … what kind of competition will it be?"

A mischievous look came over the chief's face. "One you may be quite pleased with. I understand you have already played together as a team, am I right?"

Darren also smiled and looked over to his buddies. "You might say that," he said, with a bit of bravado.

"Then you should have no problem defeating the other two teams in a little game of Pangallo."

Another hand went up, this time from Humphrey. "What is Pangallo, Chief?"

"It's a game and it's a sport. All the boys and girls here,

from the age of five or six, grow up playing Pangallo."

Collin raised his hand. "Chief, how are we to compete with recruits who have played this sport since they were little kids? That doesn't seem fair."

The chief slowly walked over to Collin and held his gaze for several long seconds before answering: "Is it fair when three Marauder-class warships lie in wait behind an asteroid, only to surprise their quarry, a small Brotherhood freighter? Firing upon that vessel and killing all crew on board? Is it fair that Brotherhood knights have been ostracized and can no longer return to their homes ... to their families?"

"No, sir, it's not."

"Do not confuse our Brotherhood values of commitment, honor, allegiance, and sacrifice with strategic necessities of war. Over the next six weeks you will be faced with what may seem to you to be contradictions ... even paradoxes. Remember, above and beyond the final scores, you will be measured and rewarded on how you conduct yourselves."

"One more thing ..." the chief looked down and began walking again, "the Brotherhood's basic training is intense, to say the least. Most Chains, over a six week period, will have several casualties."

He let that sink in. Up until then, Collin had equated the Brotherhood's basic training with something akin to the U.S. Army's. Yeah, certainly tough and even physically daunting—but no lethal consequences were typically involved. What the chief was talking about was a ten percent mortality rate.

"Take a moment and look around. The truth is, young men and women, there's a damn good chance some of you won't survive the day, let alone the full six weeks."

Chapter 25

The trek up to deck six was also an exercise in how to march. Three times the Lone Stars were ordered to return all the way back to the barracks and begin the march again. Finally, with their heads facing straight ahead, legs walking in unison, and with just the right amount of spacing between each person, the group was allowed to enter what was called the Training Field. Collin knew this because there was a placard above the double hatchway entrance that spelled the name out.

They entered the compartment, which was like a small sports arena, to the sounds of grunts and bodies hitting other bodies. The two other Chains were already there, one team wearing blue uniforms, the other wearing gray, and they seemed to be in the midst of a practice game. What struck Collin first, other than both Chains looking highly athletic—was the simple fact they were adults. Again, Bragg had thrown another curveball into the mix—increasing the odds they'd be defeated.

Collin tried to make heads or tails out of the game in progress. The field was roughly the size of a regulation football field, but probably closer in actual size to a soccer field. Each team consisted of ten players, their replacements standing by on the sidelines. The opposing players were in the process of lining up, in an inward-facing, circular formation. Now, with ten-man circles at opposing ends of the field, the players intertwined their arms at their elbows—creating an unbroken link around their own circle. A referee placed a yellow ball at the center of each circle.

A gong rang from somewhere and play started. The two

big circles began moving toward each other, gaining speed as they went. The two yellow balls were kicked between the team players on both circles as the teams moved down the field. When they finally collided, the slapping sounds of large bodies hitting other large bodies made Collin cringe. Only the circle with the gray-uniformed recruits came apart, as two of their players were thrown to the ground. A gong sounded again. Apparently, the opening play was over. Collin figured the play seemed equivalent to a kickoff in football. The two players on the ground got up and rejoined their gray-recruit circle. A referee took their ball and threw it toward the sideline. The opposing team, the blue recruits, which hadn't broken apart during the opening play, got to maintain possession of the one single ball, now in play.

"What the hell is this?" Humphrey asked. "No one said anything about f-ing adults being our competition."

Collin was only too aware that this latest surprise would take the wind out of his team's sails. He also realized this could be his first test as their chosen leader.

"Cool, huh?" he asked.

Darren spun around on him. "Cool? You think this is cool?"

Collin remained unfazed. "Do you remember last year when we played that scrimmage game? The one with those university kids … the Texan Musketeers? Most of those guys were in their twenties. We killed them. Sent them crying to their mommies."

Darren's expression changed. "I remember … yeah, they were *big* mothers too … so you think we can beat these guys?"

"I'm betting these guys and gals have played this stupid Pangallo game countless times. But are they an actual team … that's trained and played together, day-in and day-out, like we have? Do they have the kind of mojo we have? No way."

Collin turned his attention back to the game. "Hey, we need to pay attention … watch what they're doing so we can beat them." Collin pointed to the field. "Looks like each team has ten players on the field at the start of the game. Seven players are male and three are female. I guess the object of the game is to move the ball down the field, in the direction of the opposition's end zone. That much is similar to our kind of football." *But any other similarity seems to end there*, he thought.

"What the hell are they doing now?" DiMaggio asked, making a puzzled face.

Both teams now had their three female players sitting on the shoulders of three large teammates—their legs held firmly in the grasp of the male players below. One of the females, on the controlling blue team, with short, dark red hair, now held the ball. As soon as the gong sounded she threw the ball across to another shoulder-riding blue teammate, who missed catching the pass and the ball dropped to the field. The players in blue used their feet to pass the ball between them. The gray opposing team, not having possession of the ball, immediately broke apart—though first ensuring that each team player was linked to another by at least one arm. In a whipping motion, the gray team players were sent in to break the opposing team's linkage. All the while the blue team, holding the ball, continued to pass it between themselves. One of the blue male players, in a scooping motion, got his foot beneath the ball and kicked it up to one of the female players, who began passing it between the other two females. As soon as the gray opposition got close to disrupting the players closest to the ball, or around the ball, she'd pass it to another female. The blue team, as a Chain, moved the ball thirty yards towards the opposition's end zone before the gray team managed to break through their circle and take possession of the ball. Then, in a surprise move, the grays—keeping their line of players still linked at the elbows—whipped one end of their line forward; then, abruptly, they swung the other end of the line forward as well. They quickly advanced, fifty yards down the field—all the while the ball was constantly in motion. Apparently that was another rule—the ball must not become stationary. The blue team, also reformed into a line of linked players, was doing their best to disrupt the grays' advance, but to no avail. The grays' line of players crossed over the opposition's end zone. Then, in one final pass of the ball, a female positioned on shoulders just over the line caught the ball. Excited, she yelled, "Pangallo!"

Chief-in-Command Bragg was already on the field, making his way over to the two teams. With hands extended overhead, he motioned everyone to huddle around him. He turned toward the sidelines and motioned to the Lone Stars, as well as the gray and blue sidelined players: "Everyone, move in … gather round!"

Everyone circled around the chief. Collin assessed the other players and started to feel discouraged. Some of these men and women were older than he'd thought—perhaps as old as twenty-five?

"Take this opportunity to greet the other Chains, the other recruits, that you will be competing against over the next six weeks. First, under command of Fico Lucan, we have the Brave Hearts in blue."

A beefy-looking guy, with several days' stubble, half-heartedly raised a hand.

"Next, we have Commander Rocco Puma, of the Righteous Warriors in gray."

Rocco bobbed his chin once.

"Lastly, we have Commander Collin Frost, with his Lone Stars, garbed in red."

Collin also gave a half-hearted wave with his hand. "What

up!" he offered.

"Starting now, there will be the awarding, and detraction, of tributes … which will include the short Pangallo game you're about to participate in. And later today for the weapons and marksmanship training; the one-on-one close-quarters combat; and on your on-station duties. You have a full day ahead of you. Now, you will play three-team Pangallo for one hour. Take your positions."

"Chief, can I ask a question?" Collin asked.

The chief raised his eyebrows.

"Where does the third circle formation start from?"

Apparently that was a stupid question; recruits from both the blue and gray teams snickered.

The chief turned to Rocco Puma. "Commander, can you inform Commander Frost of the correct third team starting position?"

"Your choice, either end," Puma answered.

"Take your positions," the chief said again.

Collin turned to Darren. "Any suggestions?"

Without hesitation, Darren began tapping on shoulders, "Bubba, you're in, Collin in, Humphrey in, Lydia in, Tink, Karen, DiMaggio, White, you're in, and Gregg, you're in. The rest of you are sidelined." There were a few groans as the latter moved off to the sidelines.

The Lone Stars took up position at the same end of the field as the blue Brave Hearts team. Both teams moved away from each other, closer to the sidelines.

"Okay … everyone join arms," Collin said, joining elbows with Bubba on his left and DiMaggio on his right. As soon as their circle was linked together, a referee rolled a ball into its center.

Collin looked around the circle and saw apprehension on their faces.

"By the way ... I received a memo from Captain Dante Primo last night. He informed me, we only get the *Turd* back if we come out of the six-week training with more tributes than the other two Chains. To the winner goes all spoils." Collin shrugged, the news now delivered.

Humphrey looked like he was about to have an aneurism. "How the hell can he just change things like that? That's total bullshit!"

Several in the group spat similar remarks. The apprehension on their faces from moments before was now replaced with anger. Collin inwardly smiled.

At the sound of the gong, Collin shot forward for the ball.

Chapter 26

The gong came again five seconds later as the referee stopped play. Apparently Cine had wandered onto the field.

The referee raised a hand and made an unrecognizable gesture. "Too many players on the field; subtraction of ten tributes from red team!"

Humphrey screamed toward the sideline, "Get the hell off the field, freak!"

Bound arm-in-arm, Lydia and Tink, looking small and scared, stared at each other and then at Darren and Collin. Frustration was clearly evident on their faces.

"Can we just wait up a sec? I'm not like one of you football players ... or the Pangallo players. Neither is Tink. What if we drop the ball? We'll get killed out there," Lydia said in exasperation.

Everyone got ready again for the sound of the gong.

"You'll just have to buck-up, girls. We're all in over our heads," Darren told them, leaning forward, ready to attack the ball.

Gong. Darren and the two players at his side ran forward while the players across from him ran backwards. Karen lost her balance, but the players on either side quickly lifted her up by her elbows and back onto her feet. The red Lone Star circle began to make unsteady progress down the field.

"They're leaving us in the dust," Humphrey screamed. "Pick up the pace!"

Collin, positioned at the side of the circle, was doing his best to watch where he was going, yet study the other team. "They constantly move ... keeping their circle turning. I think it helps them run faster," he yelled.

154

Slowly at first, Collin's team started to move their circle counter-clockwise as they progressed down the field. They hadn't gained any on the blue team, but they hadn't lost ground, either.

The gray team was now moving close to the midfield line. The blues and grays were going to collide. Collin heard the sounds of bodies hitting bodies again and watched as two blue team players tumbled to the ground. Without hesitation, the gray team spun around and moved away from the two fallen blues. Picking up speed, they headed toward the Lone Stars.

Collin saw an opportunity. "Slow down ... stop spinning! Let Bubba hit their circle first."

Easier said than done. Their circle slowed but continued spinning for several more seconds, heading for a collision with the grays. Fortunately, their two hundred and seventy pound center, Royce White, barreled into their players. Royce, like an immense bowling ball, caused four grays to go airborne. They grunted as they hit the ground. The Lone Stars held their circle together without any links broken. The gong sounded.

Collin heard Owen Platt and Garry Hurst shout taunts and obscenities at the opposing teams from the sidelines. The referee looked ready to issue another penalty. Fortunately, the two boys quieted down.

All three circles re-formed.

Darren was back barking orders. "We have to move it! Tink, Lydia ... Karen, up on the shoulders of Bubba, White and ..." he looked around the circle, "and you, Collin."

Bubba lifted Tink onto his shoulders with one arm. Royce got Karen up on his shoulders, which left only Lydia standing, looking up at Collin.

"It's not the frigging prom here, Sticks. Just help her up," Humphrey prompted.

Collin lowered himself to one knee as Lydia climbed onto his shoulders from behind. Unsteady at first, he stood all the way up. He felt the warmth of her thighs pressed in around his neck and shoulders. He glanced up at her.

"Just pay attention to the game," she scolded.

The players intertwined their arms again.

"Wait! Which way are we going? Which way is our end zone?" DiMaggio asked.

There were more than a few confused expressions around the circle.

"We keep going the same way we started. Good God … are you all retarded?" Darren asked between clenched teeth.

The referee was back and placed the yellow ball in the middle of their circle. Each of the circles now had their three females up on teammate shoulders.

"Whatever you do, don't let go of the person next to you," Darren ordered. "I'm going for the ball … I'll get it up to one of the girls. Don't forget to keep passing it around. You got that?"

The three girls nodded, none looking particularly confident.

Collin looked behind him and saw that the players within the other two circles were quickly making plans, strategizing in hushed voices. He caught the eye of one of the opposing players. He mouthed something unintelligible, but Collin got the gist of it: He was out for blood.

Gong! Both the gray and blue teams broke apart. Darren pulled like a plow horse, both arms straining to maintain the holds at his elbows. Everyone moved in unison. The circle spun faster than before, the players somewhat more familiar with how things worked. Collin watched as Darren reached the ball and, soccer-style, dribbled it forward.

"Hey hey hey … Watch the left side!" Humphrey yelled.

But it was too late. The blue team whipped their line of players toward the Lone Stars' red circle. They had a Bubba counterpart—big and mean looking, the man at the end of the line was scary just standing still, let alone being whipped around with the accumulated momentum of a freight train. He charged at the Lone Stars with enough force to bring three of the teens down to their knees: DiMaggio, Humphrey and Gregg. Each grimaced. Collin guessed that it must have felt as though their arms were being yanked from their shoulders.

The referee scurried in and, with his hands on knees, closely inspected the fallen red players. "The Lone Stars' links are unbroken … they maintain possession … continue play!"

Scrambling back to their feet, the Lone Stars, their arms still intertwined, began moving again.

"Get ready, Lydia!" Darren said, now dribbling faster. He glanced up at her, perched high on Collin's shoulders.

"Careful … Blues are coming," Collin said, seeing their swinging line of players running full out, ready to make their swing inward.

Darren got the ball a foot into the air with the toe of his shoe, then gave it another bigger kick, sending the ball high in the air, over everyone's heads. Collin strained to position Lydia beneath the ball. She caught it with both hands and immediately tossed it over to Karen, who in turn tossed it over to Tink. Three more swinging lines of attack came from the opposing teams, as the Lone Stars' circle steadily made progress down the field.

The gray Righteous Warriors had managed to get themselves into a straight line in front of the now-approaching goal line. There was no way the red team would be able to cross into the end zone as a circle.

Collin yelled across to Bubba, "Let go of Humphrey's arm. We're going to whip you into their line. Lydia, when you get

157

the ball, pass it back to Tink." Collin's eyes met Darren's—he nodded his agreement to the plan.

Bubba let go of Humphrey's arm just as the Brave Hearts, in blue, made their own move. Their leader, Fico Lucan, was at the end of their line—ready to snap forward.

The ball continued to be passed—to Lydia, then to Tink, back to Lydia, then to Karen, around and around. In a united effort, the line of Lone Stars, ten players arm-in-arm, swung around one hundred and eighty degrees. By the time Bubba and his substantial girth careened into the line of gray Righteous Warriors, near the center of the field, there was nothing their players could do to stop him. He hit them like a bus hitting traffic cones. Lydia passed the ball to Tink, in the end zone. She yelled, "Pangallo!" With that, the referee announced the Lone Stars had scored and were awarded one hundred points, minus the ten they'd lost earlier.

While the Lone Stars reveled in being the first to score, Collin noticed Captain Dante Primo standing on the sidelines, next to the chief. Over the next forty-five minutes, the other two teams scored once. Both teams, Righteous Warriors and Brave Hearts, had earned one hundred tributes, while the Lone Stars had ninety.

Chapter 27

The march from the activity field over to the weapons range took five minutes. The Lone Stars were in low spirits. They weren't used to losing, and even though it was only a ten-point deficit, they were still angry. Collin hadn't expected them to do as well as they had against experienced, adult, opposition. Tink, Karen and Lydia were somewhat more upbeat with what they had accomplished as females on the team, but not everyone was that positive.

"We're in last place ... epic fail ... and that doesn't get us back home!" Humphrey spat.

"We'll make up the difference somewhere else," Collin said. But by the dark expressions on everyone's faces, his pep talk was falling on deaf ears.

As they approached the weapons range, the muffled sounds of energy weapons being discharged increased. The corridor had become more and more congested with Brotherhood military personnel passing by. Some glanced at them with mild interest—others, with scowling obvious annoyance.

The range was in another immense compartment. As they filed in through the double-hatchway, Collin became immediately at ease. It wasn't that it looked anything like the little rifle range he and his father frequented back home, in Middleton. Rather, it was more a feeling he got from a combination of different things: the sounds of constant weaponry fire—and something else—something that happens when there's multiple shooters with their hyper-concentration—an almost imperceptible buzz which permeates the atmosphere.

The chief gestured with a finger to his lips for everyone to be quiet. They merged into one line and slowly walked behind him. The firing range was huge, closer in size to a typical golf course's driving range. Collin noticed there were varying terrains off in the distance. With bright orange demarcations, each shooter had his, or her, own cordoned-off lane, or slice, that widened into the far distance. A dozen soldiers—some prone on the ground, some standing, and some down on one knee—were firing at a wide assortment of stationary and moving targets.

"They're like holograms," DiMaggio murmured in a lowered voice, standing behind Collin.

"The ultimate video game … I got to get me some of this," Humphrey said from the back of the line.

The chief turned around while walking backwards. His eyes found Humphrey and his cold stare conveyed his intended message: *shut the hell up.*

But Collin's attention was out on the range. The holograms were amazing. He'd actually only realized the targets were holograms when DiMaggio pointed it out. Some of the targets were armed attacking soldiers, dressed in some sort of battle suit. Other targets were hovering robots or drones, firing their own integrated energy weapons back at the shooters, who were practicing at the front of the range. He actually felt heat coming from a series of pulse shots from a tank-like hover vehicle now emerging over a distant crest. The boys looked at each other and smiled.

The chief waved everyone into a smaller compartment. The hatch slid closed behind the last teen to enter. With the exception of perhaps some big gun shows, Collin had never seen such an assortment of firearms in his life. Certainly he'd never seen this type of weaponry. Multiple rifle-rack rows lined two of the bulkheads. Another bulkhead was dedicated to smaller racks, and shelves, holding hand-held firearms.

The chief stepped up to a high metal counter holding a variety of handguns atop it. He motioned the teens to huddle around him. "You are here to learn about a variety of Brotherhood weapons. You'll learn how to fire these weapons … and to do so with precision. You'll also learn how to maintain your weapons, which, at some point in your life, might mean the difference between survival or death.

"Is there anyone here familiar with weapons?"

"Call of Duty: Advanced Warfare … Stinger M7; that'll show the Kardon Guard," Humphrey said enthusiastically, fist-bumping Clifford Bosh.

The chief looked momentarily confused by Humphrey's words when he saw Collin had raised his hand. "What's your experience, Mr. Frost?"

"My dad's a veteran soldier. He takes me to the range when he's not deployed. I've been around firearms most of my life."

The chief nodded and turned to see if anyone else had any weapons experience. "Individually, and as a Chain unit, you will need to excel, to outperform all others. Let me make one thing perfectly clear … this is not play. The weapons you'll be using can easily be set to lethal settings. A lapse in concentration, a mistake here and on the range, will get someone, maybe the person next to you, killed. There have been twenty-nine weapon range fatalities here on Nero Station. And those mishaps befell recruits with more experience, more weapons knowledge, than any of you have. So let me say this … if I find any of you acting inappropriately, not taking this seriously, I will shoot you myself." With that, the chief picked up the closest handgun on the countertop, checked it, and shot Humphrey in the chest.

The energy blast was loud enough to cause everyone to jump. Humphrey dropped like a sack of potatoes. One second he was standing beside Clifford Bosh; the next, he was splayed awkwardly on the deck. There was an acrid smell of ozone and singed fabric in the air. Wide-eyed, no one moved. They all stared down at the lifeless body—a burn-hole in his heart area.

"As I said, these weapons are fully functional." The chief looked down at the energy weapon in his hand.

Both Collin and DiMaggio started to crouch down next to Humphrey.

"Do not move!" yelled Bragg. He waited for them to stand up straight. Collin was having a difficult time keeping his rage in check.

"Now this is a Ponge 412, the standard sidearm weapon for Brotherhood forces. If you look here, at the lower left side of the barrel, you'll see that it has six micro-settings." The chief used his thumb to move the selector switch to the first position.

At this point the knuckles on Collin's two fists had turned white.

The chief droned on, "The first position is the lowest level, a stun setting. Mr. Humphrey was nailed with a setting of three: enough to burn a hole in his uniform and through several epidermal layers as well. The jolt to his nervous system was enough to disrupt consciousness … but he is not dead. I don't think." He casually glanced down at Humphrey for several seconds before the unconscious teenager's eyes fluttered open. "Someone help Mr. Humphrey back up onto his feet."

The chief scanned the faces around him. "You. Come around here next to me."

Lydia's eyes widened and she froze in place.

"I'm not going to shoot you, Ms. Bennett. Do as you're told."

Lydia took in a breath, walked around the counter, and stood next to him.

"What is this weapon?" he asked her, in an almost comforting voice.

"Ponge 412."

"How many different settings does it provide for?" he asked, handing her the weapon.

"Six," she answered. She took the gun in her right hand and looked at the selector switch.

"Good ... now change the setting to the first position."

She used her thumb as the chief had shown them and repositioned the switch. "Like that?"

The chief took the gun from her and looked at the setting. He raised the weapon and pointed it at Collin. "You tell me ... was it set to the lowest setting, or the highest, most lethal, setting?"

Lydia's expression turned to uncertainty as she searched her memory.

The chief fired once, twice, three times.

Lydia screamed, "No!"

But Collin did not fall to the deck as Humphrey had. In fact, he was smiling back at her. He rubbed at a point on his chest and said, "Warm."

"Setting position one. This is the training-level setting you will always use, while on Nero Station." The chief looked at Humphrey, who was now back on his feet. He still looked somewhat disoriented. "What is it I just said, Mr. Humphrey?"

"Setting position one is the training-level setting and we will always use that setting, while here on Nero Station."

"Correct." The chief walked to the back bulkhead and removed a rifle from one of the racks. He brought it over to the counter and laid it flat before him. "This is a Larrik 5 ... most commonly referred to as a Doubler. As you can see, there are two barrels that merge into one, here at this end. It disperses plasma … high-energy ionized gas. The plasma is created by superheating internal lasers. A very powerful weapon. This is the same weapon the Kardon Guard utilizes." He flipped the weapon over and tapped at a selector switch near the trigger guard. "And here is your power-level selector switch. Again … setting one will be the only setting ever used within the confines of Nero Station. Is that understood?"

Everyone nodded.

"Over the next hour you will learn how to dismantle and clean both the Ponge 412 and the Doubler. In the weeks to come, you will be able to disassemble and reassemble these weapons in seconds … you'll be able to accomplish this in total darkness. Any questions?"

"When do we get to shoot them?" Bubba asked.

"Maybe tomorrow. Let's see how well you do today, with the basic maintenance aspects. You're already well behind the other two Chains … you better hope you don't fall back any further. It's all about tributes and you're lacking in that regard. There are countertops situated around this compartment. Each of you must retrieve a Ponge 412 and a Larrik 5 Doubler from the racks. Go now."

Chapter 28

Chief-in-Command Bragg left the Lone Stars at the close combat gym. They'd taken a transport elevator to one of the sub-decks, located at the very lowest level of the station. Gone were the deep, rich colors, textures, and muted high lighting. This part of the space station was barebones, utilitarian, and drab. Pipes and conduits ran along gray bulkheads.

Collin, leading the way into the first of what he figured were several adjoined compartments, was almost bowled over by the hot, humid air. With the exception of a three-foot-wide walkway that encircled the thirty-by-thirty-foot square compartment, the deck was completely covered with padding. In the center of the room, standing beneath a dim overhead light, stood a lone figure. The girls giggled—both Lydia and Tink covered their mouths, embarrassed. The boys said nothing, but made faces at each other.

He was a slight man, no more than five foot seven—if that. His body, glistening with sweat, was toned and showed an astonishing amount of muscle definition. He was also naked, with the exception of a small black loincloth that covered his privates.

The Lone Stars moved around the periphery of the compartment, mindful not to tread upon the padded floor in shoes. Eyes closed, the man continued to stand perfectly still in what looked like a yoga position, or maybe a Kung Fu-type pose. Then Collin realized the man was balancing all his weight on one foot—actually, on his toes. Five minutes passed before he gracefully moved into a regular standing position.

He opened his eyes and surveyed the group. He smiled with child-like innocence, bowing his head and bringing his hands together as if in prayer, and remained still. Collin was the first to follow suit and bow in a similar manner. One by one, the others followed his lead, until everyone in the compartment had a bowed head, their two hands clasped together, like the slight man in the center of the compartment.

He stood erect and smiled again. "Welcome to this sparring room … the Roko. Thank you. I am honored by your presence here. I am honored I was assigned to train you. Please address me as Master Car." He took several steps forward and then turned and walked around the compartment, looking closely at each teenager, holding their gaze and nodding to each one. He returned to the center of the compartment.

"You must be an exceptional group of young men and women. I was retired; have not been involved in training young recruits for some years now. Note that you, alone, will be trained by me … the other two Chains have other trainers. I am one hundred and thirty-six years of age. My body does not move as it once did. I am not as quick as I once was. Please forgive my shortcomings and I will forgive yours. So let's get started. There are male and female dressing rooms. I will wait here while you dress for today's exercises. Place your garments, your shoes … everything within the cubbyhole shelves. Rest assured, no one will take your things. This is a safe environment. Go now."

Collin continued to stare at the strange slim man. He looked to be no older than forty, if even that. He projected an aura of confidence, while still maintaining an air of humbleness at the same time.

Collin was the last to enter the changing room.
"No way I'm …" Bubba was holding up a small black rectangular cloth, with longer strands of material extending from both its ends. Some of the other teens were trying to figure out the loincloth—turning it this way and

that.

Collin heard a scream and then sudden laughter from what he assumed was the next-door female dressing area. That would be Tink, he thought—he recognized her voice.

"I don't like it either. Let's just do what he wants," Collin said, removing his shoes and socks. He proceeded to place things into one of the cubbyholes. He then removed his uniform and underwear. He'd already figured out the loincloth in his head. He'd actually taken a few seconds to note how Master Car had tied his own loincloth. It wasn't all that complicated.

"This is bullshit. I'm going to be strutting around out there with only my balls covered up?" Humphrey groused emphatically. That brought a roar of laughter from those around him. Collin noticed Humphrey had a nasty burn on his chest—he'd live with that scar the rest of his life.

Collin got the cloth situated properly and the straps wrapped around his hips. The straps were so long he had to wrap them around his narrow hips twice. Royce White, on the other hand, was having a far worse time of it.

"It ain't going to fit around me. No matter what I try."

Collin turned around and saw Royce standing naked—his rotund belly hanging down close to his genitals. In each hand he held on to a strap that only reached halfway around his body.

Collin found an extra loincloth and ripped the straps from it. "Tie these to the ends. Should reach around you then," he offered.

It took another few minutes for everyone, including the three Daccians, to get properly attired. All the boys were smiling, though some of them looked ridiculous. Others, like Darren, looked like professional underwear models. Collin didn't let his mind go to the embarrassment he himself would face once he'd left the changing room.

He hesitated, then walked out of the dressing room. *Ready or not, here comes Commander Sticks, in all his glory.*

Master Car was back in the middle of the mats in a different stationary pose. The six girls were already there. They had on a different type of arrangement: their two black cloth pieces, affixed in place, weren't too dissimilar to bikinis, although they also had the same *wedgy*-strip of material running between the cheeks of their buttocks.

Collin averted his eyes from the girls, keeping them locked on Master Car. As soon as the near-naked Lone Stars were settled into place, Master Car surrendered his pose and assessed the group. He nodded appreciatively.

"Soon you will no longer feel embarrassed by your nakedness, I promise you." He was on the move now and walking the perimeter of the Roko. Collin's eyes held on to Lydia as Master Car passed by her. She stood tall, with her hands at her sides; she didn't seem self-conscious at all. *But then again, why should she?* Everything about her was pure perfection. What startled Collin back into self-conscious nervousness was the fact she was staring right back at him.

"You, the one called Ms. McBride. Please stand in the middle of the Roko."

Tink, arms crossed over her chest, moved to the center of the compartment. Her face was flushed scarlet. So tiny she'd wrapped the straps of her two cloths around her twice, maybe three times.

"And you, Mr. White. Join Ms. McBride."

As big as a Sumo wrestler, he moved into position right next to Tink. He held his head high and seemed to be coping well enough. The contrast between their two physical forms could not be greater. One of his thighs alone probably had the same weight of Tink's entire body.

Master Car stood before the two. "I will show you how to bring Mr. White down to the mat with little effort." A marker appeared in his hands, which a second before had held none. *Had he kept it hidden somewhere within the folds of his loincloth?* Collin had no idea. Now, standing directly in front of the bigger man, Master Car proceeded to draw small red circles, at different locations, on Royce's body. Barely visible against his black skin, Collin had to concentrate to find them. Car started with a red circle just beneath Royce's right kneecap, then drew one on the back of his left ankle, right above his heel. He proceeded to draw five more red circles at various anatomical locations around Royce White's large body.

Master Car then turned to Tink. "Will you assist me with an exercise, Ms. McBride?"

Tink nodded. "I guess so … Yes, sir."

"Simply call me Master Car. What I want you to do is stand before Mr. White. That's right, get close to him. As you can see, I have made small red circles all over, at different locations on his body."

"I see them."

"I have also numbered them."

Tink leaned in a little closer and squinted her eyes. "Oh, okay, I see the numbers too."

"Very good. What I want you to do is use your right index finger and, when I give the command, touch each one of the circles, in the ascending order of the numbers."

"You want me to do that now?" Tink asked, looking at Master Car.

"In one moment. Mr. White, I apologize to you in advance for the pain you are about to endure. Take solace in the fact that the effects will only be temporary. Please stay standing as long as you can endure the pain."

Collin saw Royce already taking deep breaths, trying to

prepare for whatever was about to come.

"I will place my hand on your shoulder, Ms. McBride." Master Car positioned himself behind Tink. "When you are ready, Ms. McBride, you may begin."

Tink quickly looked around the room, smiled briefly, and stepped in closer to Royce. She found the circle marked 1 below his knee and touched it.

Royce bellowed out a loud painful, "Ahhh." His breathing was fast and shallow.

Tink looked almost as surprised as Royce. She'd found the second circle and, hesitantly, touched the back of his ankle. Another scream and Royce was falling backward, grabbing at his leg in obvious agony.

Collin watched as tears streamed down the big guy's cheeks. Royce sat on his ass, rubbing his ankle. He used his forearm to wipe snot from his runny nose. "Please stop, Tink. It hurts too much." Royce looked up at Master Car. "I'm sorry, I don't want to continue."

Master Car smiled and bowed to both Royce and Tink, his hands pressed together. "You honor me and the class with your assistance. Thank you. You may return to your Chain."

The Master waited for the two to leave the mats before speaking again: "Someone tell me what just happened. How was small Ms. McBride able to bring down someone nearly three times her weight with the slightest of touch?"

No one spoke for several moments. Finally Darren said, "You had her touch nerves, sensitive areas on White's body."

"Anyone else?" Master Car asked, shaking his head.

"You psyched him out. Played mind games on him," Humphrey said.

Master Car raised his brows and tilted his head. "That may have been part of it."

"It was you ... you connected with Royce through Tink

… your hand was on her shoulder," Collin said.

Master Car pointed to Collin. "And there is your answer. By using Ms. McBride as a conduit, I communicated directly to Mr. White's mind and nervous system. It's a matter of synchronizing with your opponent's overall life force. It's not magic. You will learn the fundamentals of what I've just demonstrated. It may take you a lifetime to perfect this technique, as well as the art of Kanda Mu itself, which is the ancient, and highly secret, form of martial arts used by the Brotherhood."

Collin raised his hand.

"Yes, Mr. Frost."

"Does everyone in the Brotherhood know this … what did you call it? Kandu Mu?"

"Not anymore. The Notares' young have much more interest for the game of Pangallo, or learning how to pilot a warship. But those that have achieved knighthood … as well as those within the monarchy, learned these ancient arts from an early age. Queen Arabella Valora herself could kill any one of you with the subtlest of touches.

Collin let that sink in. Both Captain Primo and the principessa would surely be experts in Kandu Mu … something to keep in mind.

Master Car said, "You will now break into pairs. You will learn to throw a punch that has the strength of ten men behind it."

Chapter 29

When they exited the firing range, the chief was coming down the corridor with his young squire, Mr. Palermo, rushing to keep up.

The chief held up a hand. "You will now head up to the mess hall for an hour lunch break. Go ahead and get into your two-line formations."

The Lone Stars did as they were told. They'd lined up a number of times now and moved into position quickly.

"Mr. Frost, you will not be joining your Chain today … please come stand next to me. The rest of you, follow Mr. Palermo up to the mess."

As the two lines moved away, quick glances in Collin's direction showed uncertainty from several teens and even some concern from others.

"This way, Mr. Frost," the Chief said, heading quickly off in the opposite direction from the others. They walked together for several moments before they reached an elevator. The door slid open as they approached and they stepped inside.

"Eventually, you'll get accustomed to the station's layout. It's one of three … Nero Station, Astor Station, and Juno Station. Nero is smallest of the three and the oldest."

Collin couldn't imagine a space station larger than this one—and it looked fairly new to him. "Do they ever get attacked by the Kardon Guard?" Collin asked.

Chief Bragg smiled at that. "All the time. Even though Nero Station is situated on the outskirts of Notares space, in a kind of no man's land, we're still attacked fairly often. For that reason, there are never fewer than thirty Brotherhood warships patrolling local space. You and your Chain recruits will be spending significant time on those vessels as part of your on-duty apprenticeships."

Collin nodded. "Um … where is it I'm going now, Chief? Did I do … am I in trouble?"

"No, Mr. Frost, you are not in any trouble. Capitano Primo has requested the three Chain commanders to join him for lunch, at the capitano's table, on board the *Helix*."

They continued the rest of the way in silence. Collin recognized some of the station's landmarks from when they'd first arrived, but with the last turn he could tell the concourse they were now heading down was a different one.

From the series of portholes on his left, Collin was able to see the spaceship. Smaller than the *Tyrant*, it was also significantly more battle-worn. Scorch and blast marks covered the ship's port side.

"The *Helix* has been through a lot lately. Not really sure how much longer we'll be able to keep her in service."

They entered the warship's airlock compartment and waited—first, for the outer concourse hatch, and then the ship's hatch, to close. The air equalized in a matter of seconds and the Chief and Collin moved through another hatch into a ship, like the *Tyrant*, that was bustling with activity. The uniforms the crew wore were black, with a red piping that ran along the sleeve cuffs and around the collar. Chief Bragg casually returned several salutes as they progressed through the ship. They entered another elevator and Collin felt substantial G-forces as they descended downward, and then forward.

"We'll be dining in the capitano's ready room, which is directly off his quarters and close to the bridge." Once out of the elevator, they moved down another short corridor and then down a longer one.

"Here we go, Mr. Frost. In here."

Collin entered the captain's ready room and found at least ten people already seated around a formally-set table. The compartment was spacious, paneled in dark wood, and the air was thick with white smoke. Half of the men were smoking pipes. The aroma of rich tobacco, or its Notares equivalent, wasn't completely unpleasant to Collin's nostrils.

The room, loud with overbearing voices and laughter, went quiet as both the Chief and Collin's presences were noticed. Then Collin saw Captain Dante Primo, sitting on the far side of the table, in between two uniformed, middle-aged men.

Captain Primo, smiling, stood and gestured toward Collin. "Looks like we're all here now. Thank you, Chief, we'll take good care of him."

Chief Bragg nodded to Captain Primo and left. Collin suddenly felt abandoned—he was ridiculously out of his element. Not only was he just a teenager, he was in a room filled, undoubtedly, with seasoned military leaders—war heroes. Or not? There, seated at the end of the table, was Fico Lucan, commander of the Brave Hearts, and two down from him was Rocco Puma, commander of the Righteous Warriors. Collin nodded to them but got only blank stares back in return.

"Come, Mr. Frost, sit next to me." Primo patted the officer to his left on the shoulder. "Capitano Drago, would you be so kind as to scoot over one chair?"

Captain Drago slid over one seat and moved his tumbler, containing some kind of dark liquor, with him. Collin came around the table and took the chair Captain Primo pulled out for him. He sat and tried not to look too nervous.

Captain Primo remained standing. Talking had resumed and only by tapping a gold spork on his water glass could he refocus everyone's attention.

"Gentlemen … before we eat, if you haven't met them already, I'd like to introduce our newest recruit Chain commanders." Captain Primo placed a hand on Collin's shoulder. "Here we have Mr. Collin Frost, commander of the Lone Stars. He comes from many light-years away … beyond the frontier, from a planet called Earth. Captured by one of our queen's sim rover collector ships, he and his young compatriots not only survived that ordeal but found their way onto an old, abandoned, mining space vessel. Ingeniously, he used its excavation laser to punch a hole in the collector's hull and they escaped. Fortunately, or unfortunately, depending on how you view it, the *Tyrant* was there to greet their space vessel … which, by the way, they'd appropriately christened the *Turd*."

The word brought laughter from around the table. Collin smiled and saw genuine admiration in the expressions of the officers. But none from the other two recruit commanders. Collin wondered just how long the *Turd* would remain the property of the Lone Stars, once the ship's retrofitting was complete. *We're already ten tributes in the hole.*

"Tell me, Mr. Frost, on Earth, were you enrolled in a military academy, or already serving in the military?"

Collin stared back at the officer, seated directly across from him. "No, sir. I am … was … still in high school."

"And how old are you, young man?"

"Seventeen … wait … actually, eighteen." Collin was somewhat surprised he hadn't thought about it earlier—as of today—September 28th back on Earth, he'd just turned eighteen.

"You are very young to be considered for a leadership position." The officer made a sour expression as if he'd just smelled something unsavory.

Collin didn't know how to respond to that. The truth was,

the old guy was absolutely right. All Collin wanted to do was get him and his friends home, safe and sound. Playing war with these old farts was their idea, not his. Collin nodded, but kept his thoughts to himself.

Captain Primo extended a palm out to the officer on Collin's left: "Capitano Drago, tell us about your recruit."

So that's how this was working: The three Chains were each sponsored—or perhaps a better word was *mentored*—by a captain. That made sense. The Brotherhood seemed all about competition—why wouldn't that rise to the officer level, as well?

Captain Primo sat as Captain Drago stood. "I would like to introduce all of you to Mr. Fico Lucan, commander of the Brave Hearts."

Collin watched the round-faced recruit as he acknowledged the welcoming sentiments from around the table. Truth was, he looked bored.

Drago continued, "Mr. Lucan comes to us with two years of space-academy tutelage under his belt and, as we all know, he is a direct descendant of Queen Arabella Valora: a *marquis* of the House of Lucan, by birthright. Young Commander Lucan looks forward to commanding his own vessel one day soon, in the service of the Brotherhood."

At that last statement, Lucan looked at Collin—a smirk settling on his face: a face that read, *don't get too attached to that turd-ship of yours.*

Captain Drago said, "Very good, Mr. Lucan. Capitano Pritzi?"

The next captain to stand was tall and lean. He had a bright crop of red hair and an equally bright-red mustache above his upper lip.

"I am pleased to present Mr. Rocco Puma, of the Righteous Warriors. Son of a Brotherhood knight, the Duca of the House of Highcrest, this young man has already completed space academy and is well on his way toward gaining knighthood status himself. He has faced battles honorably, both in space and land campaigns."

Rocco Puma looked intelligent. He was fully engaged with those around him and Collin knew, at that moment, he was the man to beat. Fair-haired and handsome, Puma raised his chin and looked at Collin, down his perfectly straight nose.

More than merely military, these were sons of aristocrats. Collin remembered Captain Primo too was a Duca. *Was that like a Duke?* He was also a knight—and apparently still married to the queen's daughter. Collin wondered how he could ever fit into this mix of pompous blue bloods. Then, just as quickly as he'd given thought to it, he realized he didn't give a crap about any of that. Whatever didn't assist him in getting back home, screw it. He'd play along, just as long as it served him and the Lone Stars.

The food arrived on silver platters. It was some kind of duck or other fowl, covered in a sticky sweet sauce. Collin could not remember ever eating anything so tantalizingly scrumptious—so wonderful. There were the green mashed potatoes, which he'd tasted before, and several other food items that tasted good but looked unappetizing.

Captain Primo leaned in closer to Collin. "Mr. Frost, I've arranged for you to spend the afternoon here on the *Helix*, with Capitano Drago. Typically, you would spend your on-duty hours on board the *Tyrant*, but we decided to mix things up a little … just for today."

"What will the rest of the Lone Stars be doing?"

"They'll be on board the *Tyrant*. Everyone will spend a week at a different department post. Everyone, that is, except commanders. You three will spend two weeks on the bridge and four at other department posts."

Before Collin could ask a follow-up question, a loud klaxon sounded from all around them. Two uniformed men hurried into the ready room and made their way around, toward Captains Primo and Drago.

"Sirs, two Kardon Guard Marauders will be leaving Notares space and within weapons range within eight minutes."

"I'll return to the *Tyrant*," Captain Primo said, standing up. Everyone around the table then stood, several quickly leaving the ready room.

Captain Drago said, "Get back to your ship, Capitano Primo. But no assistance will be necessary. The day I can't handle two measly Marauders is the day I need to be put out to pasture. Go … I'll keep you apprised."

"And Mr. Frost?" Captain Primo asked him, stopping halfway to the hatch.

"What better way to learn than from the best, Capitano," he replied with a wry grin.

Chapter 30

As the ready room cleared out, Captain Drago stood and took several seconds to relight his pipe. He sucked in several long breaths, the bowl coming alive with bright orange embers. Collin remained standing, not sure what he was supposed to do next. The captain took several more puffs and held up his hand, signaling Collin to stand by. Reluctantly, he removed the pipe's stem from his lips and placed it in a metal ashtray on the table.

"A remarkable new blend I'm not about to waste over two little Marauders." Drago pulled down the front of his uniform jacket that only exaggerated his round paunch. "This way, recruit."

Captain Drago moved past Collin and exited the ready room. Fast on his heels, Collin followed. Ten steps down the corridor they walked into the bridge. About half the size of the *Tyrant's*, this bridge had several generations older technology. There was also significantly less attention given to customary military formality. Several bridge crew officers had their uniform's top buttons open, and there was an assortment of used cups and food items strewn about the tops of consoles. Three crewmen were standing in a group off to the side. They didn't acknowledge the captain as he entered and only when he took a seat in the command chair did they disperse, going to their respective posts.

"Take a seat, Mr. Frost," Captain Drago said, gesturing to a padded chair set slightly back from his own.

"Capitano, the Marauders have left Notares space and are on a direct course for Nero Station."

"Thank you, Mr. Capo," the captain replied.

Mr. Capo took a bite of what remained of his half-eaten sandwich before returning his attention back to his board.

"Helm, back us out of here and put us on an intersecting course. Maximum power to the thrusters."

Collin waited for the typical *Aye* or *Yes, Sir* … but it didn't come. As if reading Collin's thoughts, Captain Drago leaned back in his seat and half-turned toward the teen.

"We're like a family here, on board the *Helix*, Mr. Frost. Regs are a little more lax here than you'll find on other Brotherhood warships."

Collin nodded and saw one of the crewmembers look over and give him a shrug and a wink. The forward display was yet to be turned on. *What are they waiting for?* Collin thought, and then it suddenly came alive. In the distance he saw two ships approaching. They looked just like the other three he'd seen while on board the *Tyrant*. For a brief moment he wondered if Principessa Valora, Captain Primo's supposed wife, was on board either ship.

"Capitano, we're being hailed," a pasty-faced woman said off to the left, her fingers poised to tap on a blinking panel light.

Drago continued to stare at the screen in silence. Several seconds passed before he answered, "I'm not interested in anything they have to say. Tactical, charge forward guns."

"Guns are charged … we have a lock on both vessels."

Collin sat forward in his seat. He was finding it difficult to hold his tongue. *What the hell would the captain lose by answering their damn hail?*

"They still haven't charged weapons, Capitano. Maybe we should …"

Drago's head spun in the direction of his tactical officer. "You want to sit here, Jonto? Maybe come sit on my lap and we can command this ship together?"

The tactical officer simply shrugged. "No, that's all right. It's your bridge ... your ship."

Collin wasn't much for believing in things supernatural, but he was having a premonition—alarms going off in his head—they were all going to die on this **damn** ship of fools within the next few seconds.

"Fire both guns, Jonto ... blow them away."

Collin felt the weapons fire, each pulse like a hammer blow, emanating from somewhere below the bridge. *Thump thump thump thump ...*

The two Kardon Guard Marauders changed course at the same instant—one going left, the other going right. The ship on the left rolled, followed by an elaborate set of maneuvering that miraculously helped it evade most of the *Helix's* weapon fire. The other vessel, the one on the right, didn't fare nearly as well.

"Her shields are down. She's sucking space ... Orders?" Jonto asked.

"Finish her," Captain Drago replied.

Collin wasn't going to say anything, but the words flew from his mouth: "They're done for ... why don't we just capture them?"

"Keep your mouth shut, recruit," Drago snapped, without looking at Collin. "Vaporize them, Tactical."

Thump thump thump thump ... The Marauder exploded in so brilliant a flash that the display went totally blank for several seconds. Then, there was nothing there at all.

"**Crap!** The other one ... she's coming up our backside!" Jonto said, sounding scared.

"Charge stern guns and target—"

The captain's words were cut short by a thunderous blast from behind. Collin knew little about a warship's anatomy, but he was sure they'd just taken a devastating hit, about mid-ship.

"Shields are completely gone … we're venting to space on decks three and four."

The display changed to a port-side perspective. The remaining Marauder was sitting idle, just off their port side.

"Being hailed again, Capitano," the communications officer relayed, her fingers poised over the flashing console light.

Drago was on his feet. "What do we have left?"

"We have mid-ship torpedoes. Won't be able to get a lock, though, with the damage … I can only eyeball it."

"Load cannula tubes five and six."

Jonto shook his head and grimaced. "They'll detect it—"

"Just do it … just do what I tell you!" Captain Drago screamed, desperation in his voice.

Collin's eyes never left the display—the looming presence of the Marauder.

The Kardon Guard ship fired. The sound was like nothing Collin had ever heard, ever experienced. Explosions so loud his hearing was reduced to an ongoing high ringing in his ears. Sparks flared up from virtually every console on the bridge. The final concussive blast lifted both Collin and Captain Drago several feet into the air, then landed them hard onto the deck. The ship seemed to be coming apart around them—a wrecked ship, mere seconds from its inevitable doom.

Collin lay on his back and stared up at the top of the concave, umbrella-like struts that supported the top of the bridge. Several of the struts, or beams, were missing. Smoke was everywhere. As he slowly sat up, he almost choked on what he saw. All the bridge crew, from what he could tell, were dead. The decapitated body of the communications lady lay on the deck, near Collin's legs. One of her hands was still twitching. The beams above had fallen, crushing the entire left side of the bridge and everyone beneath them.

Collin was certain he was the only one still alive. The forward display was flickering on, then off, then on again. He could still see the Marauder, hovering on their port side.

Collin knew one thing for certain; he didn't have long to live if he stayed on this ship. Stepping over the communications officer, he made his way over to her console. Her board was a mess. Blood everywhere. He looked for the strobing light—and there it was. Collin pressed the rectangular indicator and it stopped flashing. He looked over to the display.

"Hello?" he said, his own voice sounding faint. Collin waited.

"Who am I addressing?" came a female voice.

"Um … I'm Collin Frost … Commander Collin Frost. Can you help me?"

The silence seemed to last for hours. "I'm not sure there's a way to get you out of there … even if I wanted to."

Collin saw the display flicker back on and the image of a blonde-haired officer looking back at him.

"Principessa Valora?"

She didn't reply but sat forward, as if trying to get a better view of him.

"Look, I'm just a kid. I'm not really a part of any of this—"

She scowled. "You're wearing a damn Brotherhood uniform! How can you even say that?"

Collin felt overwhelmed. How could he explain everything in time? "I was … me and my friends were abducted in a sim rover collector ship a few days ago. We escaped in a mining ship. When we got free we were found by the Brotherhood … by your husband."

"*My* husband?" she repeated, an expression of disbelief crossing her face. "What do you know about my husband?" But she suddenly looked a bit more interested.

"Capitano Dante Primo, the Duca of something or other … He helped us. Said he'd get us back to Earth if we served on his ship for a year. He's … a good guy," Collin summarized, realizing how stupid that sounded.

She stared back at him for several long beats. "Yeah, he is a good guy. Your story is too incredibly ridiculous to be anything but true." She let out a breath and shook her head. "Damn. Okay, I'll shuttle over. It'll take me a few minutes. Try to stay alive." The display went black.

Collin looked around the ruined bridge and felt his legs scoot out beneath him. He slid down the side of the console and started to shake uncontrollably. Tears filled his eyes as he took in all the carnage. *So much death! How had he survived? Why had he survived?*

Help …. me …

The voice was faint, but Collin definitely heard it. He turned his head left and then right, trying to determine where the voice was coming from. The ringing in his ears had subsided somewhat, but not completely. "Where are you? Keep talking," Collin said, getting to his feet. Unsteadily, he stepped over the dead communications officer.

"I'm … here … I'm Capt … tain."

Collin saw two feet protruding beneath one of the felled metal ceiling beams. He realized he'd have to approach from the rear of the bridge. Stumbling over something in the near darkness, he avoided falling only by grabbing onto the upturned command chair. Looking down at his feet, he saw he'd tripped over a severed head: *Ugh*, the comms lady.

Collin retched, and felt bile burn the back of his throat. Careful not to fall on the slippery deck plates, he maneuvered around to the rear of the bridge.

Captain Drago was lying on his back, his flipped-over command chair covering one of his arms, and a metal beam lying across his legs. A thin stream of blood ran out the left side of his mouth. His eyes tracked Collin as he approached.

"Help me … I'm trapped … can't move my legs."

"Hold on, Capitano. Help is on the way." Collin knelt down next to him and assessed the situation. Carefully, he lifted the command chair off Drago's far shoulder and let it flip away, onto the deck.

The captain nodded. "That's better. My legs … can't move my legs."

That was going to be a problem. The beam looked heavy. Collin duck-walked over to the beam where it crossed the captain's legs.

"This might hurt, Captain," Collin said, getting a firm grip on the beam. He pulled, but the beam barely budged and Drago screamed.

"We'll have to leave him."

Collin spun around to see the same blonde-haired woman now standing several feet behind him.

"No. I'm not going to leave him. Help me lift this beam … please." Collin tried to remember her first name. "Constantina, please help him."

She looked at the captain for a moment and moved over to the beam. "I should let him die here … I know this man. He's an ass hole."

Collin couldn't argue with that. "On three?" he urged.

She nodded. "One … two … three." They both lifted in unison. The captain screamed while the beam rose only several inches into the air and stopped.

"There's no way … what's your name again? Collin, right? We have to leave him, Collin. This ship is going to implode in a matter of minutes."

Collin looked around for something—perhaps a fulcrum—a piece of metal he could wedge beneath the beam.

Then he noticed his own wrist.

"What?" she asked, following his gaze.

"I need to get these things off my wrists." Collin pushed a finger beneath the band on his right wrist.

"I don't understand …what are you talking about?"

"They're minimizer bands."

Her expression went from confusion to understanding. "Really?"

Collin nodded, not having any luck getting the band off his wrist.

"I'll have to shoot it off. Might hurt."

"Shoot it?"

"Pull it away from your skin, as far as you can."

The principessa pulled a Ponge 412 handgun from a holster on her hip. She adjusted the setting and pointed the muzzle toward the band on Collin's wrist. He raised his arm and gritted his teeth.

"Don't be such a pussy, kid. I'm a pretty good shot … well, usually," she said with a smile, firing at the same time.

It did hurt, but the band came free. He rubbed his wrist and then held up his scorched other arm. Slipping a finger beneath that band, he pulled it away from his wrist. She fired again and this time he didn't feel a thing, except the band falling free.

Collin felt a rush of energy, which made his head spin.

"We're running out of time!" she said, gesturing toward the metal beam.

Collin took a second to think how he was going to tackle it. He readjusted his stance, bent over and placed his left hand flat on the deck, while reaching his other hand around, and under, the beam. He took in a breath—pushing and pulling. The beam came up as if it weighed nothing at all.

"Can you pull him free?" Collin asked, looking over to

the principessa.

Snapping out of her astonishment, she said, "Sorry." She placed her hands beneath the captain's armpits and dragged him free from beneath the beam. He yelped once and fell unconscious.

Chapter 31

Collin carried Captain Drago into a small minivan-sized shuttle. Getting the captain's limp body into the tiny airlock was the trickiest part. Once the three were on board, it took less than two minutes to make the trip across to the awaiting Marauder ship, a compact vessel in itself, with only a handful of uniformed Kardon Guard crew on board. Collin followed the principessa into a cramped compartment, where she gestured for Collin to place Captain Drago onto a narrow gurney.

"What is this place?" Collin asked her.

"AutoMed compartment … seriously? You've never seen an AutoMed?"

Collin did a quick look around and shook his head.

"This is a small ship … no room for a staffed, medical department. Medical procedures are administered via the AI. Watch it, now! Stand back!"

A bright white line of light moved from the top of the captain's head, down his torso, and then over his legs.

"AutoMed's now scanning his injuries," she told him.

Collin scurried out of the way when a robotic arm descended from above. Moving at sonic speed, it whirled into position, perpendicular to the captain's body. A metallic blade appeared and his uniform and trousers were cut away as a second articulating arm descended and began administering to his legs. Collin grimaced as he heard the sounds of bones being set. He was relieved for the captain that he was still unconscious.

"That thing's pretty cool," Collin said, finding it hard to take his eyes off the AutoMed in action.

"I guess … Okay … let's leave him for now. Follow me," the principessa said, not waiting for an answer.

This vessel really was small. Collin figured it was about the size of a doublewide trailer—but perhaps a little longer in length. As he followed the principessa in and around various pieces of equipment, and around several component-filled bulkheads, he passed three of her crewmembers. They stared back at Collin with interest. Then it hit him. He was now royally screwed. Now that he was in the hands of the enemy, gone were his chances of getting back home, and also of seeing Lydia again.

She took him directly to the small bridge. It was about the same size as the 777's cockpit but all similarities ended there. This ship's technology seemed to be on a par with that of the *Tyrant's*.

Drago truly was an idiot … didn't he know what he was going up against?

As if on cue, beyond the front convex observation window, the *Helix* blew apart. Collin looked for something to hold on to but the concussive wave never came. *Of course! Without an atmosphere, that couldn't happen here.*

The principessa flopped down into one of two tall-backed, bucket-like seats. She tucked a strand of blonde hair behind her ear and gestured for Collin to sit.

He sat and waited for her to say something. She looked at him for a long moment and then crossed her legs. She wore snug, black leather pants and boots that came up almost to her knees.

"If you're done checking out my legs, I have some questions for you, kid …"

Collin interrupted her: "Why were you hailing the *Helix*, Principessa? Why didn't you charge weapons like the *Helix* did?"

"I'd appreciate it if you'd stop calling me that. Stick with Captain, or Captain Valora. As for my hail … it's presumptuous for an apprentice, not yet even a squire, to be so forward as to question a superior."

Collin shrugged. "You're not my superior and as I've already told you … me and my friends were abducted. It's not like we signed up for any of this."

He watched as she rolled her eyes and shook her head. She was easily ten years older than him, but there was a youthful quality, an irreverence about her, that made her seem captivating. He could see how she and Captain Primo would be a good fit.

"The reason I was hailing that piece of BS of a ship, the *Helix*, was to leave a message for Capitano Primo."

"What about?"

She exhaled and looked annoyed. Her attention was on a curved translucent display, now hovering before her. "We've got company."

Collin watched the approaching ship. He recognized it. "Looks like you have a decision to make."

"Are you always this annoying, Frost?"

"My little sister thinks so … It's the *Tyrant*. You can't defeat her in battle, and you can't outrun her." Collin actually had no idea if this little ship of hers could outrun the *Tyrant* or not, but he wanted to keep her off-guard. "And there's another minor point … your husband's commanding that ship."

"Will you just shut up? I know perfectly well who it is. The last thing I need right now is your mouth flapping. Just be glad I haven't put you in irons."

Collin sat back and smiled. He then raised a wrist—the one with a scorch mark on it. Ever since the devices were removed from his wrists, he'd become aware of an ever-increasing amount of something—not energy, although there was that, too, but something more: it was raw power—a whole lot of pent-up raw power.

She started to say something and then closed her lips.

"You were going to leave him a message, so why not do it now, in person? What's the big deal?"

"There are things you wouldn't understand. Some of it is personal. It's one thing to have a message forwarded by a dimwit like Capitano Drago; it's another thing to—"

"… admit to your husband you were wrong?" Collin interjected.

"Maybe … probably. It's becoming clear that the Kardon Guard … that Commandant Nari lied to the queen. That his real motive was to supplant the monarchy."

"Does your mother, the queen … does she see what's happening? Does she realize that dude's been blowing smoke?"

She turned toward Collin. "Where do you get these ridiculous expressions? Yes, but what the queen knows in her heart and what she's willing to say aloud are two different things. Even now, she is a prisoner in her own castle. The commandant controls her and every aspect of the monarchy, as well as his prized Kardon Guard."

The *Tyrant* was now closing in and beginning to slow.

"They're hailing me." She sounded resigned.

"Truth is, I don't know much about any of this stuff," Collin said. "Why not just come clean about it all with Captain Primo—"

She cut him off. "You have no idea what's transpired. The gravity of it all. When the queen chose the Kardon Guard and that maniacal Commandant Nari over the Brotherhood— those who'd loyally stood at the monarchy's side for nearly a millennium—it changed everything. When she stood by and watched while thousands of knights of the Brotherhood were hunted down and killed … often right in front of their families … it's not something you can simply take back. Like, oops … sorry … I chose the wrong defenders of the realm."

Collin saw moisture glistening in the principessa's eyes. "Just tell your husband what you told me." He sat back and stared as the nearing ship filled the small display screen in front of them.

"Nobody knows we're married. It was a secret ceremony." She saw Collin's confused expression and continued, "I'm a principessa … a princess … he's a duke. Without my mother and the Council of Elders elevating him to the level of principe, a prince … it's impossible. Added to that, my mother and Dante hate each other."

She stared at the ship for a moment and seemed to come to a decision. She straightened up in her seat and composed herself. She tapped at something on the control panel— Captain Primo's face appeared before them.

He looked surprised to see her. When her lips curled into the faintest of smiles, his tight expression gave way to one of relief.

"Constantina … you destroyed a Brotherhood warship—I won't be able to protect you. Why didn't you just leave?"

Her annoyance flared: "It's not what you think. That idiot Drago ignored my hails. I didn't come here to fight. I did everything I could to open up a channel with that ship."

"That's a convenient excuse, but without proof—"

Collin interjected, "Um … it's actually true, Captain."

Again, Captain Primo furrowed his brow. The principessa tapped something on the control panel so he could now see them both sitting in the small ship's cockpit. His smile spread to his eyes and for a moment, he was speechless. "Why, Mr. Frost, I thought you went the way of the *Helix*."

Chapter 32

Collin sat back and watched the principessa pilot the Marauder back toward Nero Station. Even now, as she brought the little ship up to the designated concourse gate, she looked to be on the verge of changing her mind.

"So ... how long's it been since you've been on a Brotherhood station?" Collin asked, trying to steer her away from what he was sure was a conflicting inner dialogue going on in her head. The last thing he wanted was for her to bolt, taking him along for the ride.

She glanced over to Collin, her eyes conveying she knew what he was doing. "A few years."

Collin felt the Marauder being secured at the gate. Chewing the inside of her lip, Captain Valora didn't get up right away.

He said, "Look, my loyalties are to my Chain ... my fellow Earthlings. From what I can see, what you're doing ... is the right thing. If you're afraid they'll do something to you—"

She smiled at that. "I appreciate the concern, Mr. Frost, but that's the least of my worries. My being here is no small triviality. I don't have the monarchy's blessing and the Kardon Guard would consider what I'm doing treasonable. The simple fact of the matter is there's no going back for me, once I step onto the station."

"How certain are you of ... what's his name? Commandant Nari? That he really has ulterior motives, like taking control away from the queen?"

"Oh, I'm one hundred percent sure of that. My mother lives a secluded, protected life. I don't. It's not so much a question of if Nari and the Kardon Guard are taking control, as it is of how bad things will get once we're under their control." She stood up, now ready to leave the cockpit. "Come on, let's go."

Collin quickly stood and felt his feet start to leave the deck. He instinctively grabbed at the closest thing, the back of his chair, and watched as it bent backwards—as if it were made of rubber.

"Terrific. You owe me one Marauder cockpit chair, Frost." She walked out of the cockpit.

★ ★ ★

There were ten armed Brotherhood guards waiting for them as they exited the Marauder, who hurriedly surrounded them both. Apparently her arrival *was* a very big deal; Collin could see the nervousness in the guards' watchful eyes as they were ushered down the concourse toward the hub of the station.

Captain Primo was waiting there for them as they entered the bustling station hub. His eyes never left the face of the principessa. "I'll take her from here. Return to your duties."

It was evident the guards had received different orders. No one moved. Primo stepped in close to the one Collin assumed was the highest-ranking guard in their group.

"Sargente, I am quite capable of escorting the principessa from here. I take full responsibility. I'm giving you a direct order."

The guard saluted. "Yes, Capitano."

The men broke formation and followed the leading guard, quickly disappearing into the throngs of people. Captain Primo and the principessa flew into each other's arms. Wrapped together, neither spoke for a long time. Collin, realizing he was staring, looked away and waited.

When they finally separated there were tears on the principessa's cheeks and the captain, too, looked close to tears.

"Here's what's going to happen," the captain stated, stepping back and composing himself. "The ammiraglio is anxiously waiting for us. The implications of your being here … being here voluntarily … are big. We need to get going. I'll make sure nothing happens to you, Constantina, that you're safe."

She nodded but didn't look overly confident he'd be able to keep that promise. For the first time the captain then acknowledged Collin. "Good to see you're still in one piece, Mr. Frost."

The principessa said, "He saved Drago's life … I was there to see it. By the way, he's still in my ship's AutoMed."

"Well, it looks like the Brotherhood owes you their gratitude, Mr. Frost." Primo's glance took in the missing minimizer bands on Collin's bare wrists.

The captain and the principessa hurried along, with Collin tagging close behind. It wasn't long before someone in the crowd recognized her. Heads turned—people gawked. The three ducked into an elevator and exited at Level 20, the very top of the station hub. Like a penthouse on a goliath-sized, high-rise building, the deck was expansive and much more open than the levels below. Huge curved observation windows looked out onto the viewable part of Nero Station and at outer space beyond.

They headed for a grouping of compartments that took up the whole opposite side of the deck. A substantial-looking counter blocked further advancement. A woman in a Brotherhood uniform looked up as they approached. Collin saw a small metal sign reading *Ammiraglio di divisione Zumpanno* sitting prominently on the countertop in front of them.

"He's waiting for you, Captain Primo," the woman behind the counter said.

"Thank you, tenente di vascello, Le Monte."

The woman had a prissy, pinched face. Collin knew schoolteachers with a similarly unpleasant look. She turned a disapproving glance toward him. Before she could say anything more, the captain said, "Commander Frost is with me. We'll go right in now."

They then entered the wide open hatch into a large office compartment, which, like the deck, looked out onto the station and beyond through a floor-to-ceiling observation window. A large man, with grayed salt-and-pepper hair, looked up as they entered. Collin noticed he wore an impressive Brotherhood uniform, with gold piping detail, and a different kind of insignia on his collar.

The admiral stood and came around his desk. "There you are ... welcome, Capitano Dante Primo, Duca of the Brotherhood House of Torre."

Apparently things are a bit more formal on the admiral's deck, Collin thought. The admiral stood before the principessa, bowed, and took her left hand in his own. He kissed the back of her hand and stood up straight. "Principessa Constantina Valora, Capitana for the Kardon Guard. I am honored with your presence and so very pleased to see you again."

It was obvious to Collin the principessa would rather forgo these formalities that came with her royal standing. She politely nodded and smiled. "I'm happy to see you again, Ammiraglio di divisione Zumpanno. It has been a long time."

The admiral glanced at Collin and then to the captain, who said, "This is the young man I spoke to you about, who came to us from the frontier, Ammiraglio."

"Yes, he and his Chain have started Brotherhood basic. I look forward to speaking with you more, Commander Frost

… when time allows." The admiral brought his attention quickly back to the captain. "Capitano, you will take leave of us now. The principessa and I have much to discuss. Rest assured, Principessa, you are safe and in no way a prisoner here. You may leave Nero Station at your will. But I want to hear everything you've told Capitano Primo and then, perhaps, we can formulate a plan."

★ ★ ★

By the time Captain Primo had escorted Collin back to the barracks, the teen was exhausted and couldn't wait to get into his bunk. In the dim light, he moved silently between pods until he found his own. He was pulling off his uniform when he looked over to see the outline of someone lying on his bunk. He took a tentative step closer and squinted his eyes. "Lydia?"

He heard her stir and sit up. She'd fallen asleep there.

"What are you doing here?" he whispered, sitting down next to her.

"We heard the *Helix* was destroyed by a Kardon Guard ship. That you'd been killed. Later, we heard that maybe you'd survived. Nobody would give us a straight answer. I … I wanted to be here if … when … you returned." She put her arms around him and buried her head into his chest. He felt her begin to shake, quiet sobs racking her body.

"Hey, I'm fine. Don't cry … everything's … good."

She sniffled. When she looked up, he wiped her tears with his thumbs. She brought her arms up, taking his face in her hands, her face only inches from his own. Then she kissed him. He tasted the salt from her tears. The tip of her tongue found his as their breaths quickened. His mind was whirling—*how is this possible that this perfect person is here in my arms*? Together, they slid down the surface of the pod until they were lying down together, facing each other. She pulled her face away and brought her lips close to his ear. He felt her soft breath as she spoke, "Don't ever leave me like that, Collin. Without you here … God … I've never been so scared in my life."

Someone nearby cleared his throat in an exaggerated manner that said *hey … you're not alone here.*

To Collin's surprise the barracks lights were on and a small crowd had formed at the opening to his pod. Bubba and DiMaggio were looking down at them—both smiling. Then Collin saw that the person standing directly behind them was Darren. He wasn't smiling.

Chapter 33

The piercing sound of an alarm klaxon filled the barracks. Collin and Lydia rose to their feet. Whatever was happening was *big*. In the distance he heard multiple warnings and announcements coming over the PA. A commotion at the entrance to the barracks was followed by the unmistakable voice of Chief-in-Command Bragg.

"Everyone front and center. Move it!"

Collin reached for his uniform jacket and, along with the others, hurried to get into formation.

Bragg looked as though he'd just awakened. His hair was uncombed and his wrinkled uniform had obviously been on since yesterday. He didn't wait for the Lone Stars to get into proper formation.

"Nero Station is under attack. Thirty-four Marauders are already engaging our Vanguard warships. Four heavily armored bulk carriers, typically used to transport and deploy troops, are approaching fast. There's only one reason for those ships to come here ... The Kardon Guard is looking to infiltrate and take control of this station."

Humphrey interjected, "Let us fight, Chief ... we'll show them how Texans kick ass—"

"This station has a highly-trained Brotherhood force of four thousand men. They'll be doing the fighting, if it comes to that. With that said, you still may be called upon to support our forces."

"Why are they attacking? Why now?" Darren asked.

"We believe it has something to do with the queen's daughter, the principessa ... she may have been followed ... she may have led them here."

"No ... she came here to reach out to us. They're starting to realize the Kardon Guard's true motives," Collin told him.

"That's not for any of us to determine, Mr. Frost. Stay here and be prepared to do what's asked of you when the time comes. Is that understood?"

"Yes, Chief." Collin nodded his head.

The chief abruptly turned on his heels and headed out of the barracks.

"So what do we do now? We can't just stand around here with our thumbs up our asses while the station's being infiltrated," Humphrey said. "I say we go see what's happening."

Clifford Bosh, Owen Platt, and Garry Hurst all enthusiastically voiced their agreement.

"Our orders are to stay put," Collin said. "Let's just see what happens—"

"You know, Sticks ... I always knew you were a pussy. This proves it," Humphrey said, striding up to Collin and standing eye to eye. "You're no leader ... you're a pussy coward."

"You don't want to push me, Humph. Not now. Back off and cool down," Collin replied evenly.

Both Bubba and DiMaggio, moving in behind Collin, were staying unusually quiet. He wondered if they thought he was being a pussy as well.

"We need a leader with some guts. I say we vote again." Humphrey turned toward Darren. "We all know who should be leading us."

"That's not going to happen. I told you, back off and cool down. Let's just see—"

The punch came out of nowhere. Collin felt the blow hit his left cheek, snapping his head around to the right. It was enough for him to momentarily see stars but not enough to bring him down.

Humphrey, smiling, stood with his fists balled up. "It's

about time someone put you in your place, Sticks. I don't mind that it's me."

Collin was ready for the next punch, which was a wide haymaker—Humphrey's full weight behind it. Collin caught it mid-flight with his left hand. He wanted to punch back—wanted to pummel Humphrey into ground beef. But without those minimizer bands on, he had little doubt he could kill Humphrey with one punch. So he continued to hold Humphrey's fist in his own while slowly increasing the pressure of his grip. The first thing to go was Humphrey's smile. His full attention was focused on his hand and the increasing amount of pain emanating from it. Collin maintained his grip and Humphrey's legs went wiry. He tried to pry Collin's fingers away from his fist … crying out, "Let go! Please … let go … it hurts!"

Collin stepped in closer to Humphrey, bringing his face close to his. "You need to stop screwing with me."

"I will … I promise. Just let go."

Collin let go and watched Humphrey as he fell to his knees, cradling his bruised hand into his stomach. He noticed Bubba and DiMaggio were no longer behind him; instead, they were nose-to-nose with Darren, Bosh, Platt, and Hurst. Collin was relieved—the two did have his back after all. Then he saw the three Daccians hovering in the background—they too looked ready to step in.

The first incoming enemy fire shook the barracks so violently everyone was thrown to the deck. Sounds of thunderous explosions hitting nearby, one right after another, caused Collin to flinch.

Commander Fico Lucan of the Brave Hearts, and Rocco Puma, commander of the Righteous Warriors, ran into the barracks. Both looked like they'd run a mile and were breathing hard.

"Half the station … is gone … totally destroyed," Lucan said, gasping. "They must have known where the troops were being deployed from. Where the Brotherhood barracks were located."

"Is the station going to blow up?" Tink asked.

"I don't know … No … probably not," Rocco Puma replied. "Two of their bulk carriers have come alongside the main station hub. They're deploying their troops. Thousands of Kardon Guard forces. We need to surrender. That's the only way we survive—"

"That's not going to happen," Collin said back. "Surrendering to the Kardon Guard would mean our instant death or being held captive indefinitely." *Either way*, he thought, *we'd never get home again.* "Where did you get your weapons? Are there more?"

"The Chief left us with these. This is all we have."

Collin felt momentarily humiliated that the chief didn't have the same confidence in him as he did in these two Chain commanders to leave him a weapon as well. "Give me your Ponge for a second."

Puma shook his head. "Like hell …"

"I'll give it back. I promise."

Bubba grabbed the recruit commander's wrist while pulling the handgun free of its holster. Lucan moved to pull his weapon, but Darren moved in and wrapped his arms around him—trapping his arms in a clamp.

"What are you doing? We can't win against their forces," Lucan protested.

Bubba handed Collin the Ponge 412. Collin sat down on the deck and pulled up his left pant leg. He changed the power setting to the fifth position, pulled the minimizer band as far away from his skin as possible, and fired once. "Crap!" The heat scorched his leg. It hurt more than he wanted to let on so he

202

took a little more time with the minimizer band on his other ankle. He rubbed both ankles and stood up quickly. Without the diminishing effects of minimizer bands, Collin's feet left the ground. DiMaggio grabbed for his arm and brought him back to the deck.

"Thanks, man. Here … be careful not to shoot yourself." He handed DiMaggio the Ponge. "Darren, take Lucan's weapon and go to work on your own bands."

It took another ten minutes to shoot everyone's minimizer bands off. Collin retrieved his rucksack from his pod and was just strapping on the Glock's holster when Humphrey walked into the confined space.

Not knowing what his intentions were, Collin continued to strap on the holster and didn't say anything.

"You want to keep this?" Humphrey asked, holding the weapon out in front of him.

"No. We said we'd give them their weapons back. But thanks."

"Any idea how we're going to take on a few thousand Kardon Guard troops?"

"We'll need to arm ourselves. Let's hope the lifts still work so we can get down to the rifle range and armory."

"That sounds like a plan," Collin heard Humphrey say as he rushed out from the pod.

By the time Collin reached the others, they were getting familiar with their newfound strength. Lucan took back his weapon from Humphrey and both he and Puma left to return to their Chains.

DiMaggio, now floating five feet high in the air, waved his arms at Collin. Tink was elevated too, even five feet higher up. This could be a problem: the diminished effects of gravity's pull and how their physiology interacted in this alien environment. Their molecular structure being so different was both a blessing and a curse. A curse, if they didn't learn to control their movements.

Collin watched as both Tink and DiMaggio settled onto the deck. "Watch your movements. Running the way you normally do will send you into the air like you're on the moon. In the meantime, let's all keep our eyes on the person next to us. Have each other's back."

"So what are we doing?" Bubba asked.

"We're arming ourselves. Heading to the armory, down on deck one." His words were drowned out by the sound of nearby weaponry fire.

Chapter 34

"Let's move fast and stay together," Collin said. He looked around and did a mental head count. Including himself, they were still at twenty. He was surprised to see the cheerleaders standing together nearby, at the front of the group. Lydia looked back at him. "Are we going to do this or what?"

He smiled at her gumption, turned, and headed out of the Lone Stars' barracks. DiMaggio and Bubba were next to him, on either side. They passed through next-door-neighbor Brave Hearts' area, which was totally empty, and continued on through the Righteous Warriors' barracks. These were empty as well.

"Maybe they went to surrender," DiMaggio said.

They exited the barracks into a frenzy of activity. People were running, mostly in one direction. Some were clothed in Brotherhood uniforms; others wore regular civilian clothes. Bubba took up the lead and headed right into the oncoming masses. A Brotherhood soldier slowed and put up his hands. "You're going the wrong way ... transport is this way." He didn't wait for an answer, just kept on running, along with the hundreds of others trying to flee.

The team reached the large elevator they'd used previously to descend to the station's lower decks. As they approached, the doors opened and no less than thirty people, tightly packed together, emerged at a dead run. The Lone Stars took their place within the elevator car and waited for the doors to close. DiMaggio was quick to figure out the controls and immediately Collin felt the G-forces as they descended.

"Um ... are we sure we're doing the right thing? What did that Brotherhood guy say about a transport?" Royce White asked. Before Collin could answer, Darren said, "I wouldn't be so sure they'll ever make it. If Kardon Guard forces are infiltrating, they may be running to their own executions. Anyway, we already talked about this … we're not running from this fight."

"Don't worry, Royce, I'll protect you," Tink said, standing to the big Lone Star center's right. That brought a few nervous chuckles. At half his size, she had to crane her neck to look up at him. The interior elevator lights started to blink and then went out completely. The darkness was absolute. Fortunately, the lift was still descending at a high rate of speed. Collin briefly wondered if the car was simply free-falling down the shaft and would soon careen headlong at its bottom. But the car began to slow and everyone let out a collective breath. Apparently Collin wasn't the only one visualizing the same scenario.

The doors opened to Level 1, which was only marginally more illuminated than the elevator. The smell of smoke billowed into the car. Stepping out, there was something profoundly different about the lowest deck on the space station. As if it had been put into a massive vice, the outer bulkheads were now bowed inward. Fallen pipes and conduits blocked every corridor and numerous sparks flashed outwardly, without any regularity, in each direction.

Again, Bubba took the lead and headed toward the rifle range. He didn't get very far, stopped by a wall of metal girders. He turned back to see Collin and the group approaching. Looking discouraged, Bubba shrugged at them. Collin looked up; overhead, he got a glimpse right into Level 2 of the station, some forty feet up.

Bubba grabbed the end of one of the girders in both hands and pulled. The sound of metal against metal made a high-pitched screeching sound, but the girder was at least moving.

Collin said, "Okay … we'll pile up the debris down the corridor." Bubba passed back the first twelve-foot-long by two-foot-wide girder. Collin took it in both hands and was surprised at how light it felt. He passed it back to DiMaggio, who passed it back to Lydia, and so on. Like a bucket brigade, they moved the fallen debris away, one piece at a time, eventually stacking it all off to the side, behind them. What had amassed to metric tons of weight they'd dislodged and moved with their bare hands, and with more efficiency than a forklift would achieve back on Earth.

With the blockade removed, they moved forward, Collin again in the lead. He found the double hatchway into the rifle range, which, as he'd expected, was closed.

"Let me!" Collin and Bubba turned to see Tink making her way to the front of the group. She didn't even hesitate before placing both small hands on one of the heavy metal hatch doors. She planted her feet wide apart and shoved with all her strength; the hatch broke away from its hinges and fell forward, into the compartment beyond. Tink slapped her hands together in the gesture of wiping dust from her palms.

"Good work, Tink," Collin said as he stepped into the rifle range. Flashes and motion to his left caused Collin to reach for his Glock. He went down on one knee and aimed, his finger poised over the trigger. Three battle suit–clad combatants ran forward several steps and fired bright bursts from their energy weapons. It took Collin a second to realize they were caught in some kind of virtual, holographic loop as the three repeated the same action over and over again.

Standing up, he watched as the rest of the Lone Stars entered the rifle range. Each ducked for cover at the sight of the three virtual combatants. Like the rest of Level 1, this compartment had undergone a tremendous amount of damage. There was more debris falling down from above amid lingering black smoke. As Collin made his way toward the armory at the back, he covered his nose and mouth with his arm. Relieved when he got there, he saw the racks were still fully stocked with Ponge 412s and Larrik 5 Doublers.

No one needed any prompting to grab up weapons. Collin hadn't noticed it before, but there was a second interior hatch between the racks of 412s and Doublers. DiMaggio spotted Collin's interest and together they moved to the opening and peered inside.

"Come to Mama," DiMaggio said with a smile. Inside were several rows of black, upright, protective battle suits.

★ ★ ★

It took a full twenty minutes for Collin to figure out how to open the damn things. In his mind, the Kardon Guard was on the verge of storming their position any second, their guns blazing. In the end the most obvious thing worked. The suits opened with little effort by pulling down on a protruding cowling that ran along the back shoulders of each suit. From that point on, everything became self-evident—from stepping first into the back of the suit, then triggering the suit's back portion to automatically self-close securely, and then self-adjusting it to snugly fit one's anatomy.

By the time Collin had on his battle suit and was moving about the compartment with a level of proficiency, the rest of the Lone Stars had selected their own suits and were inserting their bodies into them.

"Can you help me? I can't get it to close," Lydia asked Collin, not fully inside her still-open suit.

Collin saw the problem. Her Brotherhood uniform had bunched up high around her torso, exposing the naked skin of her waist and hips. The suit had somehow detected the obstruction. Collin pulled the fabric down and said, "Try it now."

She triggered the mechanism and the suit quickly closed around her. Collin passed her the helmet and she placed it over her head. "Cool. A display thingy came alive."

"That's the heads-up display, called HUD," Collin said.

Bubba, Royce and Tink had problems getting their suits to properly fit. Tink was the one who soon found a way to contract and/or expand the battle suit's various jointed sections to fit virtually anyone. It was another fifteen minutes before Collin figured out the basics of his HUD enough so that the battle suits would even be usable. Undoubtedly, there were many features and functions he was still unaware of, but at least he'd figured out the means to basic communication between individuals on closed channels, as well as open channels to the group. He also figured out how to monitor such things as a battle suit's integrity and its basic physiological aspects, such as heart rate, respiration, blood pressure levels, and so forth.

"Crap! I must have done something wrong," Lydia said, now walking somewhat awkwardly toward Collin. "I'm getting all these little red icons moving around on my HUD."

"Let me help you." Collin had just figured out how to mirror another suit's HUD view in a thumbnail portion on his own HUD. It was a cool feature and something any team leader would surely find useful. He'd already allocated each Lone Star a numerical designation. Lydia was number nine. He brought up her HUD's thumbnail feed and was instantly on guard. Those little icons Lydia was talking about were small representations of enemy, Kardon Guard, forces—forces that were quickly moving into the rifle range.

Chapter 35

Collin chided himself. *Damn!* Even the lamest of commanders would have thought to leave a lookout. Looking around the confined space of the armory, his heart sank. *It'll be like shooting fish in a barrel. It'll be a massacre.*

"How did you get those icons to appear on your HUD, Lydia?"

She showed him what she'd done. Since all options and menus were selected via eye movements, it took a few seconds for her to convey the steps. What Lydia had inadvertently done was to initialize combat mode—which brought up a whole slew of other readouts and options. Using the open channel, Collin informed the others how to initialize the same combat mode on their HUDs as well.

Distant energy weapons fire erupted from outside the compartment. That would be the Kardon Guard forces being surprised by the virtual combatants. For the tenth time, Collin looked around the bulkheads. Nothing. He returned to the area holding the now-empty gun racks and scanned the compartment. Then he looked up. Like much of the first level, the ceiling on this compartment was a mess of pipes and cables. But the support girders above him, unlike those in the corridors, looked to be well secured.

He spoke into the open channel again: "Grab your weapons, ensure they are set on setting six, and follow my lead. Hurry!" Collin looked up again, found where he wanted to go, and leaped. He used a bit more force than was necessary and plowed head first into the top bulkhead. His fingers found purchase on the nearest crossbeam and he held on with his free hand, his right hand still holding his Doubler. He looked down, seeing nineteen upturned, smiling faces.

One by one the other Lone Stars followed Collin's example. Several jumped too hard and also slammed into the top bulkhead; others didn't jump high enough and needed to wait until they dropped back to the deck before trying a second time.

The last to successfully jump was Royce White. He was still in the air, halfway to the top, when the first of the Kardon Guard combatants entered the armory. Their dark-gray battle suits looked slightly different from the black Brotherhood suits. Each held a Ponge 412 at his side and carried an energy rifle.

Collin spoke softly into the open channel: "Don't fire … let more of them enter the compartment." He wondered how many that would be. His HUD indicated there were twenty guards total—five were just outside, in the rifle range, while fifteen were here in the armory. He figured they also had the same enemy-icon representations displaying on their HUDs. His high school math prowess was kicking in. These HUDs provided the Cartesian coordinate system that specifies each X and Y point separately on a plane, via a pair of numerical coordinates. Below, the guards didn't use a three point, X, Y, and Z, three-dimensional Cartesian coordinate system that would have also given them their enemy's elevation level.

Fifteen soldiers entered. Collin saw they were being hyper-alert and several were waving their arms, or their rifles, in front of them.

"They think we're down there … that we're invisible or something," DiMaggio said.

Collin caught sight of Royce White starting to squirm around. He opened a private channel to him, "What are you doing, Royce? You need to stay still for a few more seconds."

"My fingers are tired."

Before Collin could tell him to just hold on a few more seconds, the big teenager was already falling toward the deck. Collin yelled, "Fire! Don't hit Royce."

Collin let loose with his own barrage of plasma fire at three combatants directly below him. As they fell to the deck, their red icons disappeared from Collin's HUD. *Now who's the fish in the barrel?* Collin thought.

Bright energy bursts rained down all at once. Collin soon found that the enemy wasn't going down as quickly as they should have—it took at least five plasma pulses, sometimes several more than that, before those Lone Stars who had never received firearm training got their aim close enough to be effective. It didn't take long for the Kardon Guard forces to figure out where their fire was coming from, and they were now shooting back with superior marksmanship. Collin saw several Lone Stars fall down to the deck. The ten still-standing combatants were returning fire as those on the outside rifle range began moving into the armory.

"Time to drop, everyone," Collin said. He let go of the crossbeam, still firing toward the open armory hatch. He nailed two more and wounded another.

"I'm hit ... oh God ... I'm hit!"

It was Tink. Collin spotted her on the other side of the armory, holding her side. He heard several more screams but didn't know who else was shot. Right then, all he could do was keep firing. To Collin's own surprise, he was a natural. His aim was true and the enemy fell, one after another. Bubba and DiMaggio were apparently managing on their own too: They'd each taken down a Kardon Guard soldier and were looking around for others. Darren and Humphrey were moving into the rifle range in pursuit of the last three Kardon Guards who were trying to escape. Collin watched as the last of the red icons disappeared from his HUD.

Bodies lay motionless everywhere, and not all were wearing gray battle suits. To Collin's right lay the quiet cheerleader, Karen Muller. He looked down at her—into her visor. Her eyes were open but fixed—not moving.

"Oh no … Doug … Doug Summerfield's dead," Lydia said. She then spotted Karen's body lying at Collin's feet and ran to her side. "No! Not Karen." She sat down, her hands resting on the front of Karen's battle suit. "What are we doing here? We're not soldiers." The defeat in Lydia's voice surprised Collin.

"Yeah, well tell the thirty-five dead Kardon Guard guys that, Lydia," Clifford Bosh said. "Do you have any doubt that they would have killed every last one of us?" Bosh then pointed an outstretched finger at Collin. "You! That was f-ing genius. The whole thing: hanging-from-the-rafters-idea. Genius!"

Lydia was still kneeling by her dead friend. Eventually she stood up and looked at Collin. "He's right … we're all alive because of what you did. I'm just … I can't believe I killed someone today … I killed two of them; saw them fall to the deck and die."

Tink staggered over and leaned against Collin. Lydia, pulled from her inner conflict, took a look at the scorched patch on the right side of Tina's battle suit.

"It doesn't look like it penetrated your suit. I think you just got a little burned."

"Well, it feels like I got hit by a bolt of lightning. I think I'll live, though." Tina gave Collin a weary smile. "That was something … I can't believe what we just did." Then her eyes leveled on Karen's corpse and quickly filled with tears. "Not Karen …"

Darren and Humphrey reentered the armory. Humphrey's visor had a scorch mark on it, where he'd apparently taken a direct head shot.

"Rifle range is secure," Darren said.

"We also found this," Humphrey said, holding up a big weapon. Twice the size of a Doubler, the energy weapon was thick and bulbous at the middle and there were five barrels converging into one. "I'm calling it the Cinco de Mayo."

"Does it work?" Collin asked, already wishing it was anyone but Humphrey who'd found the thing.

"Oh, it works all right. It takes the head or arm or leg off someone with one shot. Tried it on a few of the dead Kardon guys."

Collin slowly nodded. The weapon certainly could be a useful addition to their team. "My only suggestion ... don't point it at any of the outside bulkheads ... or any of us."

Humphrey grinned.

Collin took stock of who was left. They were down to twenty-one. He couldn't expect them to have such continuing good fortune going up against the hundreds, if not thousands, of Kardon Guard forces now occupying Nero Station. They needed a plan.

There was an annoying blinking light showing in the top right corner of his HUD. He needed to figure out how to disable it or he'd end up going crazy. He stared at the blink for several long seconds, which caused a drop-down menu to appear just below it. There were three selection choices:

-- Join Open Command Channel

-- Join Direct Command Channel

-- Disregard

Collin selected the -- Join Direct Command Channel option.

"Frost!"

Collin recognized Captain Primo's voice immediately. "Captain Primo?"

"Yes. I see you've gotten yourselves into some battle suits. Good work. I also see you've defeated a Kardon Guard platoon. Not sure how you accomplished that but ... thank you."

"Where are you, Captain? How do you know—"

"Listen to me. I'm still on board the *Tyrant*. We've been battling the Kardon forces, mostly their Marauders ... they're all around the station. We're basically holding our own. Any Brotherhood forces on Nero Station are minimum—actually, I think all have been killed ... except the recruits."

Collin let that sink in for a few beats. "What is it you want us to do?"

"I'm glad you asked, Frost. There are close to three thousand enemy forces still on board the station. Nero Station, even when damaged, would be a tremendously strategic stronghold for Commandant Nari, and threaten the very existence of the Brotherhood. What I want you to do is blow up Nero Station ... blow it before they leave."

"If you think we're going to embark on some kind of suicide mission, think again, Captain. This isn't our war."

"Well, it has become your war; but no, it doesn't have to be a suicide mission. Not if you're smart. Listen up, there's more ..."

Chapter 36

Collin's father often talked to him about the stress of combat, from his multiple tours in Afghanistan—the debilitating loss of energy a combatant felt once the adrenalin rush from life and death situations, from battle, invariably started to wear off. That weakness was experienced now, and something else: eighteen teenagers and three *Daccian* cat creatures had all been forced to kill in order to survive. Although Collin wasn't quite sure Humphrey actually fit into that category, for the most part the Lone Stars were traumatized, in no shape to continue. The emotional toll was too much on a bunch of kids.

They moved out into the larger rifle range area where they removed their helmets and broke into small clusters—everyone talking in hushed tones. Collin asked Humphrey to clean up the mess he'd made—namely, shredded body parts from the effects of his new Cinco do Mayo weapon.

"Can everyone huddle around?" Collin asked.

With the exception of Bubba, DiMaggio and Lydia, no one moved. Even Tink stayed seated on the deck, talking to another cheerleader, Heather Primm.

"Does anyone here want to go home—get out of this place?" Bubba added, his voice loud and angry.

Slowly, at first, they made their way over to where Collin was standing and formed a semicircle around him.

"I've been in contact with Captain Primo."

"He's still alive?" Darren asked, looking somewhat more interested.

"He's alive and he says they're holding their own in space."

"Are they going to rescue us ... get us out of here?" Humphrey asked.

"No. As far as they're concerned, Nero Station's been lost to the enemy. He believes there are somewhere in the neighborhood of three thousand Kardon Guard soldiers here. For the most part, Brotherhood forces have been wiped out."

Collin saw disappointment and then fear showing on the faces around him.

"You said 'for the most part.' So there are some Brotherhood forces left?" Darren asked.

"Mostly recruits … maybe a hundred, including us. And including the admiral, too, up on the top level."

"So … what does the captain want us to do?" DiMaggio asked, already looking suspicious.

Collin hesitated, trying to think of a way to phrase things so they wouldn't sound preposterous. "He wants us to blow up this space station."

Anger erupted around him. It seemed they all had something to say now, and they weren't holding back—using four letter words to express themselves.

"He also wants us to rescue the admiral, and any others found alive, if there's time. Communications are out on Level 20, but he's pretty sure there are some still alive up there." He waited until the noise—the shouts of *no*, *no*, and *no way*, subsided—before continuing: "He also said that if we accomplish this mission, which he has almost no faith in our being able to achieve, he'll get us back to Earth … no waiting a year … just right away."

"Do you trust him?" Lydia asked skeptically. "How do we know he'll follow through with his promise?"

"He's been straight with us up to now. I think he's being honest. I also think he feels fairly safe making that promise. The odds of our succeeding are almost zero … he made no attempt to hide that fact."

"So you want to do this?" Bubba asked.

"Yeah, I guess I do. I'd rather follow a plan, even one as crazy as this, than wait around for the next platoon of Kardon Guards to find us and kill us."

Surprisingly, it was Humphrey who was the first to agree. "I'm in." He held up the Cinco de Mayo. "I'm definitely in."

Each of them said they were on board or simply nodded their assent.

"One question," DiMaggio said. "You said the captain wants us to blow the station and rescue those on the top level of the station. Isn't that ass-backward? If we blow the station first … however we accomplish something like that … then there won't be anyone around to rescue."

"That's a good point, so let me lay things out the way the captain did for me. This station is powered by three fusion reactors. They are far more efficient and safer than the nuclear reactors we have back on Earth. Getting one of these things to become unstable and eventually blow up requires specific steps."

"Won't the other two reactors just take over for the one we bring down?" DiMaggio asked.

Collin shook his head. "Once we've made the reactor unstable, it inevitably blows up … ka-boom! The other reactors will only add to the explosion. But here's where things get a little dicey. The captain wasn't completely sure how much time we'd have once we make a reactor unstable. It could be one hour, it could be three … He thinks it's closer to one hour. We'll have one hour to get to the top level and rescue the admiral and the other Brotherhood forces."

Discussion broke out between the Lone Stars. Bubba held up a hand. "Where are these reactors located?"

"Four levels up. And one more thing … the captain doesn't think the Kardon forces will hang around for very long. We need to move fast if we're going to do this."

★ ★ ★

How long before more Kardon Guards arrive, perhaps in even greater numbers? Collin wondered. Again, he prodded the teens and the three Daccians to hurry. They spent the next ten minutes swapping out drained power packs for fresh ones for their energy weapons and fine-tuning their still-rough mission plan. Together, the Lone Stars left the rifle range. It wasn't long before they reached their next major obstacle. They converged at the elevator, and Bubba slammed a big fist above the small panel to the left of the elevator doors. "Elevator's shut down. We're trapped down here," he said.

"I'm not completely surprised," Collin answered. "They know we're down here … it just makes sense they'd try to isolate us until they can assemble enough forces to wipe us out."

"What do we do?" Bubba asked.

"Come on, Bubba … we're not stuck at all," Collin said, backing away from the elevator. He pointed a finger skyward: "We've already found our way out of here."

Comprehension crossed Bubba's face about the same time it crossed the others's.

"The corridor," Tink said. "Right?"

"That's right, Tink … we're not trapped down here, not even close." Collin looked over his shoulder as he ran toward the pile of girders that had originally blocked their progress. He waited for the others to catch up, gazing up into the dark recesses of the sub-deck, and beyond it, to what was clearly Level 2.

"I'll go first. Check out if anyone's up there before we all go up," Collin said.

"Wait … I'll go. I'm the smallest … the least likely to

be spotted," Tink said, moving to a spot directly below the widest opening above them.

"You sure? How's your side feel?"

"My side still hurts but it's okay … I can do this."

Collin continued to stare at the small cheerleader. More and more he'd gotten attached to her, in a brotherly way. Protective.

"Let her go if she wants to, Frost," Darren chimed in, looking anxious to get things rolling.

Collin nodded and then held up a hand. "Reconnaissance only … just take a look and report back. Don't go all the way up onto Level 2."

"Yes, sir!" she replied, standing erect and giving a mock salute.

Everyone took a step back from her—giving her room to reposition herself. She handed her Doubler to Collin, looked up, bent her legs, and leapt.

Collin couldn't help but smile at the sight of Tink flying upward, her arms stretched out above her head.

"Super woman to the rescue!" Lydia said, smiling, and the other Lone Stars smiled too.

She easily made it up to the lowest-hanging crossbeam. She hung there, looking down for a few seconds, before letting go with one hand and waving to those below.

Collin smiled and pointed above her, a gesture prompting her to get moving. She pulled herself up like a gymnast on a high bar, bringing one leg up first, and then the other, and slowly stood. Collin could see she was figuring out her next best move—the route she'd need to take from her current position. She walked along the girder with her arms outstretched, as if walking a tightrope. From there she was able to pull herself up to another beam, or something; it was too dark for Collin to clearly see what. Then she was gone from sight.

Collin opened a channel to Tink. "How's it look up there?"

"It looks dark and kinda creepy. Why did I volunteer for this?"

He heard her straining, her breathing become more labored. "This part would have been easier for a guy," she said. "Lots of stuff in the way that I have to move. OK, I'm about to look over the edge of the Level 2 deck. Hold on."

Collin had mirrored her HUD and was able to see pretty much what she was seeing. The thumbnail image went first from almost total blackness to an illuminated view of an empty corridor. The view rotated around as Tink turned her head to look in the other direction.

Collin sucked in a breath at what he saw in his HUD. Tink screamed.

Chapter 37

The young Brotherhood recruit was obviously dead. His lifeless eyes stared directly back into Tink's visor. Collin immediately recognized the Brave Heart Chain member from the Pangallo game. He'd taken plasma fire to his throat.

Tink was on the move again. "Damn it!" Collin said aloud. He watched as she pulled herself up and onto the Level 2 deck. "Tink, hold there ... let us catch up. It's not safe—"

"No one's here. None of those little icon things are showing on my HUD," she told him.

"I can see that, but just hold up, okay?"

"Okay."

Collin was surprised to see Darren and Humphrey had already leapt. Both made it to the same girder Tink had initially clung to. Holding on to the girder with both hands, they gingerly pulled themselves up, straddling the beam. From there, they caught their Doublers, which were tossed up to them from below. They stood up then, moving across the girder, and were soon climbing out of sight, into the darkness above.

"Who's next?" Collin asked.

One by one, and sometimes two by two, they took turns leaping up to the girder above. Collin was the last to go. By the time he'd climbed up, through the jumble of beams, conduits, and pipes, and pulled himself onto the Level 2 deck, the Lone Stars already there had migrated to the far end of the corridor. He pushed his way through the crowd until he could see what everyone was looking at. A wide-open compartment spread out before them. It was some kind of huge recreation deck, with a section dedicated to what looked like game consoles;

another section had groupings of tables and chairs, while another held multiple ten-foot-wide displays—perhaps for entertainment. At present, all displays were showing the same video feed: A man wearing a fancy Kardon Guard uniform, with a long red cape hanging down from his shoulders, stood in the middle of a large room or compartment—that looked somewhat familiar. Collin then recognized just where the man was standing; it was the barracks right here, on Nero Station. The caped man was holding something in his arms that Collin also recognized: It was the same spiky, lethal-looking object that earlier had been mounted high above on the barrack's bulkhead—a knight's *cleave-sheer*—the thing used to remove an opposing knight's head from his neck in battle.

"Keep watching … it's on some kind of repeating loop," DiMaggio said.

The man smiled. "I am Commandant Nari, supreme commander of the Kardon Guard, defender of her majesty, Queen Arabella Valora, and protector of her realm … the worlds of the Notares planetary system. I have taken control of this space station. I am specifically addressing the young recruits who refer to themselves as the Lone Stars. I am aware of your attack on one of my security teams and their subsequent demise. Impressive. Especially considering you've only completed one or two days of the Brotherhood's basic training program."

The smile faded on Commandant Nari's face. "It is time for you to lay down your weapons and turn yourselves in. I give you my word that no one will be harmed … you will be treated fairly. This is a limited time offer, with dire consequences for yourselves, as well as for other Brotherhood recruits."

The video feed changed to a wider perspective. DiMaggio tapped Collin's arm. "This part is screwed up."

Sitting cross-legged in two rows were the Brave Heart recruits. Several were bleeding from their noses, or corners of their mouths. Other faces were bruised, or with eyelids swollen shut. Commandant Nari, still holding the cleave-sheer, walked between the two rows, swinging the diabolical-looking weapon back and forth near his feet. He stopped behind another familiar-looking recruit. It was Fico Lucan, the Brave Hearts' commander.

"For every fifteen minutes that transpires without your surrender, one of these fine young men will lose something dear to them." Commandant Nari pulled the cleave-sheer up, doing something with his hands that made a mechanical ratcheting noise. Collin saw that the cleave-sheer now showed two curved blades, which were pulled back in opposite directions, away from each other. In a well-practiced, fluid motion, the commandant thrust the weapon into the back of Fico Lucan's exposed neck. The two curved blades unlocked and swung around in a scissor motion. The blades sliced into the young recruit's neck from opposite sides, all in a fraction of a second. Lucan's head dropped to the deck; a gusher of pulsating blood sprayed into the air.

The recruit's body teetered and then leaned forward onto the deck. Collin saw Tink frantically grabbing for her helmet, getting it off just before throwing up. He retched and had to turn away from the displays.

"Told you, it's **screwed** up," DiMaggio said, anger in his eyes.

Commandant Nari was speaking again: "In fifteen minutes another recruit will lose his head. I'm sure you don't want to be responsible for that. I await your prompt surrender."

The display flickered and returned to the beginning of the looped feed, showing Commandant Nari's smiling face.

"I'm going to shove that thing right up his ass," Bubba

said, fuming.

"And I'll hold him down for you," DiMaggio said, looking no less infuriated.

Collin realized his fists were clenched. He didn't dislike too many people; in fact, he couldn't think of anyone—but he hated Commandant Nari. That man needed to die and Collin didn't really care who'd be the one to make that happen.

"Let's move out," Collin said. "We need to find a way up to the next level."

They all moved into the recreation area and spread out.

"Something's going on over here," Humphrey said. He was moving toward a hatchway that was bulging outward. A series of yellow lights were blinking on the access panel to its left. The hatch looked precariously close to blowing into the compartment. Collin kept clear of the hatch, as did the others, and walked over to the porthole windows on the adjacent bulkhead on his right. What he saw caused his jaw to drop. A significant portion of Nero Station's center hub was gone—blown away, leaving a jagged gap, as if a gigantic bite had been taken from it. He looked up and saw that half of Level 3, all the way up to the top two levels, was gone. That meant the fusion reactors on Level 4 were on the undamaged side of the hub structure. Commandant Nari and his forces were up on Level 7—also on the unharmed side of the hub—within the recruit barracks.

In the distance, Collin observed a large ship, one of the big bulk carriers the captain had mentioned, moored to one of the spokes, near the station's outer ring. Collin wondered if that was the piece of crap the commandant had arrived in, or if there was another bulk cruiser that he couldn't see from his present perspective.

A flash out in space caught his attention. Then he saw there were a number of small vessels out there—Kardon

Guard Marauders and Brotherhood Vanguards—still going at it. He turned his attention back to the ragged section of the hub. From where they were situated on Level 2, he counted up two more levels. That was where they needed to go, where the reactors were located. Undoubtedly, they'd be guarding Level 4 at the elevator shaft. He squinted his eyes. He'd been looking at the contours of the three reactor tanks for several seconds before he actually realized it. They looked surprisingly like the big mushroom-shaped water tower back in Middleton. The truth was, it might be necessary to access the reactor from space. *Was that even possible?* He wondered if their battle suits were space *safe*.

He opened a direct channel to Captain Primo.

"A bit busy right now, Frost," came a hurried voice. "Get up to the reactors, yet?"

"Um … no, not yet. Looks like we'll need to approach them from space. Much of the center hub is blown away."

"You're talking about a whole new level of complexity, kid."

"Do these suits work in space?"

There was a long pause while the captain swore at something at the other end of their channel. "Of course they work in space. Each suit has enough oxygen for two hours. But moving around in space is tricky. Easy to find yourselves flailing around, adrift, until your air runs out. Be careful."

"I will."

"Also. Just spoke to the admiral. They're not doing so well in holding off the Kardon Guard. Time's running out, Mr. Frost."

Collin heard the desperation in his voice and then it hit him … it wasn't just the admiral the captain was concerned about. The principessa—his wife—was also still up there. No wonder he'd renegotiated the terms of their return home. The captain was desperate to save her.

"I won't let you down, sir." Collin cut the connection and hurried over to the hatch.

"I wouldn't get too close to that thing," DiMaggio said. "Looks like it could blow any time."

"We'll need to accelerate that timeframe. Everyone, look for something we can use for a rope."

Chapter 38

The most nimble of the Lone Stars, Orman, Cine, and Pack, returned to the open section between Levels 1 and 2. There they found a type of optical cable that was both strong and plentiful enough to fit Collin's requirements.

By the time the three Dacci creatures returned to the recreation compartment, with Cine holding the large spool of cable over one shoulder, Collin was nearly ready to blow the hatch.

"I'll take that ... good job," Collin said. He quickly tested the strength of the cable, pulling it between two hands and seeing that it had sufficient strength for his purposes.

He divided the cable into four equal long sections and now, using far more strength, ripped the cables apart. He then took one of those sections and began to make smaller four-foot-long sections. "Everyone take a piece of cable and make a strap for your Doubler. We're going to need both hands for what comes next."

Collin tied one end of his own small cable around the muzzle of the Doubler and the other back towards the thinnest part of the rifle's stock. It wasn't perfect, but it did the trick.

Collin picked up the remaining three long sections of cable. "Okay, we're breaking up into three seven man groups. Tie yourselves together with no less than ten feet between."

Collin's group consisted of DiMaggio, Bubba, Tink, David *the Brick* Burk, Gregg Panichello, and Lydia. Collin noticed Darren was watching to see whose group Lydia would join. He'd purposely tried not to think about the apparent love triangle situation going on between Lydia, Darren and himself. There was no time for something so trivial—not when so many lives were at stake. But Collin couldn't help feeling a tinge of guilt when he saw the hurt in Darren's eyes as Lydia moved to stand in his group.

It was no surprise who had joined Darren's group. It consisted of Mike Humphrey, Clifford Bosh, Owen Platt, Garry Hurst, Heather Primm, and Dan St. Ama. That left the third group with Melody Sawyer, Dana Stoker, Royce White, Brian Owens, and Orman, Cine, and Pack.

Darren's group moved over to the bulkhead, near the hatch, where his group found handholds on vertical support struts that were present every few feet along the outer bulkhead.

"Standing there's not going to work, Darren," Collin said.

Humphrey said, "What now, mister boss man. You going to micro-manage every step we take?"

Collin shrugged and gestured toward the rest of the entertainment area, where chairs, tables, and other large miscellaneous items lay scattered around the deck. "Once that hatch is blown and the compartment is open to space … the vacuum of space … everything in this area is going to shoot through that hatch like a bullet. You want to be in front of that?"

Collin saw sudden realization brighten Humphrey's face, as well as everyone else's. All three groups moved to the back of the compartment and began looking for handholds on the vertical struts. Collin looked to make sure everyone was holding on okay.

"Bubba, can you hold on to me … while I shoot?"

Nodding, Bubba put his arm around Collin's waist. "Okay, man. I got you," he said.

Collin confirmed the setting on his Doubler, aimed the weapon at the set of hinges to the right of the hatch, and fired. The *thump thump thump* of plasma fire continued until the hinges, and much of the hatch itself, turned from pink to red. The hatch was taking more punishment than he had counted on. He stopped firing, taking the Doubler away from his shoulder. He'd need to rethink this—

Startled, Collin nearly jumped out of his battle suit when he heard the unmistakable roar from the Cinco do Mayo. Humphrey was firing toward the hatch and it took less than five seconds before the hinges began to disintegrate and, in a tremendous *swoosh*, blow outward. Just as Collin earlier described, everything not secured to the deck immediately flew toward the open hatchway. Tables, chairs, a large multi-sectional couch, blew outward, like crap through a goose.

Once pressure equalized, it didn't take long for the compartment to become still.

"Let's go," Collin said to his group. He saw they'd slung their Doublers over one shoulder and were cable-tethered properly together. The first to approach the open hatchway, Collin wasn't sure what to expect. He looked out and was struck by the clarity, the sharpness of everything beyond. As he reached for a handhold along the outside of the bulkhead, he was able to get a better view of the damage done to the station's main center hub. He could see what had actually happened. Off to the left was what looked like the remnants of a bulk carrier. It was torn in half, large pieces of debris suspended around it. Charred blast marks on what remained of the fuselage made it clear the ship had taken tremendous Brotherhood fire. Collin guessed the massive troop carrier lost navigational control and had careened into Nero Station—taking a chunk out of the center hub, and a significant portion of the outer ring as well.

There was still some gravity here. It made sense, now that he thought about it. As long as they were in close proximity to the station, its artificial-gravity generators would extend out into space—probably several yards, at least. Collin didn't waste any time and began climbing toward the upper decks. It was slow going, using utmost care to avoid protruding bulkheads and girders, most of which were torn and shredded—sharp and dangerous. He wondered how much time had elapsed since Fico Lucan had lost his head. Who would become the next victim of Commandant Nari and his cleave sheer if they didn't find a way to rescue the recruits in time?

Collin's Lone Star team was now out of the rec room and climbing upward. As Collin cleared what he determined was the third level, he found that he could now stand and wait for the others on a wide, cantilevered section of the deck. He gave Bubba a hand up and moved out of the way; Bubba, in turn, helped DiMaggio, who helped Lydia, who helped the next, going down the line until those in his group were all up and standing. For a moment, the vastness of space pulled everyone's attention. Standing there, Collin was struck by the absolute quiet. That, and their tiny stature compared to the enormous space station and the vast open space beyond. As if on cue, everyone turned toward the wrecked center hub. *How had the station survived such incredible damage?* Collin looked up, craning his neck. *And how many lives here were lost in this one cataclysmic event?* Sparks flared at various points and a steady stream of steam sprayed from some indeterminate location, several levels up.

Collin headed toward the inside recess of the hub structure. Eerie; when he'd first climbed up onto this level, he'd noticed dim lighting emanating from a porthole or observation window. The seven Lone Stars moved as a group and Collin signaled them to stay to the side, out of sight of the window.

Seeing the outline of a wide, double-hatch to his left, Collin figured that it was indeed an observation window; that they were standing in what previously was some kind of airlock—perhaps for maintenance personnel to access the outside of the station. Staying close to the bulkhead, he peered inside. There was movement and he quickly moved back, out of view. He gave it ten seconds before peering in again. He saw four armed Kardon Guards, in gray battle suits, turning the corner, just leaving the compartment. They were looking for the Lone Stars—checking every inch of the station.

By now the other two groups had also reached the cantilevered section of the deck. Collin spoke, via the open channel: "You need to stay clear of that observation window. Let's keep climbing."

★ ★ ★

Pack was the last one to arrive at Level 4. Once there, with no convenient cantilevered deck to stand on, everyone needed to find a place to stand. Several stood upon a lone, exposed, girder, while others chose small protruding sections of sheared-off, ragged-looking, exposed deck plating.

The three fusion reactors were huge and situated back where much of the outside of Level 5 was sheared away above. The entire group now stood near one of the bulbous, mushroom-like, seventy-five-foot-tall tanks.

"So we're here," Darren said, looking up. "What did the captain say to do next? How do we start that chain reaction you mentioned?" He looked over at Collin.

"I'll need to get inside. Get to the control room, which, according to the captain, is on the other side of these tanks."

"I don't see any hatchways, or other ways in."

"I'm going to check the top of this reactor tank." Collin looked up and pointed. "See that? What looks like the remnants of a catwalk with railings? There's barely room for one, maybe two, of us up there, so I'll check it out and report back … when I have a better vantage point."

"I'll go with you," Darren said.

Collin couldn't come up with a valid argument why he shouldn't go too. He nodded and started to untie the umbilical cable cord from around his waist.

"What's the plan?" Bubba asked from his perch, seven feet away.

"Darren and I are going to check out the top of this reactor tank for a way in. Be back in a few minutes." By his expression, Bubba wasn't too pleased that Darren was the one joining Collin.

It took several minutes for them to climb up and around the side of the tank. Collin gave Darren a hand up onto the catwalk. It swayed under their combined weight and vibrated beneath their feet. Collin briefly wondered if that vibration would transfer into an audible clang, somewhere inside the station.

Darren went first and held on to the two railings as he walked along the catwalk. Sure enough, it led to a hidden, inset, hatchway. To the right, halfway up the bulkhead, was a glowing touch-screen panel. Yellow lights blinked over the hatch. Like in the rec room, it probably indicated a warning that one side of the hatch was open to space.

"You know the code ... how to open this thing?"

"Nope," Collin said. "Maybe it's time we see just how strong we really are in this environment."

Darren looked skeptical but nodded anyway. Both found firm handholds on a ridge that ran along the inside rim of the hatch.

"We pushing in or pulling out?" Darren asked.

"Um ... probably best if we pull out ... once the seal is broken, this hatch is going to fly open, anyway. We'll have to be careful of that ... and anything else that flies out.

"On three?" Collin asked.

Darren counted it off, "One ... two ... three ..."

They pulled and pulled and pulled again. Nothing happened.

They let go and caught their breath. "Again," Collin said, getting back into position. "One ... two ... three."

Something shifted—starting to give way. Still holding the hatch, Darren repositioned his feet flat against the bulkhead. Collin followed suit as he walked up the side of the bulkhead, his fingers gripping into the ridge, and felt the effect of their combined pulling on the hatch. The seal suddenly broke, the vacuum of space sucking the air out from around the dislodged hatch. With another combined yank, the hatch blew out.

The hatch missed Collin's head by an inch. As the inside atmosphere, with the force of a hurricane, depressurized—objects began to fly out: first a chair and desk, and then several red-uniformed bodies. Collin gasped, fearing his actions had just caused the death of two Brotherhood crewmembers. One body got caught on the catwalk railing behind and Collin realized the man had died sometime earlier. A round, black scorch mark in the middle of his forehead made that all too clear. Almost as quickly as it started, the depressurization stopped. It was only then Collin realized Darren was no longer next to him. He opened a direct channel.

"Darren?" No answer. Collin quickly changed his HUD settings to show both friendly and enemy icons. He first saw himself and then the twenty others, waiting below, where he'd left them. Then he saw a single icon in what he assumed was open space. *Crap!* Collin tried again: "Darren?"

"Yeah ... I'm alive."

"You hurt?"

"Yeah ... banged my shoulder on something."

"What happened?"

"I guess I forgot to let go of the hatch. In fact ... I'm still holding on to it."

"Don't let go of it … at least not yet," Collin yelled, probably louder than advisable.

"Why … It's not like it's going to do me much—"

"Just hold on to it; be quiet and listen to me. How far out are you?"

"Maybe one hundred feet … something like that."

"Okay … Newton's third law: For every action there is an equal and opposite reaction."

"What are you talking about, Frost?" Darren asked, sounding irritated.

"You are going to either push or kick that hatch away from you with all your strength, but only when your back is facing exactly in the right direction … toward the hub."

"My back's not quite facing the hub and I can't maneuver around. There's nothing to push off against. I'm in space, remember?"

Collin thought about that for a second. "Without letting go of the hatch, with your right hand pull your Ponge 412 from its holster. Do it really slow."

"Okay, done."

"Now, use your thumb and ensure it's set on six."

"Done."

"Here's the tricky part. You're going to have to try things … test to see what works."

"And if it doesn't I could go flying off into deep space!"

"No … no, that won't happen. Any recoil from an energy weapon is practically non-existent, remember? What you want to do is fire in small, one-shot bursts. Just enough to spin your body around in the right direction."

"Yean-yeah-yeah … I got it. Just shut up a sec while I try it."

Collin waited and was about to ask what was happening.

"Crap!"

"What?"

"Nothing … spinning in slow circles now … feel like barfing."

"Don't barf in your helmet. You may have to fire in the opposite—"

"Just shut up … I know! Hold on … I think I'm getting the hang of it. Crap … I'm not going to be able to stop. It's either spinning in one BS direction or in another. I'll have to try to just time it."

Collin didn't like the sound of that. Judge it wrong by a fraction of a second and he'd miss the hub completely. Maybe he should let go of the hatch and use the Ponge to propel him back. It would be ridiculously slow … but—

"Here we go … I'm kicking away the hatch."

Collin heard Darren's expulsion of breath and watched as his green icon started to move. It was several seconds before Collin could determine if he was heading in the right direction. The HUD showed the faint outline of the surface of the station hub. It would be close. *Oh no—he was going to miss it. He was moving in the wrong direction.* Before he could say anything, seven green icons were on the move.

"What's going on?" Collin asked into the open channel.

"We're going to get Darren," DiMaggio said.

It was now apparent what they were attempting to do. While Bubba securely holding onto the hub, still tethered to the others, DiMaggio, Bubba, Tink, Burk, Panichello, and Lydia began floating off into open space. All Collin could do was watch the wavering snake of icons.

He made it back down to the catwalk and could then see what was happening. Lydia was at the farthest end of the line. She'd be the one attempting to grab Darren. To get the right angle, the group had to first climb halfway up the side of the tank before jumping out, into the void. It would be close. Darren was moving fast and Lydia was still twenty feet away from him. At this distance, their tiny lifeline cable wasn't discernible. The six Lone Stars seemed to be floating rather aimlessly in space.

"Talk to me, Lydia," Collin said.

"I don't know if I'll reach him before he passes by. He's moving fast."

"Darren … can you use your Ponge to alter your direction?"

"I could if I still had it. I let go of it when I kicked off from the hatch."

"You still have your Doubler strapped around your back. Maybe you can use it to …" Collin shut up. Lydia was no more than four or five feet from Darren. This was it, either way. Her arms were thrust forward, fingers fully extended. Darren wasn't facing her and he was flailing, trying to reorient himself, unsuccessfully. First, one leg passed beyond Lydia's fingers and then the second one. She caught hold of the tip of his heel and his momentum changed. Darren's body pivoted and his upper torso swung back around. Lydia grasped Darren's helmet in her outstretched hands, as if catching a highflying football.

Excited screams filled the open channel. Collin watched as Lydia pulled Darren to herself, into her embrace.

Chapter 39

Collin stood at the same open hatchway he and Darren had yanked open fifteen minutes earlier. One by one the Lone Stars filed in. Bubba and DiMaggio held back, staying at Collin's side until everyone had passed by. As the last pair crossed over, Collin averted his eyes, having glimpsed Lydia still holding on to Darren's hand.

"Shoulder okay?" Collin asked.

"It'll be fine," Darren said.

The Lone Stars kept moving until they entered a semi-circular compartment that had three hatchways; each of their overhead lights was blinking yellow. Collin was the last to enter the compartment. Humphrey, standing next to Darren and Lydia, glanced down and saw the two still holding hands. He looked over at Collin, a smug smile brightening his face.

Collin kept his expression neutral. He turned and assessed the position of each hatchway. Based on the reactor tank's location, it was his guess they'd have to open the left-most hatch. But before he could say or do anything, the lights above the hatch went from a slow blinking yellow to a rapidly blinking red.

"Up—flat against the bulkhead," Collin yelled into the open channel.

Everyone moved fast, which was good, because the hatch swung open five seconds later. There was no outrushing of air—no tables or chairs or bodies flew outward. Collin held up his hands in a gesture for everyone to remain still.

Then he saw the muzzle of an energy weapon. Whoever was holding the weapon was moving slowly, not taking any undo risks. What was confusing to Collin was that the color of the icon showing in his HUD wasn't enemy red—it was green. Humphrey had the Cinco de Mayo up and pointed at the hatch. Collin held up both palms in his direction and spoke softly into the open channel: "Don't shoot … at least not yet."

An arm was visible now, and it became evident its owner was wearing a black Brotherhood battle suit. Collin stepped away from the bulkhead and into the combatant's sightline. Ten feet away from each other, Collin recognized the recruit through her visor. Pretty with short red hair, she'd been one of the Pangallo players, sitting atop another of the Brave Hearts' shoulders. Her eyes widened in mutual recognition and then showed relief. There was a streak of blood on one cheek and tears were filling her eyes.

She rushed forward, practically flying into Collin's arms. She stayed there for several moments. Collin didn't move, but spent a second trying to figure out how to add her into their communication group.

He thought he had it figured out. "What's your name?"

She pulled away and looked up into his visor. "Gaetana."

"You're with the Brave Hearts?"

She nodded. "I escaped before they'd rounded everyone up. I heard them talking about you, the Lone Stars. I've been trying to find you ever since."

She quickly acknowledged the other Lone Stars as they approached.

Collin asked, "Are they, the Brave Hearts, still being held at the barracks? Do you know if any others have been … beheaded?"

"Beheaded!" she screamed. "They beheaded someone … from my Chain?"

Collin glanced over to Tink, who shook her head and rolled her eyes.

"I'm sorry ... I thought you knew. Commandant Nari—he's executing a recruit every quarter hour."

"You said he beheaded someone. Who?"

"Fico Lucan."

Suddenly Gaetana dropped her weapon, going weak at the knees. Collin was barely able to grab her before she dropped to the deck. She was sobbing, gasping for air. "No ... no ... no, not Fico. You're not sure. Maybe it was someone else, one of the other recruits." She looked up into Collin's eyes—her eyes pleading with him to say it was someone else—somebody different.

"I'm sorry. I did meet Fico several times. It was him. Nari broadcasted the ... execution. We all saw it."

Despair quickly turned to anger. "I'm going to kill that bastard. I'm going to rip his heart from his chest and make his slimy Kardon Guards eat it."

"We need to move fast. I'm sorry. Do you know your way around the station?"

She looked at him in confusion. "Of course I do. I'm stationed here."

"We need to get into the reactor control room. Can you help—"

"No! We're going back to the barracks. We're rescuing the Brave Hearts before we do anything else. Do you understand me? Before anything else!"

"I have my orders, Gaetana."

"Orders from whom?"

"Captain Primo."

"Well, I don't report to him. I report to Captain Drago."

Collin simply shook his head.

"I'm ordering you. I have seniority."

"Collin's a commander," Tink interjected. "Help us and we'll help you." Standing firm, Gaetana looked like she wanted to strangle Tink. She turned her attention back to Collin. "You realize they may already have executed other Brave Hearts, right?"

"The Kardon Guard has killed hundreds, if not thousands, of Brotherhood forces here today. I'm sorry, but Captain Primo has a plan and we're going to abide by it."

Gaetana's stare continued to bore into Collin until she finally said, "Fine. I'll get you into the control room. But let's hurry. Follow me." Tink handed back her Doubler and Gaetana took it without saying a word. She held back at the open hatchway, letting the Lone Stars file past. Collin stayed back with her and watched as she closed the hatch. She then proceeded to enter a code to reseal it.

"We need to re-pressurize this compartment before we can get into the control room," she said. She entered another series of digits and waited for the short response to show on the screen. "Okay, the pressurization sequence has initialized." She turned and headed down the corridor. The others were waiting at a juncture that split off into three separate directions. She took the left-most corridor and picked up her pace. Collin stayed right on her heels. They passed through two more hatchways and ended up in another circular compartment. This one had mostly deck-to-ceiling glass panels. Through them, Collin could see sited beyond them one of the big reactor tanks. Stepping closer to the glass and looking to the right, he saw the other two tanks, farther off to the right.

"That's the control room, but I don't know how to get in there. Have no idea what the code is to get inside. They don't want just anyone off wandering around in there."

"I'll get us in there," Humphrey said, raising the Cinco do Mayo.

Both Collin and Gaetana simultaneously yelled, "No!"

"You'll blow us into molecules," Gaetana added.

Collin continued to look for a way past the glass panels.

Gaetana pointed to the middle panel. "This one here opens." She touched the glass and a portion of the glass came alive with a display panel. "But I don't know the code."

Collin pushed on the twelve-foot-high door panel. It didn't budge.

"It's as hard as metal … you're not getting in there," she said.

Collin eyed Bubba: "Want to give it a try?"

Bubba moved forward from the back of the group and took up a wide stance in front of the panel. He placed his two large hands at chest level and slowly began to push in.

"This is a waste of time! People's lives are at stake," Gaetana said in exasperation.

The panel gave way, crashing to the deck, into the control room. Bubba was the first to step inside. "What's next?"

Collin checked his HUD timer. More that thirty minutes had passed since the Fico Lucan beheading. Potentially, two more recruits had been executed. "We need to move quickly."

"You think?" Gaetana spat back in frustration.

Collin moved to the first tank and looked up. "This shouldn't take long. From what the captain said, to start the chain reaction we just need to disrupt the cooling process. The fusion reaction is cooled by the induction of super-chilled titanium oxide." He pointed to the top of the big bulbous mushroom tank. "There are five ten-inch diameter hoses feeding into the top of the tank. We need to—"

"Well, good luck with that. Do you see any ladders around here? Let's just cut our losses and get to the barracks."

Collin was really starting to get annoyed with this chick. Without saying another word, he leapt. He'd judged the distance fairly well, sailing up just past the widest protruding flange to the incline of the tank's dome-like section. He held there for several seconds to ensure he wasn't going to slide back down the slope. He glanced down at an astonished Gaetana and smiled. Bringing his attention to the job at hand, he saw that another eight or nine feet away, over the crest of the tank's dome, were five hoses—each feeding into the tank.

First Bubba, and then DiMaggio, suddenly joined Collin at his side. DiMaggio said, "Thought you might need some help up here."

Collin gestured toward the hoses. "We need to figure out which hose carries the titanium oxide."

Crawling on hands and knees, the three carefully ascended to the top of the tank's dome. Collin carefully inspected each of the five thick hoses.

"They look identical to me," Bubba said. "Does it matter which one we disconnect? Maybe we just disconnect all of them?"

"No. For us to have sufficient time to rescue the others, and get the hell away from the station, we need to determine which one of these hoses is feeding the titanium oxide and disconnect it ... that's what the captain told me to do. Doing anything else will get us all dead in a matter of seconds."

"Okay ... so which one is it?"

Collin continued to stare at the hoses. "He said we'd have to figure it out."

Looking at the identical hoses, he knew there was simply no way: There was a one-in-five chance he'd choose wrong. "Help me out of my battle suit."

Both Bubba and DiMaggio looked alarmed.

"Who knows what shit's in the atmosphere here? It's maybe like ... radioactive or something," DiMaggio said.

"Have to chance it. Help me get out of it." Collin rose to his feet and removed his helmet. They did as he asked and within a minute he stepped free from the back of the suit.

Bubba held on to the suit while Collin crouched down, next to the hoses.

"What are you doing?"

Collin rubbed his palms together rapidly and then, one at a time, placed them onto each of the five hoses. "I'm checking their temperature. I'm sure there's a was to do this keeping the suit on … like with HUD readings … but how to do it was eluding me. Anyway, since the titanium oxide is chilled to unbelievably low temperatures, I'm hoping I'll be able to distinguish—" He stopped talking and smiled. "It's this one." He placed his palms on the five hoses again, then returned to the one in the furthest-back position. "This is the only one that's cold. This is it!"

With the help of Bubba, Collin quickly got back into his battle suit. "Do you think you can break that hose, Bubba?" he asked.

Bubba looked at it—tried moving it with both hands. "The thing's substantial." He stood and placed a foot on the hose at its elbow, where its direction became horizontal. He put his weight down onto it.

"Just kick the damn thing!" DiMaggio said.

Bubba did just that. First, he gave it a single solid blow, then continuous, full-weight, thunderous kicks.

It became evident fairly quickly that his kicks were working. A misty-white geyser erupted from the side of the hose, where it met the top of the tank. A shrieking alarm klaxon reverberated from all directions.

"Just keep going!" DiMaggio yelled.

"But don't get near that spray. You'll freeze your foot," Collin added.

Four more colossal kicks and the hose broke completely free of the tank. The hose was expelling frigid mist at an astonishing rate—to the point it was getting difficult to see through the fog.

"We need to get out of here now," Collin said, already feeling the chill through his battle suit.

Chapter 40

"How many men were guarding the Brave Hearts when you escaped?" Collin asked Gaetana.

"Somewhere between twenty and thirty. I don't know for sure … I was trying to escape, not play a counting game."

"Look, we're all going to be blown to bits within two hours, give or take. Knowing what we're up against matters."

"There are thousands of Kardon Guard forces on the station … what difference—"

Collin cut her off: "It matters because we'll be long gone from here before they're able to get reinforcements."

Gaetana gestured for Collin to turn right at the next corridor intersection. The two strode in front of the rest of the Lone Stars. Gaetana told him there was a narrow, seldom used, stairway running alongside the elevator shaft. She'd only found out about it when Fico took her there to make out in private. Collin figured the two were quite close, given her emotional response when she heard about his death.

Gaetana slowed and indicated with a raised hand for everyone to come to a stop. They were approaching the open colonnade, where the Level 4 elevator was located. "I don't see a thing; nothing that looks like a stairway," Collin said, scanning the surrounding bulkheads. Hearing footsteps, he and Gaetana quickly ducked back into the corridor. He caught sight of a formation of Kardon Guard soldiers double-timing it off to their left, fifty yards away. Once they were clear, Gaetana looked both ways and darted forward, toward the thick vertical column that held the elevator.

What the hell is she doing? Collin wondered, running after her. *We don't want to take the elevator … we've already established that!* But Gaetana veered right and scooted into a narrow alcove that Collin hadn't noticed before; there was one on each side of the elevator. A simple open space, no wider than shoulder-width, that at first seemed merely a design element of the vertical support column. As they continued forward, headed toward a dead-end bulkhead, she turned left and disappeared from view. If Collin hadn't seen her disappear with his own eyes, he would never have guessed there was actual space hidden behind the elevator support column.

Collin felt Bubba's presence coming up behind him and looked back to see the rest of the Lone Stars closely following. He made an abrupt left turn and found Gaetana waiting for him.

"In here," she said, ducking into an opening that led directly to a two-way stairwell. She headed up, taking two stairs at a time.

"What makes you so sure Commandant Nari's forces don't know about this?" Collin asked her.

"How do you think I've been evading them all this time? Take it from me, he has no clue these stairs even exist. Oh … and tell your group of idiots to tread lightly. This won't stay a secret very long with all the racket they're making."

Collin spread the word, over the open channel, for everyone to tread quietly. They passed the opening leading into Level 5 and continued up the stairs. If only he'd known about this stairway earlier, the whole spacewalk fiasco could have been avoided. He caught up to Gaetana: "Talk to me about the barracks … exactly where everyone's being held … where the guards are positioned, that sort of thing."

"I was coming out of the head when all hell broke loose. I hid at the first sight of the Kardon forces. They were already rounding everyone up. I saw several Brave Hearts being beaten senseless. That's when I headed for this stairwell. I made it down to the rifle range and the armory. I saw dead Kardon Guard forces so I knew Brotherhood combatants were still alive and I needed to find them. There were several battle suits and weapons available ... the rest you know."

Before Collin could say anything, the distant alarm klaxon was disrupted by a repeating announcement. He stopped for a second and listened.

Abandon Station ... Abandon Station ... Abandon Station ...

He checked his HUD, astonished that twenty minutes had already passed since they'd left the control room. He hurried to catch up to Gaetana.

They passed the Level 6 opening and continued upward. Collin, working on several possible rescue plans in his head, answered an incoming hail from Captain Primo.

"Captain?"

"I see you got to the reactor. It's highly unstable. Readings tell us it's already overheating."

"We did what you asked. We—"

"Just shut up and listen!"

"You don't have two hours ... maybe not even one. There's a mass exodus going on, the Kardon Guard ... they're all abandoning the station. Get up to Level 20 and rescue the admiral!"

"And the principessa?" Collin asked, annoyance clear in his tone.

"Yes, and the principessa."

"There may be some Brotherhood recruits still alive down here. We're supposed to just leave them?"

"You want to get home, Frost? I mean ever? If so, you'll do what I say. There'll be a Brotherhood ship arriving in fifteen minutes. I hope the reactor hasn't blown by then. Now get moving."

The captain cut the connection.

They were approaching Level 7's opening. Gaetana looked back over her shoulder with a scowl. "What was that about?"

"We've run out of time, Gaetana," Collin answered. "The station's on the verge of blowing up. My orders are to get us to Level 20 now ... no stops along the way."

"You can't. You have to help the Brave Hearts!" she said, looking on the verge of losing it.

Collin turned around to the line of Lone Stars, standing behind him in the stairwell. "Bubba, DiMaggio ... lead everyone to the top, Level 20. Get to the admiral and the principessa and anyone else still alive up there. A rescue ship's en route."

"What are you going to do?" DiMaggio asked.

"I'll be right behind you. I'm going to check on the Brave Hearts."

"Why don't we all just do that together?"

"There's no time. We're wasting time now ... just go! Take Gaetana with you."

"That's not going to happen," she said. "I'm going with you."

"Fine. Whatever." Collin pointed up the stairs, "DiMaggio ... get going ... the stairwell goes all the way to the top."

"What the hell's going on up there?" came Humphrey's voice over the open channel.

DiMaggio and Bubba gave Collin a nod and quickly got moving up the stairwell. Collin waited for all the Lone Stars to pass.

"What are you doing, Collin?" It was Lydia. She was coming up the stairs, her eyes locked on his. Darren wasn't with her, had already passed. Collin saw the worry in her eyes for him and knew they still were ... *what? Something?*

"We'll catch up ... I promise."

Gaetana's patience had run out. She grabbed Collin by

the arm and pulled him through the Level 7 opening.

They exited the narrow alcove into Level 7's colonnade. Like a ghost town, it was completely deserted. The *abandon station* klaxon alarm was louder and seemed to be repeating at a faster rate than before.

Gaetana sprinted toward the entrance to the barracks.

"Wait!" Collin yelled after her. She disappeared around a bulkhead as he rushed to catch up.

Her screams foretold what he saw for himself, three seconds later. Finger poised on the trigger of his Doubler, Collin came around the corner ready to fight. The barracks were now open into one large compartment. It was clear that Commandant Nari was gone—the Kardon Guards were gone. Gaetana was on her knees—her screams continuing. Blood was everywhere—as were headless bodies of the Brave Heart recruits.

Her screams suddenly stopped. She came at Collin like a wild animal. Her eyes were wide and crazed, her fists clenched into tight balls. "This is your fault!" She plowed into Collin with enough force to knock him off his feet—which wasn't particularly difficult to do given his comparatively reduced gravitational properties. Unhurt, he steadied himself as fists pounded down on his visor and chest. "You had to go to the control room … you had to waste all those precious seconds … you killed them … you killed Fico!"

She was on top of him, straddling him. Collin let her rampage continue. The punches landed, but didn't hurt. He watched her face as the tears streamed down her cheeks. As the punching slowed, her eyes gently closed and her body softened as she leaned forward. Her arms came around him—and his arms around her—as she silently sobbed.

Abandon station … Abandon station … Abandon station.

Gaetana pulled herself up and off Collin. "Let's get out of

here," she said, her eyes taking in the carnage.

"This won't go unanswered, Gaetana. I promise you," Collin said, scurrying to his feet.

"Just shut up." She picked up her Doubler as Collin slung his around his shoulder. Without another word they ran from the barracks.

Chapter 41

Leaving the barracks, Collin saw Gaetana disappear into the narrow alcove and yelled after her, "Let's try the elevator!"

She came right back and met Collin at the elevator doors. "I didn't even think of it." She tapped on the small access panel. "It may not be working." But the doors suddenly opened and the two rushed inside. She set the destination to Level 20. "It's not accepting Level 20. Whoever is up there has it blocked."

"Get us up to Level 19, then." Collin opened a channel to DiMaggio: "Where are you at?"

"We're just passing Level 12. What happened at the barracks?"

"Nari and the Kardon Guard are gone. But the Brave Hearts are all dead. Hold on a second."

Collin asked Gaetana to stop the elevator at Level 13.

"DiMaggio, the elevator's working. We're coming up to Level 13 now."

The doors opened and Collin tentatively looked out onto Level 13's colonnade. Deserted. He checked his HUD clock—forty-five minutes had passed. They had fifteen minutes—probably less.

The Lone Stars came around the corner and filed into the elevator. Eyes darted to Gaetana and her blood-streaked battle suit. No one said anything while the doors closed.

The elevator slowed and came to a stop at Level 19. The doors opened to a barrage of plasma fire. "Get the doors shut!" Collin yelled.

Gaetana was already at the panel. "They're locked open!"

Collin, DiMaggio and Bubba quickly returned fire, not knowing what they were firing at. Level 19 was pitch black.

This was a trap and they were sitting ducks. The first hit was Dana Stoker. She took two consecutive hits to her visor.

"Out! Everyone out!" Crouching down, Collin put his free arm around Dana's limp body and, returning fire with his right hand, carried her off the elevator. He took two hits to his left thigh and felt the superheated section of his battle suit start to scorch his skin. Two more bolts hit him, one in the upper arm—the other to the back of his helmet. His legs were failing and he dropped Dana. Falling forward, Collin watched as his fellow Lone Stars rushed by, all firing weapons into the darkness beyond.

Collin was conscious that he was being dragged. "Dana … wait … don't leave Dana."

"She's already gone," he heard Darren say as he was dragged for another minute—maybe two. Finally, he was propped up, sitting against a bulkhead. Collin saw in the dim light several other Lone Stars next to him. All were returning fire, shooting between narrow vertical gaps in the bulkhead.

"How many are there?" Collin asked, feeling his senses slowly start to return.

"No more than fifteen. They're well protected by some kind of barricade," Darren answered.

Collin checked his HUD. He couldn't believe that an hour had almost passed. They were living on borrowed time. Feeling somewhat better, he got to his knees and peered through the same slat Darren was shooting through, just above him. "What is this place?"

"I don't know … looks like some kind of open space that's still under construction."

Darren was right, and that could have worked to their advantage, but not now—they simply didn't have time.

Collin recalled his father telling him about a firefight in Kamdesh—what he'd described as a god-forsaken craphole in northeastern Afghanistan. Outnumbered, his father's small Special Forces team had two choices—continue to shoot it out until one side or the other was killed off, or take the offensive and hit their flanks. Even though their military numbers were small, it was better than getting picked off one by one. Collin had heard the story often—it was when his father had earned his silver star.

Collin cleared his throat and spoke into the open channel: "We're not going to beat them just returning fire, going back and forth like this. And we've run out of time." He looked down the line and saw Humphrey. "Humphrey, take Bosh, Platt, and Hurst and come at them from the other side of Level 19 ... flank them to their right."

"Give us a minute to get in position," Humphrey affirmed, quickly heading off with the others.

"Tink, Brick, White, Melody ... start moving to the right, the area opposite the elevator column."

"The rest of you, follow my lead." He quickly got to his feet and nearly lost his balance as vertigo overwhelmed him.

Darren put an arm on his shoulder. "Easy there, man."

"I'm all right." Collin looked around for his Doubler. It was gone. He pulled his Ponge 412. "What's their distance from us?"

"Fifty feet ... maybe sixty," Darren said.

Collin estimated the same. "Let's take these guys out."

"Yeah, we're already trying to do that."

"No, from above."

Darren looked up to where Collin was staring. The top of the compartment reached thirty feet above them. Multiple exposed, arching girders spanned across, from one side of the compartment to the other, like a giant rib cage.

"Why didn't I think of that?" Darren asked in a flat voice.

Collin went back on the open channel. "Move it ...

flanks … make your attack!" He was already on the move, still running parallel with the bulkhead. He cleared the corner and saw flashes from energy weapons coming from virtually every direction. Even when a plasma bolt hit his torso, his forward progress wasn't impeded. Two more running steps and he leapt, firing down at the enemy combatants below him, as he sailed over their heads into the air. Behind their barricade, Kardon Guard soldiers clad in gray battle suits stared upward in surprise.

He holstered his Ponge and reached out with outstretched arms. His fingers grabbed for the edge of the girder, but his forward quick momentum caused him to lose his left hand's grip. He hung for several moments, legs swinging down, thirty feet above the enemy. There were twelve below him, fully occupied as their right and left flanks came under assault. Collin reached for his Ponge and began firing down.

Within seconds they returned his fire. *Maybe that wasn't such a good idea.* He'd already taken five shots to his battle suit. *Wasn't that about the suit's limit?*

Out of the corner of his eye he saw movement—five bodies flying up through the air. First to join him was Darren and, soon after, Bubba, still holding his Doubler in one hand. Bubba grabbed for the girder with his free hand and somehow managed to hold on. He wasted no time before the *thump thump thump* of plasma fire was heard, showering down on the Kardon Guards below.

The Lone Stars held the proverbial *high ground* and, one by one, the enemy fell to the deck—assaulted from the right, left, and overhead.

Collin looked for an open area on the deck and dropped. He didn't even glance at the elapsed time on his HUD. *What was the point?*

Royce White, standing on the deck, his Doubler held at

an angle in front of his chest, greeted Collin as he approached. "That was outstanding, man ... way way way outstanding!"

Collin was at a dead run. "Do a head count, Royce. Make sure we don't leave anyone here behind." He saw Dana's sprawled body to the left of the elevator column but kept moving toward the right, where he'd entered the alcove. Fast on his heels were DiMaggio, Bubba, Darren and Humphrey.

Collin made the abrupt turn to the left and then again into the stairwell. Practically flying, he took the stairs four at a time—his feet barely touching the steps in the process.

Another turn in the stairwell and Collin tripped over a dead soldier. Apparently the Kardon Guard discovered the hidden stairway. Up ahead, dead bodies lay everywhere, piled on top of one another. Slower going now, Collin had to climb up and over the bodies. He stopped counting them at twenty. A mountain of gray battle suits.

It took ten minutes to reach the end of the stairwell and an opening out to the alcove. Here it was even worse. Bodies stacked high into what amounted to a four-foot-high wall.

"Let me," Bubba said, chaffing at the bit behind him.

Collin switched places with Bubba and let the big defensive tackle barrel his way through the thicket of bodies. As the last of the dead fell away, and they reached the open expanse of Level 20, energy weapons erupted from four separate directions. Bubba took two hits and stumbled down to one knee. Collin raised his arms high over his head, in what he hoped was a universal sign of surrender, like on Earth.

The plasma fire halted. Collin leaned down next to Bubba. "You okay?"

"I'll live." The big guy rubbed at a scorch mark on his chest.

Collin looked up to see armed, gray-uniformed recruits moving forward. They were the Righteous Warriors. Five of them stopped. Nearly unrecognizable, Rocco Puma approached. Blood covered most of his face, and his left sleeve was torn away at his shoulder. As the rest of the Lone Stars entered the alcove, Rocco and his few Righteous Warriors didn't try to hide the tears welling-up in their eyes.

Rocco said, "We couldn't escape … too many Kardon Guards … they just kept coming up from Level 19."

"They're no longer a problem. The admiral … the principessa?" Collin asked, fearing they'd arrived too late to rescue them.

Rocco gestured to the far side of the compartment— to the reception counter, which was pocked with hundreds of blast marks. Both the admiral and principessa were there, pointing their Doublers in their direction.

The principessa smiled and said, "What the hell took you so long? You do know the station's about to blow, right?"

Collin smiled back. "Um, yeah, we're aware of that. How do we get out of here?"

"Level 17. There's a maintenance airlock still viable. Now that you've moseyed up here, maybe we can leave?"

Chapter 42

Admiral Zumpanno hurried around the reception counter. His head was bandaged and he moved with a slight limp. He tapped something on the elevator control panel and, within a few seconds, the doors opened.

"In … Let's go!" he barked, standing outside the doors while everyone else piled in; only then did he step inside the car and move beside the principessa. The admiral turned his head to assess the Lone Stars behind him. He was face to face with Orman, the cat-like Daccian. They held each other's gaze for a brief moment before the admiral looked away.

Collin had his visor up and was talking to the captain via his helmet comm: "We're heading down to Level 17 now … yes … the principessa is alive and unharmed," he said, looking over at her. She continued to stare straight ahead, but he saw her lips turn up slightly at the corners of her mouth.

The elevator came to a stop and the doors opened. Collin felt heat on his exposed cheeks and quickly closed his visor.

"The reactor's gone critical … the lower levels below us are literally melting," the admiral said, taking the lead through the hazy, smoke-filled Level 17 colonnade. He suddenly turned toward Collin. "Which airlock?"

Stunned, Collin didn't know what to answer. "Um … there's more than one?"

"There's two … and we don't have time to get it wrong, recruit. Ask the captain where he's parked, damn it!"

Collin tried to reestablish his comm link to the captain. There was nothing—dead air. He'd heard his father say it a thousand times … *when in doubt, go right.* Collin gestured to the right, not really knowing what the hell he was pointing to.

"That's what I thought," the admiral said, picking up his pace. Collin looked down and to his right, catching Tink staring up at him through her visor. She was smiling and mouthed the words *you better be right* ... He shrugged.

The lights flickered out and suddenly they were moving in near-total darkness.

"Stay close to me. I know this station well, with or without lights," the admiral said with confidence.

Collin found and activated the HUD setting, turning on his helmet light. Suddenly, a wide swath of light cast illumination several feet ahead. Steam or smoke, or both, was rising up from the deck. From the tight expressions on the Righteous Warriors' faces, they were feeling the blistering heat through their shoes.

The admiral made another series of left-right turns before lifting a hand, gesturing for everyone to halt. He repeatedly tapped at a panel to the right of a double-hatch, but it became quickly apparent the panel was unresponsive. "Crap ... no power ... no access."

"We can get it open," Collin said.

"Well, you better be able to close it again too. This is an airlock, remember? Look around you. More than a few of us don't have battle suits on," the admiral said.

"Take our suits," Collin said, already removing his helmet.

"I appreciate the gesture, Mr. Frost, but that won't solve the prob—"

"Actually, it might," Collin cut in. "Remember, sir ... we're not from around here. Different molecular structure ... and all that. I think we can last longer." Collin felt the back of his battle suit fall open as Bubba pulled the flange down from his shoulders. Before Collin could ask for other volunteers, Bubba, Darren, Humphrey, Lydia, Tink, and Royce White were already in the process of extracting themselves from their own battle suits.

"Crap, it's hot!" Humphrey exclaimed, looking as though he were having second thoughts. Reluctantly, he helped the principessa into his now-vacated battle suit. The admiral fitted himself into Collin's suit and, within minutes, other suit exchanges were also completed.

Bubba, Humphrey and Collin positioned themselves in front of the hatchway—each grabbed a firm hold along the inside edge. "Pull it towards us," Collin directed.

They pulled in unison. The threesome's combined strength caused the hatch to creak and groan as it soon began to give way. Collin felt the soles of his shoes starting to melt and stick to the deck plating.

"Hurry, my fricking toes are on fire," Humphrey cried out between clenched teeth.

The hatch came free with a loud clang. They hefted the wide double hatch out and away and placed it against the bulkhead, off to the side. First the Righteous Warriors, next the principessa, and then the admiral filed in.

Tears were running down both Tink and Lydia's cheeks. The rising heat was becoming unbearable, and Collin wondered if they could survive much longer.

"Lydia, Tink, and you, too, Royce … Inside." The temperature was significantly cooler within the airlock. Collin surmised it was due to its proximity to the open space beyond, but he wasn't really sure. With the exception of Bubba and himself, the rest of the Lone Stars quickly hustled into the small airlock.

"Help me prop the hatch back into its opening, Bubba," Collin said. He was now feeling a sizzling on the soles of his feet. He thought he could smell his own flesh burning. They got the hatch propped back on.

At the far side of what now was aptly an airlock chamber,

a ship could be seen as it maneuvered into position, through a series of small portholes halfway up the bulkhead.

The space station began to shake, making it difficult for anyone to stay on his or her feet. A distant rumble grew in intensity, to the point they could no longer hear anything else. Nero Station was on the verge of total annihilation.

Collin stood at the back of the airlock; he and Bubba had found vertical struts to pull themselves onto—just enough so their feet were several inches above the scalding deck plates. Both Tink and Lydia jumped onto the backs of two other Lone Stars still wearing battle suits.

"What the hell's taking them so long?" Humphrey yelled; he was one of the few to look out through a porthole. "We're being cooked alive in here and all they can do is point to the hatch?"

Then it hit Collin like a freight train. *Of course!* The power was out. The only way the outer hatch could open was if it was pried open from the inside. Collin, Bubba and Humphrey were in no shape to physically pull another hatch free. No way. But apparently the same conclusion came to Clifford Bosh, Owen Platt and Garry Hurst. The three positioned themselves much the same way Collin, Bubba, and Humphrey had earlier, when removing the other inner hatch.

The outer hatchway broke free and immediately the vacuum of space's atmosphere was sucked from around the outer hatch. The inside hatch, behind Collin, began to flutter but kept holding. Other Lone Stars, fighting the sucking-out of the atmosphere around them, moved in to get handholds on the outer hatch; together, they moved it out of the way. Collin could now see the other ship several feet out from the space station. Two men in battle suits were frantically gesturing for everyone to jump over. As the inhabitants within the airlock's confined space jumped over, one at a time, to the waiting ship,

Collin found he couldn't move. He hadn't anticipated the frigid cold—and, without any breathable air, he simply wasn't going to make it. The last thing he saw, before blacking out, was Bubba's still body flying toward the outer hatch.

Chapter 43

Collin was somewhat aware that he might be having the same dream again, but that was alright—that was good. His father had just tossed another southern cypress branch onto the fire. The forest had come alive with the sounds of night creatures, and one particularly noisy owl, with its repetitive *hoo hoo hoo*.

His father settled onto a stump next to his son and stared into the flames. "You did good today, boy."

"How can you say that? I didn't even get one shot off, Dad."

His father took a sip from his steaming cup and smiled. "That's not important."

Collin's eyes found the outline of his father's old F150 parked thirty yards away, in between two ancient oaks. The four-pointer his father brought down with a clean shot, from sixty yards away, was now secured in the truck's bed beneath a tarp.

"It's usually the how ... not the what, that's important."

Collin didn't always understand his father's musings. Sometimes it would take him a few days for their meaning to become apparent. Sometimes he never did figure them out. Asking for clarification was pointless ... his father would simply answer with a blank stare. A stare that said ... *figure it out, kid.*

Collin brought his attention back to his father and wondered what he was thinking about. Was he half the world away, in the scrub tundra of Afghanistan? Back when he was Second Lieutenant John Frost?

The dancing flames played across his father's blue plaid

shirt, which suddenly morphed into the subtle green-and-tan camo pattern of his army combat uniform. Now, a combat helmet sits on his head, where only a moment before rested a faded, Houston Astros baseball cap. Collin's heart began to race … he knew what was happening because he'd had this same dream a hundred, no, a thousand times before. Second Lieutenant John Frost was now standing, his M4 rifle coming up in slow motion. His index finger moved, ever so slowly, into the trigger guard. The sounds of night creatures turned to the *thump thump thump* of automatic-weapon fire. Explosions echoed off in the distance. The first of four 7.62x39 AK47 rounds pierced Second Lieutenant John Frost's chest, just below the collarbone, on his left side. The other three rounds moved downward, diagonally, the last shot piercing his heart. Collin's father was looking at him now, with an expression holding a mixture of curiosity and sadness. Perhaps he was wondering what life had in store for his sixteen-year-old son, and how he'd never be a part of it… that he wouldn't be returning home from this Afghanistan tour.

"Collin …? Hey, Collin … you're dreaming."

As the dream with his father faded away—back to where dreams settle down—patiently waiting to revisit in some future time, Collin opened his eyes.

Lydia was looking down at him, a look of concern on her pretty face. She reached down and wiped the moisture away from the corner of his left, and then his right, eye. She really was heart-stoppingly beautiful, he thought.

"We made it," she said, a smile crossing her lips.

"I blacked out. What happened? Where are we?"

"Astor Station."

"Is Bubba …"

Lydia gestured to his right. "He's in the bed next to yours. He'll be okay. You both had third degree burns on the soles of your feet. You were both moved into AutoMed-things and now you're recuperating."

Collin glanced down at his bandaged feet. "They didn't cut off any toes, or anything, did they?"

She laughed. "I don't think so. They say you'll be up and moving around in a few days." She placed the palm of her hand on Collin's chest. Their eyes held each other's for several beats before she said, "You know … you saved us. All of us, Collin."

He shook his head. "No more than Bubba, or Darren, or even Humphrey."

She shook her head and smiled again. "We all know what happened. Some might not say it out loud … but we all know."

Collin wondered if Lydia knew how ridiculously head-over-heels in love with her he was. Maybe someday he'd get up the nerve to tell her. His thoughts were interrupted with the pounce of Tink, flopping down on his bed.

"Scoot over!" she said.

Collin pushed over to give Tink room. She wiggled next to him and put her head on his shoulder. "Did she tell you?"

He looked down at her with a furrowed brow and then up at Lydia. "Tell me what?"

Tink said, "We can go home … go back to Earth as soon as we want."

"That would be nice," Collin said, watching Darren and Humphrey approach them, moving to stand on the opposite side of the bed, across from Lydia.

"Well, well, Sticks … you finally decide to wake up?" Humphrey asked, with a crooked smile.

Collin didn't answer; he was too busy noticing the bands on Humphrey's wrists—both wrists. He looked down at his own wrists and then at Tink's and Lydia's.

"They didn't waste any time slapping these things back

on us," Darren said. "I guess we make them nervous."

"When we get home, we've decided to throw a big party," Lydia said.

"You know, the kind you were never invited to," Humphrey added.

Tink sat up. "Be nice ... Collin will be the guest of honor. You, on the other hand—"

Her words were interrupted with the approach of Captain Primo and Principessa Constantina Valora. They were both smiling as they stood at the end of Collin's bed. The captain was dressed in a fresh uniform; the principessa was wearing a long gold and silvery gown. She looked like a princess in every sense of the word.

"May we have a moment alone with Mr. Frost?" the captain asked.

Tink let out a dramatic *huff* and scooted off the bed. Lydia, who still had her hand placed on Collin's heart, stood back and winked at him. "See you later."

Once Collin was alone with the captain and the principessa, they came around and stood in Lydia's vacated space.

"We owe you much," the captain said. "*I* owe you much," he added, glancing over to the principessa. "You're an amazing young man, Mr. Frost. I suspect you're the result of a good upbringing."

Collin didn't say anything to that. The principessa leaned over and kissed Collin on the forehead. Smiling, she said, "Collin, I want to be honest with you. You deserve that much." She and the captain exchanged another quick glance and the two became serious.

"The collector ship that abducted you and your friends was sent by the Notares, by order of the queen, and carried out by the Kardon Guard. Since the return of the sim rover you were first held in, three more have been dispatched to

Earth. Earth has a rich and diverse quantity of metal … metals with a molecular composition not found anywhere in our own galaxy."

Collin was having a hard time listening to her words. The devastation caused by a single sim rover was cataclysmic—three would, most assuredly, destroy much of the Earth he knew. And what of the populace?

"I'm so sorry, Collin," she said.

"How do we stop them? How do I stop them?"

"Even a week ago I could have halted the plunder of your world. But I'm no longer in the queen's good graces. Not as long as Commandant Nari has my mother's ear. I've been branded a traitor to the monarchy and a bounty's been placed on my head."

"I'm sorry to hear that, Principessa, but I don't understand why we can't travel back through the portal and defend Earth? Or just let me do that."

"I made you a promise, Mr. Frost," Captain Primo said. "I can return you and your Lone Stars to Earth within a few days."

Collin felt relief hearing that, but he knew a *but* was coming.

"What will you attempt to do to defend your planet against those highly advanced collector ships, not forgetting there are a small fleet of Marauders too, now encircling Earth's upper orbit?"

Collin closed his eyes, suddenly feeling very tired. He didn't have an answer. He didn't know how to save his planet, let alone his mother and little sister. "What do you suggest?"

"In five weeks your ship, the *Turd*, will be retrofitted. You've earned the right to command that vessel. What I propose is this … spend the next five weeks completing your basic. You, and your Chain, finish what you began and become true warriors ... warriors who'd have some semblance of a chance defending their home world."

Collin let that sink in. "Is that all you'd ask in return? Five weeks of our time and we're free to return to Earth with a warship?"

The captain shrugged. "This is war, Mr. Frost. You'll need to ask yourselves this: what can we do that will ensure the long-term survival of our people ... our planet?"

The End

Thank you for reading Lone Star Renegades. If you enjoyed this book and would like to see the series continue, please leave a review on Amazon.com — it really helps! To be notified of the soon-to-be released next **Lone Star Renegades - Book 2**, *contact* **markwaynemcginnis@gmail.com**, *Subject Line:* **Lone Star Renegades - Book 2**.

Acknowledgments

I am grateful for the ongoing support I've received for my latest novel, *Lone Star Renegades*, as well as for the other books I've written. This book, number eight, came about through the assistance and combined contributions of others: First, I'd like to thank my mother, Lura Genz, for her tireless work as my first-phase creative editor and a staunch cheerleader of my writing. I'd like to thank my wonderful wife, Kim, for her endless support. I'd like to thank Mia Manns, for her phenomenal line and developmental editing … she is an incredible resource! Eren Arik produced an amazing, fun, cover design. I'd also like to thank pilot Mike Wilson, who provided the technical information for scenes regarding the Boeing 777-328 wide-body jetliner. I'd also like to thank those in my writers meet-up group, who have brought fresh ideas and perspectives to creativity, elevating my writing as a whole. Others who've provided much appreciated support include Lura and James Fischer, Sue Parr, and Chris DeRrick.

Other books by Mark Wayne McGinnis:

Scrapyard Ship
(Scrapyard Ship series, Book 1)

HAB 12
(Scrapyard Ship series, Book 2)

Space Vengeance
(Scrapyard Ship series, Book 3)

Realms of Time
(Scrapyard Ship series, Book 4)

Craing Dominion
(Scrapyard Ship series, Book 5)

The Great Space
(Scrapyard Ship series, Book 6)

Mad Powers
(Tapped In series, Book 1)

Lone Star Renegades
(Lone Star Renegades series, Book 1)

www.ingramcontent.com/pod-product-compliance
Lightning Source LLC
Chambersburg PA
CBHW072235190626
46809CB00018B/2269